I drummed my fingers on the ME's desk. "What's the good stuff?"

"Remarkably, her adrenaline and adrenochrome levels are off the chart."

"What does that mean, doctor?" Helen asked.

"There is no doubt she was frightened to death."

"I'm sure she was scared. She had been kidnapped," I said.

"No, you're not catching my drift," the doctor said. "She was absolutely frightened so badly that she died from fear."

"My god," Helen said. "That's horrible."

"Yes, it would be a horrible death for anyone to suffer."

"Where does that leave us, doc?" I asked.

"I don't want to do your work for you, but I've done a little research since receiving this report this morning. I think you should be looking for a cult. Remember what I told you about the blood moon? It all just ties together. I think the little girl might have been sacrificed to the blood moon by a cult of people who drink human blood. They may be practicing vampires. And I don't mean the type you find in the movies. I mean people who enjoy drinking blood for sport or ritual. The blood of a young virgin would be highly valued, especially if it was full of adrenochrome and adrenaline which would give them a high."

Praise for Edward S. Baker

Author of four published sci-fi novels and one police mystery, Edward S. Baker once again forges into the police detective genre with a second Bartholomew Jones murder mystery. With each successive novel we learn more about Jones' unique personality and the possibility that he and Helen may have "a thing."

Blood Bath

by

Edward S. Baker

Bartholomew Jones Series
Book Two

Blood Bath

COPYRIGHT © 2023 by Edward S. Baker

Cover Art by *Debbie Taylor*

The Wild Rose Press, Inc.
PO Box 708
Adams Basin, NY 14410-0708
Visit us at www.thewildrosepress.com

Publishing History
First Edition, 2023
Trade Paperback ISBN 978-1-5092-4942-8
Digital ISBN 978-1-5092-4943-5

Bartholomew Jones Series, Book Two
Published in the United States of America

Dedication

I dedicate this novel to my wife Edna, whose gentle guidance keeps my writing on the straight and narrow.

Prologue

July 24, 1492

Pope Innocent VIII lay silent on his back under a thick red and gold bedspread. Crystallized tears clung to the outer edges of his closed eyes. His breathing was shallow. Seated beside him, a young woman unlaced her cotton bodice and leaned over a silver goblet. Dark brown ringlets of her hair brushed gently across her cheek. She squeezed her breast with her right hand. A dozen drops of breastmilk spilled into the goblet. She sat erect, then poured a few drops of milk into the Pope's open mouth. The old man sputtered and pushed her away.

Dr. Giacomo di San Genesio touched the young woman's shoulder. "Enough."

She rose from the bedside and covered herself. Then she bowed to the doctor and walked quietly from the room.

San Genesio turned to Cardinal De Medici. "That is three times we've tried to give the pontiff nourishment. But a few drops is all he has consumed each time. It is not enough to sustain life."

Even before he had stopped eating solid foods, Pope Innocent VIII had become emaciated. He had never been a large man, but his sickly pallor and the atrophication of his arm and leg muscles had become evident to all who saw him. The Pope was wasting away and the ailment consuming his body was a mystery.

Dr. San Genesio felt the pontiff's forehead. The pope had developed a fever. "Fetch the Captain of the Guard."

"As you request," the cardinal replied.

A few minutes passed before Captain Larosa appeared, followed by De Medici. "You have need of me?" he asked.

"Yes, Captain. Have you held the three young boys, as I instructed?"

"Yes, Doctor. They are ages eight, eleven, and thirteen."

"Have you ensured they are all virgins?"

"Yes, according to their parents."

"Bleed them all and bring me the blood in a copper vessel."

"All?"

"Do you question me? What do you know of the medical arts?"

"I apologize, Doctor. I meant no disrespect. I had hoped not to have to explain the deaths of three sons to their grieving mothers."

"They will rejoice when they learn the sacrifice of their sons' lives has saved the life of our glorious pontiff."

****

At three o'clock, an enlisted soldier entered the pontiff's chambers carrying a copper urn. "Captain Larosa ordered me to deliver this urn to you."

"At last," San Genesio replied. "Place it here, beside the pontiff's bed."

The soldier did as instructed, bowed, and departed.

San Genesio waited until he was certain the soldier would not return and then he collected the items he needed from his large medical satchel: a sealed jar of leeches to bleed the bad humors which plagued the dying pontiff, and a funnel with a long, thin copper tube to feed him an iron-rich liquid meal. And last, a copper cup from which to pour the warm blood collected from the three young men, in hopes it might give the pontiff's frail body the vitality of the youth from which it came.

Sadly, on July 25, 1492, the bells of the Vatican began their mournful dirge. Pope Innocent VIII was sleeping with the saints.

Almost immediately, Dr. San Genesio was accused of having performed a blood transfusion which caused the pope's death. Nothing was further from the truth, because no blood had been passed directly from a host into the pontiff's bloodstream.

However, unbeknownst to the medical profession at the time, ingestion of large quantities of human blood can cause haemochromatosis, or iron toxicity, which leads to liver damage, fluid in the lungs, and dehydration. Given the pontiff's weakened condition, Dr. San Genesio's treatment probably did, in fact, deal the fatal blow which sent the pontiff to his heavenly reward.

Chapter 1

Little Laura Moretti was playing in her back yard. Dressed in green corduroy pants, a white long-sleeved top with a penguin print, and an orange down-filled jacket, she was prepared for the cool weather outside. Every few minutes her mother looked from the kitchen window to be sure her daughter was safe. Rumors that feral hounds were roaming the back alleys of Willow Falls fed her uncertainty that the family's back yard was safe from any number of evils. But Laura had begged and, with winter just a few weeks away, her mother could not deny her daughter the joy of the family's backyard playground.

First running to the rope swing and then moving to the wooden playhouse her father had built for her, Laura dwelled in a world of make-believe. The borders of her little world included high white vinyl fences on both sides, and a tall burning bush hedge which protected her yard from the back alley.

She pretended to cook a meal in her playhouse, stirring imaginary stew with a wooden spoon in an aluminum pot. Then, from the window over her play sink she saw movement at the bottom of the family's hedge. At first, Laura was afraid it might be a wild animal, but then she saw its entire form. It was a puppy. A white puppy, wearing a collar, and perhaps a leash was attached. She could not be sure.

She ran from the playhouse and fell to her knees in front of the puppy. At first, the puppy took two steps toward her. But then it lurched backwards, as though being pulled.

"Come, puppy," she cried. "Come here."

The puppy moved backwards again.

Laura crawled forward on hands and knees, brushing acorns away as she moved toward the puppy.

The puppy whined and pulled against its leash toward Laura. Then, it moved backwards, its feet pawing the ground as it was drawn away into the thick bushes by an invisible hand.

Laura fell to her tummy and crawled under the branches of the red burning bush, following the puppy as it was backing away. She reached with both hands and tried to grasp the puppy. Her fingertips touched its soft white fur. But the puppy moved away again.

Laura put her head to the ground and squeezed under the prickly bushes. Her hands reached the cool grass on the other side of the hedge. Suddenly they were grasped, and Laura felt her body being pulled out from under. Before she could see who had helped her through the bushy hedge, an arm wrapped around her waist and a soft cloth was held against her face. Her nostrils burned at an odor like the nail polish remover her mother sometimes used. Her head began to swim, and in a few seconds, she lost consciousness and fell limp in her assailant's arms.

****

Imogene Moretti looked out her kitchen window. She could not see Laura. She hurried to the back door, opened it, and called out, "Laura?"

There was no response.

"Come inside, honey. I've made you some lunch."

She heard no response.

Imogene grabbed her coat from a hook behind the back door and pulled it on as she walked outside. She looked inside the empty playhouse, then her eyes quickly scanned the yard. At the hedgerow she saw marks in the dirt where something had been dragged through the thick brush. Could it have been Laura? Was she taken by a feral hound?

Behind the wall of burning bushes, a car door closed. Then the sound of tires digging into the gravel road. Imogene pushed into the bushes. Its sharp branches tore at the skin on her arms, legs, and face. She could not push far enough to see the vehicle which was hurriedly driving away. She stumbled backwards, branches of the hedge now tearing at her clothing. Then she fell to her knees and screamed. Her beloved little Laura was gone.

Chapter 2

I had just popped the plastic lid on a Styrofoam coffee cup when the telephone at my desk rang. Before answering the call, I quickly sipped at the coffee and scalded my tongue.

I opened my mouth in surprise. A small stream of hot coffee ran down my chin and onto the thin brown carpet beneath my desk.

I lifted the receiver. "Bart Jones here."

The husky voice gave away the speaker's identity. "Claiborne here."

Charles Claiborne was the Willow Falls District Attorney, at least for the moment. The city fathers were still deliberating his removal in the aftermath of the BabyX case, a case where Claiborne had pressed charges against a West Virginia judge before he had gathered enough evidence to obtain a guilty verdict. The resulting lawsuit cost the city almost twelve million dollars. The city's comptroller had not been so lucky. He lost his job immediately because he had failed to renew the city's liability insurance and, as the result, the city council was obliged to borrow the money to cover the settlement via a twenty-year loan at seven percent interest. The papers had had a heyday with that story.

"I need your help, Bart," Claiborne stated. "I got a couple of close friends coming to see me. Their kid has gone missing. They think she was kidnapped."

"How old?"

"Seven."

"Then she's probably not a runaway, is she?"

"Not this kid. She's just a sweetheart. She's never given them a lick of trouble. Cute and smart—maybe got a little rascal in her, like one of those sitcom kids. But she'd never run away from home. She's got everything a kid could want."

"When did they notice she was missing?"

"Just this morning. The kid was playing in the back yard while her mom was fixing lunch. One minute she was there playing in her playhouse, and the next minute she was gone. Her momma heard a car pull away down the back alley, but she never got a look at it."

"What time are they coming in?"

"Should be here any minute. Could you come down to meet with them? I've asked Chief Comstock to assign little Laura's missing person's case to you. I need you on it, pronto. We gotta find that little girl before…well, you know."

Mirroring the DA's conclusion, I knew the probable outcome of so many missing person cases involving children. When they were abducted into the white slave market, they were silently whisked away to who-knows-where and then they served a brief lifetime of drug addicted horror. If they were abducted by a self-serving pervert, they often suffered sexual abuse and, if the body was ever found, it offered evidence the kid suffered an agonizing death. Either scenario would likely destroy all but the strongest of families.

"Laura is her name? I'll be right down."

"Oh yeah, Bart. I've also asked Helen Martin to join us, too. You seem to work well with her. This case might benefit from a woman's perspective. You don't mind, do you?"

"No. Helen's a good detective and she's good people. It'll be a pleasure to work with her again."

"Good. See you in a few."

****

I stopped briefly at the men's room to ensure I looked presentable. Fortunately, I hadn't dribbled any coffee on my white shirt or red and blue striped tie. I emptied my tanks, then dabbed some cold water on my face, and wiped it dry with a paper towel. I paused to look in the mirror at the thinning brown hair on the top of my head and the small but noticeable spare tire I had been developing from my desk job. Back when I walked a beat, I was lean and strong, but nowadays my work as a police detective was more mental than physical, and I had not adjusted my eating habits to account for the lack of exercise. I made a mental note to start exercising on a regular basis…maybe starting next week…or the week after.

I met Helen near the women's restroom on the second floor of the police department. She was dressed to the nines this afternoon in a leopard-print blouse, black slacks, and leopard spotted flats. Several gold tone necklaces dangled above her breasts, and her wide black belt was accented by a large square gold buckle.

"When I saw you weren't at your desk, I thought you might be in the john swimming laps," I joked. "Looks like I was right."

"You think I got a small bladder, Jonesy?"

"No, but I know your habits, and you don't go to any meetings without making a pitstop first."

"How about you…though I s'pose I already know

the answer."

"Been there. Done that. And how would you know?"

Helen pointed at my khaki trousers. "You got leopard spots by your barn door."

I fanned the spots with my hand. "Damn. No wonder you made detective." While I finished flailing my hand back and forth, I changed the subject. "The DA tell you what this is about?"

"Yeah. Don't sound like something gonna be fun."

"I'd like to find that little girl in one piece and unscathed, but the chances are slim."

"If she's alive...and if she's been abused...she's gonna need a lifetime of therapy. She's too young to deal with it without professional help."

We took the elevator to the fourth floor and found the DA's office. His secretary told us to go on in. "The parents are already here."

I opened the door and followed Helen into Claiborne's office. Claiborne was sitting behind his gray metal desk in a white shirt with a blue plaid tie. The venetian blinds on the window behind him were partially closed, their dusty blades in need of cleaning. Seated in front of him were a man and a woman, both in their mid-thirties. They looked up as Helen and I came in, but neither smiled. The woman was dressed in blue slacks and a pink blouse. Her eyes were puffy and red. Her husband wore blue jeans and a wool shirt in a green tartan plaid. His face was stressed.

Claiborne told us to sit in the two chairs to his right. He introduced us to his friends, Wayne and Imogene Moretti, parents of the missing child.

"We're so sorry this has happened to you," Helen

began. "Mr. Claiborne gave us brief details. Would you mind retelling them to us?"

Imogene provided most of the details. They were no different from what the DA already had described, although her tale often was interrupted by tears and sobbing. To summarize: She did not see her daughter being kidnapped and did not see the vehicle which sped away from their home. Her husband Wayne was at work when the incident occurred and came home immediately after his wife called his cell phone in hysteria over the probable loss of their daughter. He was in the dark, except for the details Imogene had managed to share with him in between sobs.

"What do you do for a living, Mr. Moretti?" I said.

"I run Sammy's Sundaes."

"The ice cream place down by the river?"

"Yeah, that's it. With the cold weather on us, I'm starting to shut down for the winter. We don't sell enough to remain open after the middle of October."

"Do you have any problems with the mafia or with street gangs?"

"Trouble? Like what?"

Helen jumped in. "Do you have to pay anybody a portion of your profits in order to stay open? You know, like collection men representing a gang of any type or even the mafia?"

"No. None."

"Have you ever been approached by anyone asking for that sort of thing?" I asked.

"No, never."

Helen jumped in again. "Do you gamble or have outstanding debts which might cause someone to kidnap your daughter to hold her for ransom?"

Imogene Moretti burst into tears. "Could it be that gang from Long Island, Wayne?"

Wayne Moretti sighed. "Maybe, but I don't think so." He looked at Claiborne for a moment and then at Helen and me. "We moved up here ten years ago from Riverhead, where I owned a similar business which catered to summer clientele...pizza and ice cream. I was approached by a Hispanic gentleman..."

"He was no gentleman, Wayne. He was a thug," Imogene blurted.

Moretti gave his wife an annoyed look and then continued. "I was approached by a man of Hispanic heritage who explained he represented a group who would ensure my business would never be burglarized or burned down. All I had to do was give him a thousand dollars per month. He would come by and pick it up on the last day of each month, and I would be protected for the next thirty days."

"What did you do?" I asked. "Did you report the shakedown to the police?"

"Hell no. Back then everyone knew the local police were paid off to look the other way when they encountered gang-related business, especially if it was MS-13."

"So, what did you do?" I repeated.

"I shut down the business, sold the building, and we moved up here. I haven't experienced anything like that up here...at least not yet. Do you think Laura's kidnapping could be related?"

"Possibly," Helen offered. "Do you remember the man's name?"

"I'll never forget it. Diego Esperanza. He had a tattoo of a black widow spider on his neck. The hourglass on the spider was bright red, and there was a drop of red blood dripping from one fang in the spider's mouth."

Helen jotted down Esperanza's name. "This was in 'Riverhead?'"

"Yes. Riverhead, New York. Out on Long Island."

"Do you have a picture of your daughter with you?" I asked.

Wayne Moretti nodded. "Yes, Charlie...I mean Mr. Claiborne...asked us to bring one, preferably recent and preferably in color. I just took pics of her yesterday. I printed some from my cell phone." He handed Helen a stack of pics. Each photograph was a close-up of Laura wearing a new outfit she and her mother had purchased for the family's upcoming Thanksgiving trip to Disneyworld. Little Laura's chestnut hair, blue eyes, and radiant smile were infectious.

"She's adorable, Mr. Moretti," Helen said. "She has your nose and smile, Mrs. Moretti, and your husband's eyes."

I nodded. My mother once told me no matter how ugly the creature in the picture is, you have to say something positive because the owner of the picture loves the kid.

Imogene Moretti's hands were shaking. "Do you think you can find her, Detective?"

"We hope so," Helen murmured, not wanting to share her personal fear that it was already too late to find anything but a cadaver. "We'll do everything humanly possible."

"We'll get these pics out on an Amber Alert," Claiborne stated. "And to the news media. Hopefully, someone will have seen her."

"We'd also like a list of her best friends," I said.

"Sometimes there's a connection."

Wayne Moretti tilted his head. "You mean, like, one of her friends' parents might have stolen our little girl?"

"Yeah. Or maybe an older sibling. Or maybe they have suspicions or have noticed suspicious people watching all the children when they're playing together outside."

"They don't even know she's missing yet," Imogene sobbed.

"They will shortly," Claiborne promised.

An hour after the Morettis went home from the police department, every cell phone in Willow Falls sounded an emergency warning, followed by a child abduction announcement asking all citizens to watch for Laura Moretti, age seven. Following the alert, all cell phones received a color photograph of Laura. If she were being held locally, there was a good chance someone had seen her and would immediately alert the police.

Chapter 3

I started the motor on my city-issued tan sedan. "You know, I thought she'd have had more close friends."

"She's only just started second grade, Jonesy," Helen replied. "By the time she's in middle school she'll have dozens of them."

"And by the time she's in high school, dozens of boys will try to be her favorite."

"Yup, that's the way it works. Pretty girl like Laura ain't gonna have no trouble attracting gentlemen...if she's still alive."

"Yeah, I kind of put that out of my mind." I backed out of my official parking space. "Who's first on the list?"

"Says here it's Meghan O'Rourke. Lives on Danielson Drive, over near the Crosstown entrance."

"Got a number?"

"4205."

We drove for five minutes, turned onto Danielson Drive, and found the O'Rourke's home. It was a two-story orange brick fortress with a white addition on the left side. The afternoon was waning, and the yellow glow of a lamp illuminated the curtains on the side porch.

I pushed the doorbell, but when I didn't hear chimes inside, I knocked. A little girl answered. Her red hair and abundance of freckles gave away her Irish heritage.

Before I could say anything, she was pulled away from the door by her mother, a husky woman with rust-colored hair, pulled into a bun.

"Can I help you? You aren't Seventh Day Adventists, are you?"

"We're with the Willow Falls Police Department, Mrs. O'Rourke," Helen replied. "We're hoping you may have some information on a missing child case."

"Oh, you must be here about Laura Moretti. That's a shame, isn't it? I learned about it when my cell phone went off like a fire alarm. Never heard it do that before."

"Can we come in, ma'am? We'd like to ask you a few questions. Also, is Meghan home? We have a few for her, as well."

"Oh, I'm sorry. Yes, please come in. Meghan's upstairs. She had school today." She turned to the little girl who had greeted us at the door. "Why don't you go into the den and watch the Muppets, Shannon?" Shannon did as her mother had instructed.

Helen and I stepped into the slate-floored foyer. It struck me Laura Moretti should have been in school today, too. "How did your daughter become acquainted with Laura Moretti?"

"Brownies. They started a Brownie Troop at the elementary school last year. Nice group of girls, all from good homes. They rotate meetings. You know, meeting each month in a different girl's home."

"Laura wasn't in school today," I stated. "And she was kidnapped from her own backyard."

"Yeah, it's that COVID thing. The district broke the classes up so there's never more than a dozen kids in the classroom at a time. When they're not in class, they watch the class online. Meghan and Laura attend on alternate days this year. Meghan doesn't like that because they were good friends, but there isn't anything to be done about it."

"So, Meghan and Laura don't attend class on the same days?"

"No. they don't. The teacher divided the classroom up by the alphabet. Moretti is in group A, which goes to school on Mondays and Wednesdays. O'Rourke is in group B, which goes to school on Tuesdays and Thursdays. We call them 'apples' and 'bananas' so it doesn't sound so awful."

"What about Fridays?"

"That's now a planning day for the teachers. They have a lot to do to get ready for each week's lessons.

"To the point of our visit, ma'am," Helen said. "We're trying to learn if anyone might have any idea about who might have kidnapped little Laura."

"I haven't a clue."

"When the Brownies were outside playing, did anyone notice a stranger watching them?"

"No, Brownie meetings are always indoors."

"Do any of the Brownies have older siblings, maybe in their early teens?" I asked.

"Just the McCabes. They have a son who's fifteen, but he's in a wheelchair. Even if he wanted to kidnap a little girl, I don't think he could have done it."

"What about any of the fathers? Have you ever seen one of them take special interest in Laura? Maybe inappropriately touch her?"

"Nope. It's a girl's world when we're doing Brownie business. Gentlemen are not permitted."

"Is that a rule established by the national organization?" Helen asked.

"Of course not. Over in Marshfield a couple of men are Junior troop leaders. They do different things with the girls than women leaders do. Their girls earn merit badges for different things, like basic automotive maintenance, fly fishing, shooting...those sorts of things."

"But there aren't any men leading Brownie troops?"

"Not that I know of, but there could be. It's not against policy."

I jotted a few notes on my legal pad.

"Can we speak with Meghan?" Helen continued.

"You won't frighten her, will you? She's upset over Laura's disappearance."

"Why don't you stay with us while we ask our questions? If anything frightens her, you let us know."

Mrs. O'Rourke went to the stairwell and shouted up the stairs. "Meghan, would you come downstairs for a minute?"

As Meghan thumped down the stairs, I smelled something burning in the kitchen. "Do you have something on the stove?"

"Oh, God, I have spinach on the burner!"

Mrs. O'Rourke hurried into the kitchen, removed a pot from the stove, and doused it under cold water. Then she opened the kitchen window to let the cloud of smoke dissipate.

She came back into the foyer wiping her hands with a dish towel. "I guess I ruined the side dish. I'll have to open a can of peas."

"We're sorry for interrupting your preparations, Mrs. O'Rourke," Helen said.

"That's okay. My husband will be home in a few minutes, and he'll be happy I deep-sixed the spinach. He hates it."

Helen turned to the brunette child who had come down the stairs and was hanging onto the end of the banister, perhaps shy of the two strangers who were chatting with her mother.

"Meghan," Mrs. O'Rourke said, "these two people are police officers, and they are here to ask us both a few questions about Laura Moretti. We're not in any trouble and it is our civic duty to help them try to find Laura."

"Hi, Meghan," Helen said. "My name is Miss Martin, and this is Mr. Jones."

Meghan simply nodded.

"Is Laura Moretti one of your friends?"

Meghan nodded again.

"We're hoping to find her. Do you have any idea where she might be?"

"Maybe at Sammy's with her daddy."

"I guess we'll go there next to see if we can find her," Helen replied. She dropped to one knee and held Meghan's hand. "Now this is really important. Did Laura ever tell you she was afraid of somebody…anybody?"

"She was afraid of the principal. He sends people home who are bad at school."

"Was Laura ever bad at school? Did the principal ever send her home?"

Meghan looked at her mother and then back at Helen. "No, she was a good girl, not like some."

"Thank you, Meghan. That's all we needed to ask you."

Helen and I thanked Mrs. O'Rourke again and apologized for diverting her attention from the spinach she burned.

Once we were back in the car, I started the motor,

but before asking for the next address, I turned to Helen. "Maybe little Meghan was onto something. How about we go check out Sammy's Sundaes, just to see if she's being held there?"

"Are you thinking the father is guilty of kidnapping his own child?"

"Wouldn't be the first time."

"You know you can't go snooping around there unless we got a search warrant. And you know no judge is going to issue you a search warrant without cause."

I drove to the river and followed Shore Drive until I came to Sammy's Sundaes, the warm weather business which was the Moretti family's principal source of income. It was a cinderblock building, painted white, with small slider windows where patrons could place orders and servers would hand them cones and bowls of many assorted flavors of frozen treats. On both sides of the building sat round picnic tables with colorful aluminum umbrellas and fifty-gallon steel trashcans. A dozen seagulls perched on the flat roof of the building, half of them facing the river below. The building's lights were off, and the place looked deserted.

"Probably looks abandoned because it's cool weather and almost dark," Helen said. "And besides, Wayne Moretti is probably at home living this horror with his wife."

I got out of my sedan and peered into the windows. A container of spray bleach and a balled-up rag sat on the stainless-steel sink. The worktables were in disarray with assorted cardboard boxes scattered on top of them.

I returned to the car. "Yup, Moretti is closing down for the winter, just like he told us."

Across the street, the marquis lights of an

independent gas station came on. I started the motor and drove across the street, filled the gas tank, and then went inside. Helen followed me in. The man behind the counter was Indian or Pakistani. I couldn't tell which. I paid for the gasoline and while I waited for my change, I asked, "Who owns this business?"

"I do," the man replied with a heavy accent. The hair on his head and his moustache were jet black. His skin was olive, almost brown. He wore khaki trousers and a white shirt with no name tag.

I flashed my badge. "My name is Detective Bart Jones with the police department. Have you been here all day?"

The man's expression turned to concern. "Yes. My daytime assistant manager called in sick. Young people today are so undependable."

"We're looking for a little girl. Someone told us she hangs around the ice cream stand across the street. Just wondering if you might have seen her over there today?"

"Is she the one the police are looking for? I jumped when my cell phone went off earlier today."

"Yes. We're trying to locate her."

"Nobody's been there all day. The owner closed up yesterday afternoon, and he hasn't been back."

"How do you know?" Helen asked. "You could have been busy with customers when he arrived."

"When he's here, the lights in his building are on. He usually stops in for coffee and the paper around eight in the morning, and then he comes back for a refill around ten, just before he opens for business. But I haven't seen him at all today. He's been skipping Tuesdays since the schools opened. I think he must have a child at home who needs help with schoolwork."

"So, nobody at all has been at Sammy's today?" Helen asked.

"That's what I said."

I handed him a business card. "Thank you for your time. If you can remember anything else or if you see a little girl at Sammy's over the next few days, please give me a call."

Helen and I walked back to the car and got in. Helen was the first to speak. "Well, now we know Wayne Moretti lied to us this afternoon."

"Yeah," I replied. "He told us when his wife called, he came directly home from work to console her."

"So, put him down as our number one suspect. It's often the father who abuses the daughter."

"He didn't seem the type when we met him this afternoon, but you never know." I started the car. "Where to next?"

"Amber Penrose. Lives on Fremont Place, on the east side. Gotta go past Moretti's and take Ulster Street for eight blocks according to my phone's GPS. Good opportunity to check out the back alley at Moretti's."

I drove back the way we had come, up Shore Drive to Genesee Street then away from the river. Two right turns and one left turn later I saw the Moretti's home. Wayne was getting out of his car, so I honked the horn and pulled over to the curb.

Wayne approached the car, bending over to see who was driving. When he saw Helen roll down the window, he stooped down.

"Oh, hello," he said. "Got any news for us yet?"

"Yeah. We thought you should know you're our number one suspect, Mr. Moretti," Helen said.

Wayne stood upright with a shocked look on his

face. "How dare you accuse me of kidnapping my own daughter. Are you insane?"

I climbed out of the car, leaving its door open. I walked past the front of the car, hopped onto the grassy yard, and pointed at Moretti's face. "You told us you came home directly from work when your wife called you this morning."

"Yes, that's exactly what I did."

"You didn't go to work this morning, Wayne."

Moretti's expression turned to one of guilt.

Helen opened her door and stepped out of the car. "Where's your daughter, Mr. Moretti? What have you done with her?"

Moretti looked behind himself at the front door of his home. It was closed. "I have an alibi, but you can't let my wife know. She'll kill me."

I figured Moretti was going to spin a wild yarn, something hard to believe.

"I've been having an affair with a woman here in town. It just started five weeks ago, when schools reopened. We meet one or two days each week when my daughter is at home and my wife is helping her with the online instruction."

"And today is your regular consensual sex day?" I asked.

"Yes. And when my wife called about Laura, it interrupted us before we had really begun. We had just opened a bottle of chardonnay and poured two glasses. Of course, I was really concerned about my daughter, so I hurried home."

"You know we're going to have to check this out," Helen said. "What's her name?"

"I'd prefer not to tell you. It could cause her

problems at home. She says her husband carries a pistol and he's a bit of a hothead."

"If you were having an affair with my wife, I could become a hothead where you're concerned, too," I said.

"What's her name?" Helen asked again.

"Look, I'd really rather not say. But we checked in at the Marshfield Inn. You can verify that by asking them if I checked in. The hotel room was in my name. I paid by credit card."

"You didn't use a 'John Doe'?"

"Honestly, I'm new at this. This is my first time doing something like this, like cheating on Imogene. I didn't even think about using a 'John Doe.'"

"You know we're going to verify your alibi," I said, "and if even one little detail of it doesn't check out, we're going to drag you down to the department and grill you for more information. Maybe you ought to stay home and spend some more time with your wife."

Helen and I got back into our car.

"Too dark now to examine the alley. We'll have to do it tomorrow," she said.

"You see every detail, don't you?"

"We sisters are sharp when it comes to details."

Chapter 4

I asked Helen to pull out her cell phone and punch in directions to the Marshfield Inn.

Helen did as I asked. When her phone found its location, she hit the "go" button and the phone began giving oral directions. I followed the instructions given by the phone's female voice until I saw the Marshfield Inn.

"Shut her up, would you?" I complained. "Her voice is annoying."

"She got us here, didn't she? I could have asked her to do it in Spanish, but I figure you flunked foreign language in high school."

"I took French. And if you'd had her give me directions in French we'd be lost. The only French phrase I can remember is from that song, 'Voulez vous couchez avec moi, ce soir?'"

"You ain't really asking me that question, are you, Jonesy?"

"You know better than that, Helen." I shut the car's motor. "Let's go check out Wayne Moretti's alibi."

The Marshfield Inn was a small four-story hotel, nestled among two rows of giant oak trees. Customers got to it by navigating a circular, one-way gravel driveway which arrived at the front door. There, car keys were handed to parking attendants who found an unseen parking spot somewhere away from falling acorns and who returned with the proper vehicles when called for, always extending a hand for a tip.

The inn itself was stately red brick with a gray stone foundation and a five-step granite stairway which led from the driveway to the entrance. Inside, the walls were adorned with red and purple wallpaper, and adjacent to the registration desk, the main room was home to four seating areas, consisting of gray leather sofas and matching stuffed chairs. Coffee tables were nestled in between and tall plants added a discreet curtain of privacy.

Helen and I approached the front desk. I asked to speak with the manager. When the sole receptionist left to get him, Helen nudged me. "Them white people on the sofas don't think I belong here. See them staring at us?"

"Don't pay any attention to them. They're probably wondering why an attractive Nubian goddess like you would be hanging around with a schlep like me."

"Come to think of it, you may be right, Jonesy."

The receptionist returned and asked us to follow him to the manager's office. It was a small room, not even eight by ten, containing a desk and two leather chairs for guests. Behind the desk sat a young woman, barely thirty. She was brunette with hazel eyes. When she stood to greet us, I noticed her navy skirt was snug around her hips and rump. Her white blouse was unwrinkled. If I were unattached and five or six years younger, I'd consider acting on the interest I was feeling.

"Yvonne Spenser." She held out her hand.

I flashed my ID and badge. "We're Detectives Jones and Martin from the Willow Falls Police Department. We need your assistance in verifying the alibi of a suspect in a child kidnapping case. "

"How can I be of service?"

"Can we check your registration book for a name?"

"Certainly. I can do it right here."

"It would be a registration this morning. Wayne Moretti. Paid by credit card."

Yvonne clicked a bunch of keys on her keyboard. "Yes, he and Mrs. Moretti checked in at ten o'clock. Room three-fifteen, overlooking the golf course."

"Are they regulars?"

Yvonne clicked her keyboard a few more times. "Yes, this is their fifth visit with us. Always one day. Interesting…always on Tuesdays."

"How would you know that?" Helen asked.

"Each registration is exactly seven days apart. Today is a Tuesday, so counting backwards seven days is another Tuesday."

"Do you have security cameras so we can verify it's actually Mr. Moretti and not someone claiming to be him?"

"Yes, we do have video cameras recording everything that happens here all day and night, but it would take hours to scroll through the tapes. We'll be happy to do that for you if it's necessary. However, I think we can do better. Whenever a customer registers, our hidden desk camera silently takes their photograph so we can attach a name to a face in case of trouble."

"Same thing as my bank," Helen said.

Yvonne made some more clicking sounds on her keyboard. Then she smiled. "Yes, I have a nice picture of the Morettis." She grasped her computer monitor with both hands and turned it around so it faced us. "There they are. Is that Mr. Moretti?"

"Yes, it is," Helen said. "I guess his alibi checks out.

Thank you so much for your time."

Helen noticed I was strangely quiet, almost frozen as I stared at the picture. "Come on, Jonesy. No need to take up any more of this nice lady's time."

"Yeah," I said. "Thanks for helping us out. We learned a lot. Maybe more than we had hoped."

Helen stood to leave and waited while I got up slowly.

"Let's get moving, Jonesy. I still got time to get home before *The Voice* comes on. I'm hoping that little girl from Selma, Alabama makes it to next week."

We stopped at the front desk, where I asked for my car to be brought around. The receptionist made a call and then told us to wait at the front door.

When the car arrived, a bellhop opened the front door, and Helen and I walked down the granite stairs. The parking attendant tried to hand me the keys, but I handed him a five-dollar bill and pointed at Helen. "Give them to the lady."

"What?" Helen said in surprise. "You always drive."

"Not right now. You drive."

We climbed into sedan and fastened our seat belts.

"What's wrong, Jonesy?"

"I know the woman Moretti is having the affair with."

"Well, let's go see what she knows."

"She's my wife Rachel."

Chapter 5

Helen drove me back to the police department, where she parked my sedan in its numbered parking space.

"Want to talk?" she asked.

"About what?"

She patted me on my thigh and gave me a peck on my cheek. "Good luck with whatever you decide to do tonight. If you need to talk, just give me a call, Jonesy."

After Helen turned the car over to me, I tried to drive home. My right foot shook so badly I had difficulty keeping it on the gas pedal. My forward progress was so slow several cars behind me blew their horns repeatedly. The drivers flashed their headlights and waved their arms out their windows, urging me to pull over. Eventually, I did.

I sat silently for half an hour, staring at the blood moon which filled the sky, completely distraught Rachel would cheat on me. She had kissed me goodbye this morning and had headed out the door smiling, supposedly going to work. She had seemed upbeat and happy. Why not? She was going to meet Wayne, to have him kiss her, to have him fondle her, to feel him inside her, and then to come home and cook supper as though it had been a regular day at work. When I asked, "How was work today?" Rachel would have fabricated some scenario, a lie which never happened so her secret rendezvous would go undetected. And that night, if I sought something amorous, she would have feigned an excuse, a contrivance to put me off so my fluids would not mix with the warmth of Wayne's.

I crept home, pulled into the garage, and felt myself enter the door to our kitchen. Rachel was cooking porkchops. After tears and angry accusations and wailing and sobbing, the porkchops plopped into the white plastic trash bag which lined the plastic trashcan in the cabinet under the sink. I slept uncomfortably in the guestroom.

Wednesday morning started quietly. I remembered the long conversation with Rachel the night before. In light of her recent betrayal of our matrimonial promises, we decided a trial separation was called for. I called in sick to work. Because I had more options than she did, I decided I would be the one to move out of our two-bedroom cape cod in Willow Falls. I had no idea where I would go, and no idea how I could afford to move out. But I felt I had no other option.

I felt miserable. I felt betrayed. I felt defeated. And I felt alone. I played my marriage over and over in my mind. What had I done well? What could I have done better? What little things had I done to annoy her, to drive her into the arms of another man…Wayne Moretti of all people…an ice cream salesman? The only challenge to our relationship had been the miscarriage of our child, a daughter, who departed the earth a year ago at five months of age. Maybe Rachel had never gotten over it.

I slept only two hours Tuesday night, those coming between three-thirty and five-thirty in the morning, and my sleep was fretful at best. At seven-thirty in the morning, I walked out the back door of my home, suitcase and suit bag in hand, and into the garage, where my official city vehicle, a seven-year-old sedan waited for me. I started the motor, then backed out of the garage and onto the street. I paused for a moment to look at the home Rachel and I had purchased, scraping together the down payment and praying we could continue to make the monthly mortgage payments until my next pay raise. That was four years ago. We had faced lean months together, sometimes existing on ramen noodles for several days, until my next paycheck arrived. Finally, she took a part-time job with a local doctor, where she was trained to be an MRI technician. Her paychecks had given us breathing room, the flexibility to buy better cuts of meat, to splurge on an occasional blockbuster at Movieland, and to save for an annual vacation to the Adirondacks or Cape Cod. I flipped the finger at my own front door and drove away.

There was so much to be decided and the details played over and over in my mind like a broken record. Of course, I would continue to hand over most of my monthly paycheck so Rachel and I could keep the house and so Rachel could keep her leased Hyundai Accent. After all expenses—the mortgage, insurance, power and gas, food, and credit cards—we had a little more than two hundred dollars per month to put away for special holiday functions and for our annual vacation. I knew I could not live on that. Maybe I would take a part-time job, if I could get the Chief's approval. Maybe Rachel would have to do the same, a second part-time job. I felt that would be fair, especially since it was her infidelity which had brought this new reality down upon us. But the first order of business was determining where I would live. With so little money, there was only one option: the YMCA, where I would be surrounded by the deadbeats of society, many of whom I had arrested in the past for various infractions of society's penal codes. The thought of dwelling among them was a living nightmare.

At eight-thirty in the morning, while I was sitting outside of the YMCA unsettled about renting a room there, my cell phone rang. It was Helen.

"I know you called in sick, but you've got to come in. There's been a development in the Laura Moretti case."

"I can't. I haven't showered. I'm in blue jeans and a tee shirt. I didn't sleep all night and I look like hell."

"The little girl has been found."

"Thank God. How's she doing?"

"She ain't doing nothing. Two pheasant hunters found her body by a creek out in a field near Esperance. The recovery team is bringing her in, and Dr. Foster is prepping to examine the corpse after her parents identify her. Thought you might want to come see how she died."

I started my car and drove across town to the police department. Somebody had parked illegally in my parking space, so I jotted down the license plate number and went inside to Helen's office. She was not there, so I texted her:

--*What's ur 20?*--
--*DA's. Parents r here.*--
--*Be right up*--
--*Going to ME now. Meet there.*--

I took the elevator to the basement, where I saw Helen behind a small group of people entering Dr. Foster's medical examination lab. It had to be Claiborne and the Morettis. I walked quickly down the hallway, its floors and walls covered shoulder-high in dull red tiles.

I opened the door and walked in, just as the black body bag was being unzipped.

Mrs. Moretti gasped and then nodded. Mr. Moretti turned his face away.

I looked at Helen, who motioned for me to come look at the cadaver. I stepped forward and glanced down. Laura's face was framed by the black plastic of the body bag. Her brown hair was dirty with leaves and twigs. Her skin was ghastly white, as though all the muscular structure had been removed and the skin had been pulled tight against the bone of her skull. The cartilage of her nose created a yellow line from its pointed tip to the skull. Her eyes were wide open, possibly wider than a child could open them, and her mouth was contorted, frozen in an expression of absolute fear. I had seen plenty of cadavers in my career, but her face offered the grisliest expression of horror I had ever seen. Although I was exhausted from lack of sleep, I hoped I would be able to sleep tonight without that face haunting me.

Claiborne spoke first. "The medical examiner is going to examine Laura's body to determine cause of death and to see if any evidence can be discovered that will help us identify the killer."

"Please don't damage her body," Wayne Moretti pleaded. "We'd like an open casket,"

"I'll do what I can," the ME replied, "but I can't make any guarantees."

Imogene Moretti burst into tears and pressed her face into her husband's chest. "I can't bear to look again. It must have been so terrible for her."

Wayne Moretti pointed at Claiborne. "Promise me you'll find her kidnapper. Nobody should sneak into a man's yard and steal his child."

"I was thinking the same thing, Mr. Moretti," I said. "Nobody should sneak into another man's home and steal the one thing he values the most."

Moretti looked at me for a moment and then turned his face away. He knew I had figured out whose wife was his tryst partner.

"Cancel your sick day, Jones," Claiborne ordered. "You and Martin need to solve this case as soon as possible. Every day that goes by is a day the perpetrator might strike again. We gotta put this bastard with the fishes."

"Shoot on sight?" I asked.

Claiborne gave me a look which meant, 'You know you can't do that,' but he did not say it aloud.

"We'll do everything we can, Mr. and Mrs. Moretti," Helen said. "We know you want Laura's killer brought swiftly to justice."

After leaving the ME's lab, Helen went back to her office to make some calls to the parents of Laura's Brownie friends. But I drove to Zack's Gym, where I signed up as a ten-dollar per month member. Since I still had no place to spend the night, I thought I might start working off a little of my spare tire on the exercise machines and I could shower and dress at Zack's every morning before work if I had to sleep in my car. At least it was a workable option for the short run. After signing up with Zack's, I went back to the office.

At one o'clock on the dot, I was called by the medical examiner. "I've completed my examination and thought you'd like to see what I've discovered. Bring Detective Martin with you."

"Be right down."

I stepped out of the elevator at the second floor and found my way to Helen's office. "ME's finished his examination of the Moretti girl. Want to come see what he's found?"

Helen forced a lungful of air out through her mouth. "Not sure I want to see her face again. Reminds me of a few horror movies."

Helen followed me to the elevator, shuffling her flats as she walked, losing ground against my fast pace. "Hey, slow down, Jonesy. I got a couple of questions for you."

"Like how's my love life? It sucks right now."

"Well, I did want to ask you how it went last night. I know it wasn't easy seeing Rachel standing next to Moretti on that computer screen. Nice picture of her, though."

I stopped at the elevator and punched the DOWN button. Helen caught up with me. "I heard what you said to Moretti in the ME's lab. Did you intentionally send him a message?"

"You betcha. If I ever find him alone, I'm gonna punch his lights out."

"But what about Rachel? You didn't hit her, did you?"

"No, she's still the love of my life. But she's deeply hurt me and we're separating. I moved out this morning. That's why I called in sick."

"I got a fold-out couch if you need a place to stay tonight."

"How would that look to your neighbors? It would ruin your reputation, Helen."

"Might push me up a few rungs, a nice white guy spending the night with me."

"Your neighbors might think I'm paying you. I don't think it's a good idea."

The elevator door opened. I held it and let Helen walk in first.

"Learn anything on your phone calls this morning?" I asked.

"Just what you might expect. Nobody knows anything. Everybody's mostly concerned with how Laura's kidnapping and murder is gonna affect their own daughters. And nobody's letting their daughters out of their sight."

We exited the elevator at the basement and went directly to the ME's lab. As usual, because he was barely five feet four inches tall, Dr. Foster was standing on his apple crate, continuing to examine Laura Moretti's corpse through the pink lenses in his glasses. His blue lab coat was splattered with a mixture of blood and body fluids.

"Thanks for coming down, folks," he said when we entered the lab.

"Whatcha got for us?" I asked.

"Bizarre shit." He pointed at Laura's neck. "Two big puncture wounds in her carotid arteries, one on each side. The one on the left looks a little like a vampire bite, but it's not. Somebody missed the target the first time he jabbed her. The wounds were made by a twenty-four-gauge intravenous cannula. Don't know why there were two entry points, unless it was to empty the cadaver more quickly. The victim's veins were almost completely void of blood."

"Are you saying a vampire bit her?" Helen asked.

"Not at all. Somebody put IV tubes in her carotid arteries for the purpose of draining the blood from her body."

"Who the heck would do something like that?"

Foster pulled up the bottom of the sheet which covered the cadaver. "Let me show you more…Look at her ankles."

"They're rubbed raw," I said.

"Yes. She was either dragged for a long distance or she was hung by her ankles to expedite the blood drainage, the way a hunter would hang a deer. Given her abdomen and back show no signs of dragging, I would say she was bled out like a steer in a slaughterhouse."

"Ghastly," Helen said. "What about the question Jonesy asked a minute ago…?"

"What's that?"

"Who would do something like that?"

"I did a little research. Do you know what occurred last night?"

Both Helen and I shook our heads. I wanted to say my wife and I split up, but the ME's conversation was not headed in that direction.

"Last night was a blood moon. Did either of you see it?"

"Yeah, I saw it from my car," I said. "Didn't know what it was. Didn't really pay attention to it."

"Is that when men turn into werewolves?" Helen asked.

"You're making a joke," the ME replied, "but you aren't far off. There are some cults whose members believe the blood moon is the time for human sacrifice."

"Modern cults?" I asked.

"Yes, they're mostly in Europe and Scandinavia, but a few exist in certain places in the United States. They're underground societies and they do ritual sacrifices. Most don't really sacrifice human beings, but a few…"

"Do you think we have a group like that in Willow Falls?" Helen asked.

"I'm not saying we do, but there's another possible explanation."

"What's that?" I asked.

"The UFO conspiracists believe space aliens steal cattle, then drain them of their blood and remove their sexual organs to conduct hybridization programs. Perhaps this little girl was kidnapped by space aliens…except she still has her sexual organs."

"I'm opting for something closer to home, doc," Helen replied. "Jonesy, it's time we start searching for one of those weirdo cults."

"I may have more for you in a few days," Dr. Foster said. "I've sent some of her blood to the State lab in Albany. Perhaps it will show traces of what they drugged her with. Maybe other things. I'll bring you up to speed when I get the results."

****

Still shaken by the ghastly expression on Laura Moretti's face in death, Helen and I left the department at three in the afternoon and drove to Saint Bartholomew's Roman Catholic Church on Sinclair Street, four blocks away from the Moretti's home. I had called ahead, so when I parked in front of the church, a middle-aged gentleman waved from the two giant front doors and then stepped back inside. I guessed he was Father Michael Lofton, the priest I had called an hour before so he would be expecting us.

"Guess he knows we're here," Helen said.

The afternoon air was crisp and refreshing, and our feet made crunching sounds as we walked across a layer of dried leaves covering the worn granite stairs which led to the church's entrance. The church was newer, apparently built when its original structure burned to the ground in the nineteen sixties. Some suspected arson, but there was never enough proof to drag the head priest into court at the time. Most parishioners thought it was a form of punishment when he was transferred to a smaller parish in the mountains north of Fort Edward shortly after police questioning began.

I pulled open the heavy oak door and let Helen enter before I did. Once inside, we waited for a few moments until our eyes adjusted to the dark.

Fr. Lofton shook Helen's and my hands. "Hello, hello."

He was a tall man, and uncharacteristically strong, judging by his handshake. His white hair was medium in length and was swept back over his ears. His steel blue eyes were piercing, making me think he could see into my soul, and I felt child-like guilt while standing before him. I had not been to church in several years, and I was afraid he knew it, somehow.

"Father, I'm Bart Jones and this is Helen Martin," I said.

"Ah, you were named after the saint whose name our parish carries."

"Yes, I guess I was."

"Were your parents among our parishioners?"

"I don't think so, but I'll ask my aunt. Maybe she'll know."

"Father, we're here about little Laura Moretti," Helen said, getting down to business.

"Oh, what a tragedy." He crossed himself. "May her soul find peace in our Savior's arms."

"Father, can you tell us anything about the family that might help us find her killer?"

"They are a nice family, somewhat quieter than most. Mr. Moretti always donates the ice cream for our annual church picnic in City Park. And they always meet or exceed the amount they pledge to tithe. Other than that, I don't know much."

"Do you know if the family was threatened by anybody, or do you know if the Morettis were in any sort of financial trouble?" Helen asked. "You know, like with a loan shark or somebody who might have taken out revenge on the parent by killing the child?"

"Oh, no. I can't imagine such a thing. They're model citizens. And the child was, well, an absolute joy."

"Are you aware of any cults in this area which might drain blood from a human being for sacrificial purposes?" I asked.

Fr. Lofton took one step backward and made the sign of the cross. "Mother of God, you don't suspect we have a blood-drinking cult in the city, do you?"

"If we had one, we thought you might have heard something through the ecumenical council," Helen said. "That sort of information might be shared between the clergy of the various religions in spite of differences in beliefs."

"I swear to you I would be the last person to know." Fr. Lofton paused for a moment and then gave us a stern look. He raised his right hand in the air, pointer finger extended. "If you find any of those sickos are in this city, let me know so I can warn my parish."

We promised we would, and then we said goodbye to Fr. Lofton.

In the car, Helen rolled down her window and spit

her chewing gum onto the pavement. "I think his reaction to your question about cults was a little overplayed, wouldn't you say?"

"How the heck would I know? I'm basically afraid of priests and nuns. Always have been."

Chapter 6

Four days went by before memorial and funeral services were held for young Laura Moretti. Helen and I attended the viewing and memorial services, hoping to spot someone who did not belong, someone who might be the kidnapper or murderer. We took turns kneeling and saying a prayer beside the open casket. The mortician had done well in applying makeup to Laura's face, and he had dressed her in a high collar so the puncture wounds on her neck were not visible.

I saw nobody suspicious in the crowd of friends and neighbors who had come to offer condolences to the Morettis. I nudged Helen. "I'll go ask the funeral director for a copy of the guest book signatures." It was one way I could stop my eyes from drifting to Wayne Moretti and my brain from wondering what Rachel ever saw in him.

"Are you heartless, Detective?" the funeral director replied. "It certainly is nothing you should ask the family for today. Perhaps you might approach Mr. Moretti in a few weeks, after the peak of the family's mourning has passed."

"Yeah, I guess I can wait a day…but no more."

I found Helen sitting at the end of a row of chairs and told her the funeral director's response. "No problem," she replied. "My cell phone camera already took care of that problem."

"Good thinking."

"That's why the DA put a woman on the job, Jonesy."

We skipped the funeral mass at St. Bartholomew's Roman Catholic Church, preferring to jot down the license plate numbers of attendees and, again, to look for someone who simply did not belong. Nothing raised our suspicions.

As the mourners lined up outside the church for the procession to the cemetery where the interment rites would be delivered, Helen and I stayed at the very back of the procession and did not put a small funeral flag on the hood of my car. Instead, we followed the cluster of cars from one hundred yards back, once again watching for someone suspicious to join the procession. When the procession entered the cemetery, we held back, idling five rows away.

After twenty minutes, we watched mourners place flowers on top of the casket, and then the casket was lowered into the grave. Mr. and Mrs. Moretti stepped forward and threw handfuls of dirt into the grave, the priest raised his hand in a final blessing, and the crowd began dispersing. It was then I noticed a black four-door BMW parked outside the cemetery walls. A woman was seated in it, dressed in a black hat and sunglasses, taking pictures of the burial through the open window. I could not make out the license plate number.

"Strange someone would do that," Helen said.

"Let's go," I said.

I put my car into DRIVE and followed the winding cemetery pathway toward the exit, negotiating the curves as quickly as I could without drawing too much attention to my car. At the same time, the BMW lurched forward and turned left at the first stoplight.

"We've been spotted," Helen said. "So much for stealthy police work."

I exited the cemetery and turned right. At the first intersection, I took a quick left onto Lincoln Avenue, hoping to catch the BMW. It shouldn't have been more than three blocks away. Helen put a flashing blue light on the sedan's dashboard, and I hit my horn as I entered each intersection, weaving through the vehicles and pedestrians who stopped to let me pass. Two blocks ahead, a black BMW came to a stop at the red light. I hurried up to it and then screeched to a stop behind it. I jumped out and ran to the driver's door.

When I knocked on her side window, the driver looked at me in surprise. She rolled down her window, but only two inches. Her face showed fear. "What do you want?"

"Weren't you just outside of St. Anthony's Cemetery taking photos?"

"No, I'm test driving this car."

I could see she was not wearing black, and there was no hat in the car. "Sorry, ma'am. Wrong Beemer."

I hurried back to my Sedan, slammed the car into DRIVE, and drove several more blocks.

"Probably took a side street," Helen said.

I took a left and swerved between cars as I sought any black BMW.

Helen pointed to the opposite lane. "There's one up ahead." It was coming toward us. The driver was a young man with long hair, wearing a green tee shirt.

"Wrong gender and in his parents' car," I said.

"Probably down here to score some drugs or strike a deal with a prostitute," Helen said.

I turned left again and flew down four blocks before

I saw another black BMW. I hit my horn and pulled to a stop beside the Model M6. Helen and I hopped out. I went to the driver's side door, and Helen went to the opposite side. Its windows were tinted, and we couldn't see who was inside. I flashed my badge and made a motion for the driver to lower his window.

A moment later, the driver's side window slowly descended, revealing a gentleman, probably in his late fifties. He seemed unflustered by the sudden interest in his car.

"Can I help you?" he asked calmly.

"Yeah. Please roll down the passenger side window so my partner can hear what we're saying."

"Certainly." The man pressed a button on his console and the passenger side window slowly descended. He nodded to Helen. "Good day, Officer."

"I'm police Detective Jones and to your right is Detective Martin. A BMW fitting the description of yours was involved in suspicious behavior across the street from St. Anthony's Cemetery. Have you driven down there recently?"

"Why, no. I've just been driving the streets looking for real estate for sale by owner. I'm always on the lookout for properties I can fix up and flip."

"I see you have a camera in your car," Helen said.

The man turned his head to face her. "Why, yes, to take pictures of properties I might be interested in purchasing."

He lifted a digital camera from the passenger seat, turned it on, and showed Helen the first three pictures on his two-inch square screen."

"Yup, they're houses," she told me.

"And a few buildings, too. Want to see them?" the

man asked.

"That's okay," I replied.

"Would you happen to have seen a vehicle similar to yours being driven by a woman wearing a black hat?" I asked.

"Why, no. But I'll keep an eye out. Should I call you if I see her?"

"No, it's our job to find it. Sorry we bothered you."

"No bother whatsoever. In fact, if you hadn't stopped me, I'd have driven right by that small brownstone right over there."

I turned. Behind me was a dilapidated three-story brownstone with a hand-scrawled sign in its left front window: FOR SALE BY OWNER. The gentleman raised his camera and took three quick pictures.

Back in my car, Helen removed the flashing blue light from the dashboard. "Something I don't like about that guy," she said. "It was like he was expecting us or something."

"Yeah, like he enjoyed playing with us. Almost taunting us."

"Think we should haul him in and ruin his afternoon by playing 'fifty questions'?"

"We got nothing to charge him with except 'suspicious behavior.' And if he has a good lawyer, we could both find ourselves with a letter in our file."

"Yeah. But I took a photo of his license plate. I'm going do some snooping about him. I don't like him."

Chapter 7

Helen sat at her desk with a tuna salad sandwich, a bag of Cape Cod potato chips, and a diet Pepsi. She turned on her computer. "Here goes nothing. This thing is slower than whale poop."

The department's computer network was old school and needed updating, but city funding always seemed to target other needs, like whatever new social program would help drive more state funding in the city's direction. And, in light of the "Defund the Police" protests which had been capturing national attention, she knew no new funding of police infrastructure would be coming the department's way. In fact, with recent rumors about police layoffs, she hoped her position would not be cut because she didn't know what other form of employment she could possibly enjoy.

Helen moved her cursor to the Google search bar and typed in "bloodless body." Her computer screen changed when the results arrived, but they were not what she had hoped for. Instead, Google had pulled up articles about "bloodless surgery" and "hemodilution," a surgical process in which blood is removed from a patient shortly after he receives anesthesia.

She returned to the search bar and typed in "victim found with no blood." Her computer went to work again. The results were more promising. One described the recent demise of a woman in Hartford, Connecticut, who was found dead in her bathtub. Her body had been stabbed multiple times, and she had apparently bled to death. It was gruesome, but not close to the details surrounding Laura Moretti's death.

Another article told of five bulls a rancher found dead, mutilated, and bloodless in Salem, Oregon. Each animal's tongue and sex organs had been surgically removed, but there was no evidence to indicate how the bulls died. Not even any signs of struggle.

"This is what the Medical Examiner was talking about," Helen muttered, "space aliens killing animals and draining them of their blood. This is some weird shit."

However, a third article described the death of Lilly Lindestrom, a Swedish prostitute who was found dead in her apartment in the 1930's with her clothes neatly folded beside her. Also found was a ladle, presumably used by her murderer to drink her blood. The local press nicknamed her killer "the Atlas Vampire."

"Now we're getting somewhere," Helen said, jotting down notes and sending a copy of the article to her computer printer. "Jonesy will be interested in this one."

Her desk phone rang.

"Martin here."

"This is Dr. Foster. I have the results of the blood analysis done on the Moretti girl. Can you and Detective Jones come down?"

"Yeah. One of us will be there in a few minutes. Don't leave on us."

Helen called me.

"Did you get a call from the ME?" she asked.

"Nope."

"I guess he called me for some reason instead of

you. The results of the blood analysis are in. Thought I'd go down and see what he's learned. You coming?"

"Yeah. I'll meet you in the basement."

When Helen's elevator door opened in the basement, I was standing in the hallway waiting for her. "You look more rested today," she said. "Those bags are gone from beneath your eyes and your shirt is pressed."

"What took you so long?" I asked.

"Stopped by the ladies' room."

"Did the ME give you any indication of what the report says?"

"Not an inkling. We're both going to hear it from the dude firsthand."

We walked down the hallway, and I opened the door to the Medical Examiner's lab so Helen could walk in first. Dr. Foster was seated at his desk on the left side of the room.

"Come in, come in," he said, almost anxious to relate the discoveries in Laura Moretti's blood. "I have some interesting stuff to share with you."

"I'm all ears," I said.

"Her blood shows all the signs of good nutrition. Her red and white cell counts are appropriate for someone her age."

I drummed my fingers on the ME's desk. "What's the good stuff?"

"Remarkably, her adrenaline and adrenochrome levels are off the chart."

"What does that mean, doctor?" Helen asked.

"There is no doubt she was frightened to death."

"I'm sure she was scared. She had been kidnapped," I said.

"No, you're not catching my drift," the doctor said.

"She was absolutely frightened so badly that she died from fear."

"My god," Helen said. "That's horrible."

"Yes, it would be a horrible death for anyone to suffer."

"Where does that leave us, doc?" I asked.

"I don't want to do your work for you, but I've done a little research since receiving this report this morning. I think you should be looking for a cult. Remember what I told you about the blood moon? It all just ties together. I think the little girl might have been sacrificed to the blood moon by a cult of people who drink human blood. They may be practicing vampires. And I don't mean the type you find in the movies. I mean people who enjoy drinking blood for sport or ritual. The blood of a young virgin would be highly valued, especially if it was full of adrenochrome and adrenaline which would give them a high."

"Sick bastards," Helen muttered.

"My thoughts exactly, Detective Martin. Your investigation may uncover a local 'Pizzagate.'"

****

Helen's phone rang at two in the afternoon. She had been online reading about 'Pizzagate' and decided the medical examiner had been making a casual reference to groups of people who organize to sexually abuse children.

"Martin here," she said.

"Detective Martin, this is Nadine in Technical Support Services. We ran that plate you asked about. Just wanted you to know we emailed you the results."

"Thanks, Nadine. How's your father?"

"Better, thank you. Doctor says he'll be able to walk

without a walker by the end of the week. Then he'll use a cane for a while. He's healing much faster than I thought he would. Knee replacement surgery has come a long way since it first started."

"Yeah, I guess it has. Just the thought of somebody sawing through my leg bone gives me the willies, but I guess if I were knocked out, it wouldn't make much difference until I woke up."

"Daddy said it was easier than having a tooth pulled, especially since they got better pain medicine nowadays."

"Well, give him my best when you see him. Tell him to get better quickly so he can make me some more of those delicious buckwheat cakes."

"Will do, Helen. Bye now."

Helen checked her email and opened the results of the license plate search:
--MSS-002
HORACE MODERN, owner
MODERN SCIENTIFIC SUPPLY
BALLSTON AVENUE
WILLOW FALLS, NY--

She called me. "Didn't Modern say he was some kind of real estate developer?" she asked. "That was a crock of manure. He owns a scientific supply company, whatever that is."

I met Helen at her car, and she drove us over to Modern Scientific Supply on the north end of town. It was a retrofitted three-story red brick middle school on the fringe of the city, situated on a huge lot with a football field of grass to mow each week during warm weather. We parked beside ten cars in what might have been the teachers' parking back in the school days, and then we walked into the building. A security guard greeted us and asked us to sign in. We jotted down our names and time of arrival and then asked to see the owner of Modern Scientific. The guard called someone and within a minute a door to our left opened. Out walked Horace Modern, looking as chipper as he did the day we stopped him for questioning. He was dressed in black slacks and a white shirt but wore no tie or suitcoat. His face bore a wide grin.

"Oh, I remember you. How are you officers? Did you catch the bad guy?"

"Maybe," I said.

"We need to talk," Helen said.

"Certainly. Please follow me into my office."

Modern turned and escorted us through the doors which led to administrative offices. "Coffee?" he asked.

"Not while we're on duty," I replied.

Modern's office was a converted classroom, filled with sunlight from the tall windows which once brightened students' lives. The walls were painted the same color as his khaki pants and were adorned with aboriginal artwork, perhaps from Australia or Africa. I didn't know which. His desk sat at the front of the room, as a teacher's would, but where one would expect student desks, he had fashioned a living room with two sofas and half a dozen comfy chairs.

"Thank you," Modern replied. "I do most of my work at the desk, but the casual area is where I hold staff meetings and entertain guests, such as yourselves." He motioned to one of the sofas. "Please sit and let's chat."

'Chat?' I wondered. He was treating us like old friends rather than police officers pursuing the killer of a child. But, I suppose, he didn't know that.

Helen and I sat on a sofa which would hold three people comfortably, and Modern sat opposite us in a recliner.

Helen is better at interviewing than I am. She just eases into the questions without alarming the person of interest. "Mr. Modern," she began, "I thought you told us you were a real estate developer, but here you are the owner of a science company."

"Yes, when we spoke, I was pursuing real estate offered for sale by owner. For me, real estate is a part-time hobby, something I do after hours and on weekends. The day you stopped me was my day off. Even company owners are permitted a day off, aren't we?"

"How many homes have you purchased thus far?" I asked.

Modern shuffled in his chair and crossed his legs. "So far, I have to admit I haven't purchased any, but if you've checked public records, you already know that. I've been watching some of those television shows where people purchase old homes and then rehab them either for habitation or sale. I want to try my hand at it. You know, they make it seem so easy, but every city has special zoning and construction codes which can cause a person to lose his shirt if he's not careful. I'm still trying to find just the right property here in Willow Falls to make the investment worthwhile."

"Exactly what does Modern Science do?" Helen asked.

"Modern Scientific Supply," Modern said, correcting Helen. "We supply scientific equipment and specimens to high schools and colleges around the world for use in their science classrooms and laboratories. Occasionally, we secure a governmental contract for specific supplies, but mostly we serve schools and colleges."

"How's business?" I asked.

"It was great until COVID hit, although recently we have produced individualized experiment packets for kids who are studying biology, physics, or chemistry at home. Sales of those packets are increasing rapidly. Schools order a certain number of packets, and we distribute them directly to students at their home addresses as given to us by the schools. It keeps us hopping as the demand increases. I mean, can you imagine shipping thousands of pickled frogs to individual homes so kids can dissect them on their kitchen counters? We have to juggle the manufacturing of packets with shipping, so each student receives his packet prior to the lesson's start date. The post office sometimes can be undependable, you know."

"I thought schools were using digital dissections nowadays," Helen said.

"Yes, many are. But a lot of kids don't have access to computers or the internet. We fill in the gap wherever there's need. Besides, there's nothing quite as exciting as actually feeling a scalpel cut into the flesh of a frog's abdomen or a sheep's eyeball. Wouldn't you agree?"

"I can't imagine," Helen replied with a look of disgust.

Modern stood and motioned for us to do the same. "Come, let me show you our production facilities."

We walked out of his office and down the hallway to a newly installed elevator, one large enough to hold ten people comfortably. I figured it set him back a bundle.

At the top of the building, we stepped out onto the

third floor. Modern escorted us room-by-room into labs where scientific supplies were being raised or cultivated. The walls had been removed from many adjoining classrooms so that two or three classrooms had been converted into one large space for specific functions. Inside each space, shelving permitted the doubling and tripling of floor space. In one such space, technicians were raising white laboratory mice for use as live experimental subjects. It smelled strongly of cedar chips. In another, tadpoles were being hatched into bullfrogs. In others, South American tree frogs were housed in glass aquariums with signs which boldly warned, "DO NOT TOUCH." In yet others, nightcrawlers, goldfish, and leeches were being raised by the tens of thousands for school children to dissect.

We turned down another wing of the building and were shown labs where certain fungi were being grown. In others, Modern rattled off the names of plant species I had not heard since high school biology -- angiosperms, liverworts, mosses, lichens, Marchantia, and sphagnum.

More gross biological stuff was grown on the second floor—planaria, Platyhelminthes, and common fleas, which were used for genetic studies. The second floor also contained rooms full of powdered and liquid chemicals, jars and beakers, dissection kits, and supplies used for time, rate, and motion experiments in physics. Another wing contained live snakes, lizards, and spiders -- all specimens for schools and colleges to exhibit for educational purposes.

Before we rode the elevator to the first floor, Helen gasped when she looked through a glass door. "Are those really full skeletons or are they fake?"

"Let me assure you they're real, although imported,"

Modern said. "It is common for men and women in eastern countries to sell their body parts upon death as a means of providing their families with the equivalent of a good life insurance policy here in the USA. Why, a body can fetch as much as six or seven hundred dollars in fair trade."

"Is that all?" Helen asked.

"In countries where the average family lives on less than four hundred dollars per year, it's a small fortune," Modern replied. "In fact, we have no difficulty in obtaining body parts from the East. They're just dying to sell us their bodies. Ha. Ha. Ha."

Neither Helen nor I laughed at his tasteless joke.

The four wings of the first floor contained rooms where special orders were processed and prepared for shipping. Clusters of workers filled, vacuum-sealed, and affixed an individualized mailing label to each order. Packages were then placed into large bins for shipping by USPS, UPS, or FedEx handlers who arrived twice per day at the facility's back door loading docks.

Modern escorted us past his office and the security guard and to the front door. "If you officers have no further questions, you can see I have a business to run."

"Well, we thank you for your time, Mr. Modern," Helen said.

"Yeah," I replied, "you have some weird stuff, but I guess it's all necessary for the education of our kids." I paused for a moment. "Give us a call when you buy your first 'For Sale By Owner.' I'd like to see how a renovation takes place."

Modern gave me a look of annoyance and then smiled. "You can count on it."

We walked out the front door and climbed back into

Helen's Hyundai. As she drove us back toward the department, Helen opened up. "There's something about Modern that gives me the creeps. He's friendly enough on the outside, but he's not altogether forthcoming. We gotta figure out what he's hiding."

"Yeah, I agree. He's some kind of slimeball. I don't trust him."

"Think he might have been the woman who you saw taking pictures at the cemetery?"

"Possibly. We never searched his car. We just saw he had a camera with pictures of brownstones."

"If he was wearing a wig, he had plenty of time to dispose of it."

"Yeah, and he had control of the camera and only showed us what he wanted us to see. No telling if the pictures of the burial were on there, too."

"We're a couple of pretty lousy detectives. Should have thought of all this stuff when we were questioning him at the traffic stop."

"I haven't been thinking too clearly."

"I know. That shit with your wife and Moretti would screw up anybody's analytical thinking."

"Tell me about it."

Chapter 8

Helen shut down her computer and rubbed her neck. She had been searching through the results Google had retrieved on her search for "blood drinking cults." Google had found more than she had anticipated, and she had compiled a small notebook of possibilities.

She called me. "How's your search going, Jonesy?"

"Just getting started. How about you?"

"I'm done for now. Gotta get away from the virtual world. I'm maybe going to take a couple of aspirins."

"What did you learn? Anything new?"

"Well, the big thing is this: The ME has us looking for cults, but blood eaters don't necessarily belong to a cult. Some people have a physiological or psychological need for blood and their friends allow themselves to be cut so the needy ones can suck a few mouthfuls. They call it 'feeding'."

I shook my head. "That's an ugly picture. If I knew a friendly tape worm was hungry, I don't care how good a friend he was, I don't think I'd swallow him just so he could find a home and good meal in my intestines. That feeding stuff you described is not something I'd do for anyone, Helen. Not even for you."

"I know. It's bad enough we girls always got some guy trying to hang off us, wanting to get his jollies, you know? Can you imagine some dude hanging around just so he can cut you and suck your blood? Gives me the willies."

I needed to cut the call short. "Listen, I have a couple of calls to make, and the day is starting to slip away. How about we debrief over dinner? Maybe at the fish place you like?"

"Sure. Six o'clock-ish?"

"Yeah, six o'clock…fish. You drive."

I went back to my work looking for local people who had disappeared mysteriously. I assumed if there was, indeed, a cult operating locally, then more than one person, adult or child, would have gone missing or would have been found drained of blood. After half an hour of fruitless searching, I shut down my CPU and picked up my desk phone.

My strategy was to call friends in the "big three," the neighboring cities of Albany, Schenectady, and Troy. From there, I would branch out to smaller cities, Saratoga Springs, Amsterdam, and Glens Falls. I began each call like this:

"Hey, this is Bart Jones from Willow Falls. Yeah, it's been a long time. I'm working on a case, and I need your help. Have you had any cadavers show up with their bodies drained of blood? Yeah, like a vampire sucked them dry…"

The responses to my first two calls were speculative. In Albany and Troy my friends had heard rumblings of such things, but they had no specifics. They were not even sure if the rumors were about murders in their own cities or in others nearby.

But, when I called Schenectady, Detective Eric Petronis was quick to reply, "Yeah, we've had two like that in the past eighteen months. One was a kid…a ten-year old boy. And the other was a young woman, maybe in her late twenties. Why are you asking?"

"We've just had our first case…a little girl. I'm trying to find similarities. Can you share some investigative details?"

"Yeah, I can. I'll have the files photocopied and someone here will call you when they're ready for pickup."

"Super. I appreciate it."

"Where was yours found?" Petronis asked.

"She lives here in Willow Falls and was kidnapped from her own back yard. Her body was discovered by a couple of hunters over near Esperance."

"So, the perp has stalked victims in Schenectady and Willow Falls. Maybe he's a Schenectady resident who's tired of shopping in his own back yard, or maybe he's from Troy or Albany and has just started shopping in a second market. Your guess is as good as mine. But if he's planning on taking two in each market, then you're gonna lose another one within the next few months, and then he's gonna move on to a new supermarket."

****

Helen was in the lounge during her break, sipping a cup of hot coffee with Stanley Wolff, a guard in the department's basement holding cells. Stan was a tall black man with white hair and the bulging stomach shared by many men in their early sixties. His uniform shirt was faded from too many cycles in his wife's washing machine and his tie was stained, probably from coffee or ketchup or both.

Helen handed him a napkin. "You got powdered sugar on your lips, Stanley."

He took the napkin and clumsily wiped his mouth with his large right hand. Then he held up a white paper bag with the Willow Falls Bakery logo. "You want one? They're pretty good...and my wife's favorites. I got two left."

"Thanks, but no. Don't want any of that sugar settling on my new red blouse. Costs almost as much to clean it as it did to buy it. Got it on sale at Penney's clearance rack."

Stan took another bite of donut, then slurped his coffee. "You must be going out to interview people, huh? Nobody dresses to the nines if they're staying here all day. Got an interesting case?"

Helen sipped her coffee and then wiped her lips. "Weird case, maybe. Blood drinkers."

Stan perked up. "Blood drinkers? Like those weirdos in Hollywood? Saw a thing on them a couple of months back. Dateline, I think. Strange dudes."

"Yeah. Strange for around here, anyway. Been reading up on cults, looking for any signs which might point to a problem here in Willow Falls. Maybe Satanic types."

"Say, I got a little lady you might be interested in, Helen. She was booked two days ago for killing a dog, but she hasn't made bail yet. Don't think she's been assigned an attorney either. Want to meet her?"

"I guess so. It might be nice to get away from the internet for a while."

They finished their coffees and then rode the elevator to the basement. Stan opened two locked doors before they reached the cell block. When they walked past the cells, some of the men let out wolf whistles and cat calls. Stan rapped his billy club on a cell door. "Shut up, gentlemen. We have a lady in our presence. Keep up this commotion and you'll answer to me."

The whistles continued until Stan and Helen had passed through the men's cellblock and entered a third door beyond which the women were held.

"Fewer cells," Helen noted.

"Fewer women give us problems. Mostly hookers and shoplifters. Maybe an occasional child or spouse abuser. That's all." He stopped at a cell and pointed to an old woman who could have been dressed for Halloween. She was wearing a dirty denim A-line skirt, a long-sleeved tee-shirt and a knitted vest with deep pockets. Her hair was brown, streaked with gray and completely disheveled. Her eyes were transfixed on something she could see in her mind.

"Then there's Miss Appleton," Stan said, "booked for killing a dog. Maybe for drinking its blood."

Helen tapped lightly on the cell. "Hi, Miss Appleton. My name is Helen. I have a few questions to ask you. Can we talk?"

Ms. Appleton's eyes crossed and then straightened. She seemed to return to the present and recognized she was in a cell. She turned toward Helen. "What do you want, Missy?"

"I'm just working on a case which I don't believe involves you, but I'm wondering if you can help me?"

"You got twenty-five thousand dollars you can lend me for bail?"

Helen smiled. "If I had twenty-five thousand dollars, I'd probably be on vacation in Hawaii."

"Figures…"

"Miss Appleton, do you know why you were arrested?"

"They say I killed a dog. I might have and I might not have. I need to talk to a lawyer before I answer a question like that. Just 'cause I'm old doesn't mean I don't know my rights."

"Well, would you tell me about the dog?"

"Pit bull. Mostly friendly, I guess. But his owner let him run loose."

Miss Appleton sighed and sat down on the steel cot in her cell. When she did, Helen saw satanic symbols had been scratched into the concrete floor of the cell, and on the wall above the cot.

"Interesting artwork. Yours?"

Miss Appleton nodded her head.

"How'd you do it? They usually don't give prisoners anything to write with."

Miss Appleton held up a small piece of concrete. "Found this under the bed. Must have fallen out of the wall over there." She pointed to a missing chunk of concrete wall at the foot of the cot.

"What's the purpose of the symbols?"

"The star within the circle fends off evil spirits, and believe me, there's plenty of them in this place. The little figures of men with spears protect me from those spirits that sneak around the star."

Helen nodded. "Are they voodoo symbols?"

"They're hex signs, taught to me by the Queen from England."

"The Queen of England? Do you mean Queen Elizabeth?"

"I told you she was bonkers," Stan mumbled.

"No," Miss Appleton said, "I mean the Queen from England. And that's all I'm saying about that."

Helen went back to the subject of the dog. "So, tell me more about the dog."

"Like I said, Mr. Brock just let him run free. I asked

him to chain the dog or else walk him on a leash, but he never did. He said it was a dog's God-given right to run free. So, I told him how his dog kept pooping in my yard. Big poops. Smelly poops. But he said to me, 'It's a dog's God-given right to poop where he wants to.'"

She cleared her throat, stood, and filled a paper cup with pale yellow water from the small steel sink in her cell. After drinking it, she returned to her bunk.

"So that damn dog came onto my porch and annoyed my cats and then pooped on my door mat. I didn't see it at first, so I stepped in it. I got so angry I went and got myself a boning knife and a hotdog. I offered the dog a piece of hotdog and when he came up to me and started eating it, I slit his throat."

"Pretty miserable death, don't you think?" Stan asked.

Miss Appleton looked at Stan. "I'm not talking to you, Officer." Then she continued her story. "So, I cut off the dog's head and left it on Mr. Brock's doorstep. Pretty soon he came running over to my porch screaming all sorts of obscenities and claiming I was a murderer and animal abuser. I just told him I had a God-given right to protect my cats and my property from marauders. And well, here I am."

"They say you drank some of the dog's blood, Miss Appleton," Stan said.

"Now if I did, wouldn't that be something? Woohoo! I can see the headlines now: 'A blood sucking vampire lady' in Willow Falls. I'd never be able to go home 'cause my neighbors would burn me out."

Stan shrugged his shoulders. "I guess you have a point."

"You ever drunk any blood?" she asked Helen.

Then, she pointed at Stan. "I know he hasn't. His belly is a testament to how many beers he's had."

"No," Helen replied, "but I've heard some people in Willow Falls do. Do you know any of them?"

"Maybe I do and maybe I don't. But if I were you, and I wanted to find out the answer to that question, I wouldn't waste my time with crazy old ladies who find their way to jail. I'd go hang around the Crystal Cantor Shoppe."

"Isn't that some kind of sex toy operation?" Helen asked. "I've driven by it, but I've never gone in."

"I expect you ought to go inside and see what's for sale, unless you're looking for a French Tickler. They don't sell items of that type in there."

"And where might I find the Queen from England?" Helen asked.

"I've said all I'm going to say about her."

Miss Appleton laid down on her cot and pulled its single green blanket to her chin. "I'd appreciate any help you can give me toward getting bail."

"I'll see what I can do," Helen replied.

They walked back through the men's holding area. "Are you really going to help that old crazy woman?" Stan asked.

Helen raised her right hand for Stan to see. Her fingers were crossed.

Chapter 9

As I had promised her, Helen and I went to dinner at Captain Mambo's, a white building with its name painted in oceanic blue across its door and its one picture window. Of course, it was in a section of town which frowned on white people frequenting the establishment. I suffered through the stares from the clientele, but the staff did not seem to mind my being there. I figured they had seen me often enough, always coming in with Helen, and my money was as good as anybody's. I ate my usual fried shrimp platter and Helen opted for fried catfish with collards and cornbread. I don't think they served anything that wasn't fried.

After dinner we did ice cream sundaes at Carvel and then she dropped me off behind my car at the police department.

"See you at ten tomorrow morning so we can go scope out the voodoo place," I said.

"Sleep tight, Jonesy. Don't let the bed bugs bite," she replied.

Hell, I was still sleeping at the Y and showering at Zack's Gym. She might have been right about the bed bugs.

The next morning, I had coffee while checking my mail and then met Helen beside my car in the parking lot. We were both dressed in plainclothes, though we were packing. I drove while Helen pointed which way to turn.

We turned onto Farley Street about a block from the Crystal Cantor Shoppe at ten fifteen. A black BMW matching the one driven by Horace Modern had just pulled out of a parking space and was driving away. We could not see the license plate number. I pulled into the empty space and we both climbed out.

The building was covered in white aluminum siding, except for its glass showcase alcove where a stone façade rose from the ground to knee level. Inside the showcase were crystals of assorted colors, books on magic and witchcraft, jars of concoctions—should I say 'potions'?—and candles and aroma therapy kits.

A little bell jingled when I opened the door. I held the door for Helen, and she walked in before me. Helen and I browsed the shelves until the proprietor asked, "May I help you folks?"

He was a thin man with a balding head and a bushy ponytail that indicated he once had a full head of brown hair. His moustache was thin and cut short. And his glasses were round wire-rimmed, like John Lennon wore.

"We're new in town…just browsing," I replied.

He nodded. "Where are you from?"

"Salem," I lied. "Salem, Oregon."

"Oh, I had hoped you were from Massachusetts."

"Everybody we meet around here seems to hope that." I picked up a jar of bee pollen, examined it, and then set it back on the shelf. "Didn't I just see Horace Modern leave here?"

"Why, yes. Do you know Mr. Modern?"

"Yes. In fact, Helen here and I toured his facility just the other day. Interesting place. Ever been there?"

"Oh, many times. He and I do business together."

"Really? I'll have to mention we met you when I see him next. In what sort of business do you partner with him?"

"Oh, we're not business partners. He's one of my suppliers. Brilliant man, you know. He went to Yale…was a member of Skull and Bones."

"That's interesting…I suppose you purchase herbs and fungi from him. It would be good fresh stuff for your clientele."

The proprietor pointed at a tank with a dozen or more colorful frogs in it. "All of that and even South American tree frogs. They're very popular, you know."

The colors of the frogs were fascinating, a brilliant green back with a bleached white belly and large black eyes. I opened the lid and reached in to touch one.

"Stop!" the proprietor warned. "They're deadly poisonous. They excrete kambo, a substance forty times more powerful than morphine. If you touch one and then touch your face anywhere near your eyes, you'll go blind."

I pulled my hand out of the aquarium and dropped its lid shut. "Tell me more about these toads. Isn't it against the law to sell such dangerous creatures?"

"It's only against the law to import them from South America. However, Horace breeds them here in Willow Falls, so they're a domestic product and bypass any importation laws. And I don't sell them to children. They're for sale to adults only."

"Do you sell many of them?" Helen asked. "I don't think I'd want something so poisonous in my home."

"Actually, they fly out of here. They're very popular among the college set and yuppies like yourselves."

"And why would that be?" I asked.

"I assume you still smoke marijuana. Most of us do. But most of us don't use cocaine or heroin because they could interfere with our professional lives. The risks of arrest are too great. However, if you rub the back of a tree toad with a rolling paper and then chew it and swallow it, you get a dreamlike rush like LSD. It lasts for only ten minutes. It's safe, quick, and there are no aftereffects. And no bad trips," he emphasized.

"No shit?" I said.

Helen slid her arm beneath mine and took my hand. "Will you buy me one, sweetheart? It sounds like it could be fun."

"How much are they?" I asked.

"Sixty-nine ninety-five each, and there's a twenty-five-dollar charge for the aquarium and a dozen meal worms to feed it. Two meal worms per day at suppertime. And I'll throw in a forked plastic log for the toad to sit on."

"Wrap up two of those little buggers," I said.

"And a buck and a half for a package of rolling papers?" he asked.

"Yeah, why not? We usually use a bong."

The proprietor began collecting our stuff -- a ten-gallon aquarium with screen lid, two foam containers of meal worms in sawdust, a plastic tree branch, and a package of rolling papers. I handed him my credit card and he rang up the sale. Then he inserted the plastic log into the aquarium and placed two frogs into it. Of course, he was wearing rubber gloves. He snapped the lid shut.

"I think this is the beginning of a long friendship between us," the proprietor said. "My name is Billy Travis, Mr. Jones."

I tilted my head and squinted.

"Your name is on your credit card."

Helen seemed interested in a large full-color postcard which was pinned to a bulletin board near the cash register. "What's this Halloween party on October 31, Billy? It looks interesting…"

"It's an annual event held at the Odd Fellows Lodge in Schenectady. This will be its sixth year. It draws all sorts of interesting people like yourselves from around the Capital District—even some members of the Willow Falls Druid Society. You'd probably enjoy it. Tickets are only fifty dollars each and it includes dinner, drinks, and entertainment."

Helen turned to me. "Druid Society? Why don't we go, honey? Maybe we'll meet some people we have something in common with."

I looked at Billy.

"I just happen to have a few tickets left," he said, "if you'd like to purchase them today. I wouldn't wait too long."

I nodded and handed him my credit card again.

"Don't forget to wear costumes," he said. "For the Druid Society and others who believe Mother Earth is a living being on whom we are merely parasites, October 31 is our Christmas."

****

When we got back to work, I put the aquarium with its two iridescent toads on my desk. Then I wrote a requisition for the Department to reimburse all my recent credit card expenses as part of the Laura Moretti investigation. I hoped the chief would not disallow them.

At noon, my phone rang. It was Joey Astor, a patrolman whose beat was on the west side of town.

"Heard you been sleeping in your car, Jonesy."

"Yeah and sometimes at the Y," I said. I was a little embarrassed that word of my separation and living predicament was getting around.

"Well, I got an option for you to consider."

"Shoot."

"My father-in-law just went into a nursing home. He's got a place out in Mariaville. It's too late in the year to try to fix it up and sell it. We'll do that in the spring. The wife and I thought maybe you'd consider living there...rent free. We just want someone in it so kids don't break in during the winter to drink or screw. All we ask is you pay the utility bills and keep the propane tank filled so the heater and stove work."

"Sounds pretty good. Can we go see it after work?"

"Yeah. Listen, Jones, I gotta warn you it's no palace. I mean, an old man has been living in it by himself since his wife died three years ago. He never lifted a finger to clean it or to repair damages. But it's gotta be a hell of a lot better than the back seat of a city sedan."

We decided to meet out front at five and drive to Mariaville in two separate cars.

****

Joey Astor was a nice guy, like most patrolmen I know. He had been a defensive lineman on the Lincoln High School football team and had graduated in the middle of his class. Then he attended community college for two years, majoring in Police Science. With a brand new associates degree, he was accepted into the local Police Academy and immediately after graduation started working for Willow Falls Police Department.

He married his high school sweetheart, Rosemarie Hurley, and they had three kids over the first five years of marriage. Twenty-six years later he was four years from his retirement goal. His eldest son was now a fireman in Schenectady and his only daughter was an LPN at a hospital in Amsterdam. His youngest son had just enlisted in the Marines and was headed to boot camp in a week or two.

I followed Joey to Mariaville. He pulled into a gravel parking space in front of a bungalow nestled fifty feet from Mariaville Lake, a small recreational lake located eighteen miles west of Willow Falls. Most of its shoreline was dotted with older vacation homes which had been stick-built in the mid-fifties from empty factory shipping crates. Most were old and looked older than their age, although about a third had been updated to meet modern electric and construction codes.

Joey's father-in-law's "camp," as small lake houses are called in upstate New York, was one of the older ones, although recently it had been updated with insulation to allow him to live there over the winter. We brushed away a spider's web and walked in. It was one story with a great room, a kitchen, two bedrooms, and a single bath. The twin beds in one room had been made, although I did not know how long ago. The bed in the master bedroom looked like it had not been made in over a year. In the living room, the lakeside wall sported a sliding glass door which opened to a deck eighteen inches off the ground. The kitchen included a small refrigerator and a three-burner propane stove. The cabinets were white metal pitted with hundreds of small rust spots and the drawer pulls were pitted chrome. The green vinyl tile floor had not been swept or vacuumed in God knows how long, but for a guy like me, it was a piece of heaven.

"This is a great place, Joey," I said. "I'll be away

from the city and out of my car. Who could ask for more?"

Joey handed me the keys. "Just change the electric and propane into your name and it's yours until spring."

"Thanks, Joey. Give my best to Rosemarie."

After he left, I inspected my new digs to see if anything edible was still on the safe side of its freshness date. There was not much worth the gamble of intestinal discomfort. So, I drove across the bridge to the west side of the lake and bought a few necessities at the small convenience store that served the lake's "campers"—a can of Spam, a small jar of mayonnaise, a loaf of whole wheat bread, and a six pack of beer. Dinner was not going to be fine dining, but I had a thing for Spam. And beer.

Chapter 10

On my way into work, I stopped in a Jewish neighborhood at a family bakery specializing in New York City style products. I bought two poppy seed bagels with cream cheese. Then I headed to the PD, where I sat in front of my computer for three hours. Well, I made a couple of phone calls, too. At noon I called Helen.

"You inviting me out to lunch?" she asked.

"Maybe next time."

"Sure, Jonesy. Next time."

"You know that guy Modern?"

"How could I forget him?"

"I was doing a background check on him and couldn't find him. And nobody ever heard of him at Yale—at least not the Alumni Office or the Registrar."

"That's interesting. So, he lied to Billy What'shisname about his credentials."

"But then I found a picture of him in an online version of his company's Annual Report. Ten years ago he registered his company down in Westchester. His name was different back then, kind of like Cary Grant."

"You mean 'Archibald Leach?'" Helen asked.

"Yeah, and Natalie Portman."

"Really? What's her real name?"

"Get this...Neta-Lee Hershlag."

"Are you for real?"

"Yeah."

"If somebody stuck me with one of those names, I'd have been right down at city hall asking to change my name, too."

"You mean you didn't?"

"Kiss my fanny, Jonesy."

I thought I should get down to business. "So, Modern used to be known as Benjamin Middleton."

"I wonder why'd he go and change his moniker?" Helen asked. "We going to go ask him about it? Maybe accuse him of a few things and see how he reacts?"

"Not yet. I want to do some more background checking at Yale...see what he was into. Didn't your new boyfriend Billy say Modern was in Skull and Bones?"

"How you gonna find out something about a top-secret sorority? They don't post the names of their members."

"Fraternity."

"Yeah, whatever. I get gender confused sometimes."

"I'm going to use my highly specialized interrogation skills...and I'm going to cross my fingers."

"Well, good luck, Jonesy. Keep me apprised."

We hung up. I found the telephone number of the Dean of Student Affairs at Yale. I had not thought to call that office before now. A young woman answered and transferred me to the dean.

"How may I help you?" she asked.

"My name is Bart Jones. I'm a detective in Willow Falls, New York, and I'm conducting a background check on a former student of yours."

"I've only been here for six months, so the best I can do is to check our official records, Detective Jones. Can you give me a name and a graduation year?"

"How about the name Benjamin Middleton?"

"Do you have a graduation date?"

"Not really."

"It shouldn't make a difference anyway."

I heard her clicking away on her computer keyboard.

"Yes," she said. "He attended Yale for three years, then stopped out for a year, and then graduated with High Honors the following year. That would be 1987. His major was Biological Sciences."

"What else can you tell me about him?"

"Actually, I'm not permitted to give you further information, unless you are a potential employer, and the alumnus has given us written permission to share further information with you…Or if you have a warrant."

"Was he a member of Skull and Bones?"

"Do you mean 'The Brotherhood of Death'? That was the group's original name."

"Sure, I suppose…or the Skull and Bones."

"I have no idea. It's a very secretive organization. Membership is confidential, even for the university staff. Some members out themselves later in life, like George Bush, Sr. and Jr., but most never let the public know they're members."

"Can you give me any more information?"

"About Skull and Bones?"

"Yeah."

"Everything publicly known can be found on the internet. Search the number '322' and their old name, 'The Brotherhood of Death.' Otherwise, you'll need to find a member who is willing to share the fraternity's secrets."

Other than confirmation that Benjamin Middleton and Horace Modern were, in fact, the same person, I had struck out with the registrar at Yale. Thus, I had to consider Modern's possible membership in the Skull and Bones Society just a piece of hearsay, perhaps only wishful speculation. Still, there had to be a reason why Modern had changed his name and I decided to double down on discovering it before this case was solved.

****

Helen and I went to lunch together, this time to Ruby's Red Hots, a place where your stomach is challenged to tolerate a healthy portion of grease and habanero sauce before passing it along to your intestines for the meandering trip to the john. There, if you're lucky, your hemorrhoids won't scream too loudly as the hot stuff exits. If they do, there's always Preparation-H.

We found two stools at the far end of the thirty-foot counter.

"How ya been, honey?" the waitress asked me. "What's it been, two days?"

"I knew you liked this place, but I didn't figure you for a regular," Helen said.

I ignored her and smiled at the waitress. "Gimme two of my usual."

Helen shrugged her shoulders. "Let me have what he's having. It hasn't killed him yet and I hear it's good protection against the flu."

The waitress nodded, then she turned toward the head chef. "Gimme four weenies with sauce and onions."

She walked twenty feet to the chef's station, reaching him just as he finished scooping meat sauce onto four hotdogs, two each on white paper plates. She took them from him and delivered them to us in short order. She handed me a bottle of hot sauce, then looked at Helen. "You want a separate bottle or will you share?"

"I ain't afraid of his cooties, if that's what you mean, girl," Helen replied. She took the bottle from me and doused her hotdog with twice as much Habanero as I use.

I took the bottle from her. "Gimme your plate," I said. "Your mouth won't tolerate what you just did to that hotdog."

"What?" Helen asked. "You think a sister ain't eaten hot sauce before? I grew up on ribs and enchiladas." She took a bite. Within a second, her eyes began watering and she plopped her hotdog down onto her plate. "Did she give us water?"

I handed Helen her water and traded plates with her. Then I cut off the end of the hotdog that had burned her palate, shoved the fresh cut end into my mouth and bit off a healthy chunk. Yeah, it was hot, but it was nothing I couldn't handle…although I did ask for a second glass of water when I finished the dog.

When my water came, I took a slug. "You got plans on Halloween night, Helen?"

"Yeah, I'm going to the Odd Fellows Hall with you. I was thinking maybe we could dress up like vampires and draw some interest from the real blood suckers."

"If we do that, we might draw too much attention to ourselves. I think we need to dress in something subtle."

"I 'spose you're right. Got a better idea?"

"How about we go as cops? Dress in beat blues and nightsticks. Maybe give a few of them folks a laugh."

"Well, I don't know how subtle it would be, but it would sure save us money on costumes. I can't imagine the chief covering the cost of a couple of fancy costumes."

"Then let's do it."

****

Before leaving work, I called the *Schenectady Herald* and used my credit card to place a personal advertisement for private investigative services:

Private Investigator
12+ years of service
Police background
Reasonable rates
(518) 999-7744

I had no idea if the ad would draw any interest. I thought of it as a "feeler." Besides, I had not asked the chief to approve my taking a part-time job. But in this case, as a private eye I would not be working for somebody else, and I would not be visible to the public. You know what I mean, I would not be working at a fast-food restaurant or a gas station, where some of my former collars would see me moonlighting.

I was surprised when my phone rang at six in the morning. The man on the other end of the line had a Hispanic accent. "Are you the private dick who put the ad in the *Gazette*?"

"Yeah. How can I help you?"

"I got an employee who might be selling my private merchandise on the side. I gotta find out if he is and who he's doing business with."

"Why don't you call the cops? Employee theft is right up their alley."

"I don't want any cops. I just need to know what's going on. I'll take care of the judge and jury stuff myself."

I was intrigued. "So, give me an address where I can meet you and we can discuss my fees."

"Come to 455 Draper Street. Be here before eight."

I knew the address, but I couldn't place where I had

heard it before. "Who should I ask for?"

"It's Cabrillo Construction. My name is Diego Cisneros."

Aha! The guy whose company dug up BabyX.

"What's your name?" Cisneros asked.

"Jones. I'll be driving a tan sedan."

Chapter 11

I pulled into Cabrillo Construction at seven fifteen in the morning. I was dressed in denim but wore a tie to impress my possible client.

Cisneros met me at the door. I looked at his hand on the door jamb and saw he was still wearing the ring which identified him as a member of the Los Equis Cartel.

He raised an eyebrow when he saw my face. "Hey, I know you. You're a cop."

"Not when I'm working as a private eye," I responded. "Two different jobs."

"How can I trust you with anything confidential?"

"I'll be happy to sign a non-disclosure agreement. I can assure you that your private business with me will not be shared with the police."

"You bet your ass you'll sign a non-disclosure agreement. What's your last name? Jones? You have that strange first name."

"Bartholomew."

"Yeah, that's it."

We entered his place of business. His secretary was at her desk, trying to look busy.

"Laverne," Cisneros said, "I need you pull out our non-disclosure agreement and make a small change to Article Six."

"Yes, sir."

She turned to a filing cabinet, opened the second drawer, and thumbed through a stack of manilla folders. She opened one and handed a piece of paper to Cisneros. He scribbled a sentence or two and returned the document to her.

"Make the changes and print me two copies."

"Yes, sir."

Cisneros opened the door to his work area and escorted me to his office. The sound of saws and drills filled the air. His office looked the same: inexpensive white paneling with ten-inch-wide pine board shelving held in place by white triangular metal supports.

"Sit," he said.

I did as he directed. Heck, he might become my client.

As I crossed my leg, I heard the office door open. It was Laverne. She handed Cisneros two sheets of paper.

"You read this and then sign it if you want to work for me."

It was a standard non-disclosure agreement, except for Article Six: *Disclosure of any information regarding Cabrillo Construction or any of its management or employees or any of its business activities will result in immediate termination.* I got the picture. A novice would assume I would be fired, but I knew better than that. He meant I would be "fired at." He was willing to work with me, but if anything I learned was passed along to anyone else, I would be executed by the Los Equis Cartel.

Did I really want to get involved with Cisneros and his gang of thugs? I signed the document, handed him the signed version, and kept the copy for myself.

"So, what's the issue requiring a private investigator?" I asked.

"Some of my most expensive product seems to be in short supply."

"You mean your cranes and bulldozers?"

"Get real, Mr. Jones. I run a legitimate construction company as a means to give my men legitimate occupations of record so they can stay in this country without fear of being hassled by your immigration authorities. But I'm sure you aren't stupid. My business consists of more than constructing buildings. I am the gateway for the distribution of Central American products desired by the people of the United States. I make a lot of money and use the construction company as a means to…how do you say it?…ah, yes, 'launder' the proceeds."

"I'm sure the authorities already know what you're up to."

"Yes, and they are rewarded handsomely for turning their eyes away from my activities."

After my first visit to Cisneros' company, I told the chief of my suspicions about Cabrillo Construction. Maybe it was a front for the Los Equis Cartel. He told me, "Don't worry about it. I got someone else on it. Just find the killer of that skeleton." To my knowledge, nobody was working on anything involving Cabrillo Construction, and certainly nobody had been arrested thus far. I wondered if the chief was on Cisneros' payroll.

"So, what's the issue?" I asked again. "Are you thinking one of your men wants his own cut of the proceeds?"

"You got the picture."

"Do you suspect anyone in particular?"

"Three, to be exact, but I don't want to accuse anyone unnecessarily because all my men have been brought into my organization by brothers and fathers who have worked for the corporation for a long time. I would like you to do your investigative thing and tell me who I should accuse and hold accountable."

"I get thirty dollars per hour plus expenses. All times and activities and receipts are kept in a log, which I will share with you on a weekly basis. However, I only conduct my investigations outside of the City's eight-to-five workday, meaning I work early mornings, nights, and weekends. And, as we agreed, all information I learn during the course of this investigation will remain totally confidential."

"We are simpatico," Cisneros said. "My primary business is conducted at those same times…outside of the Cabrillo Construction Company's workday."

Cisneros and I shook hands. Then he gave me the names and photographs of the three employees he suspected. My job was to figure out if only one, or two, or all three were pilfering product, and if they were working as individuals or as a group. Other than the fact I was a gringo and neither understood nor spoke Spanish, this job looked like a piece of cake. With luck, I could stretch it out for a few weeks and enjoy a nice payday.

****

It was seven o'clock Friday night. Halloween. Dressed in patrolman's blues, including nightstick, mace canister, and holster with a loaded nine-millimeter Sig Sauer, I was already in town cruising the neighborhood streets. Little kids in costumes were scurrying about from house to house filling their bags with assorted candies and an occasional apple. I hoped nobody would hide a razor in an apple or candy bar this year. But there was always some asshole trying to ruin an otherwise nice holiday.

Helen was waiting for me when I arrived at her place, a clapboard duplex on the east side of the Town of Glen Cove. It was in a neighborhood of ethnic diversity, but not poverty. Her home was near the bad side of Willow Falls, only five blocks away, but its crime seldom bled into her neighborhood. Helen had purchased her home from a retired police officer who moved to Florida after receiving his golden parachute, a large sum awarded after the brakes went in his patrol car, sending him careening over an embankment and leaving him slightly paralyzed on his left side. She got the home for a less than full value, and the rent from the next door neighbor more than covered her mortgage payment.

When I rang the doorbell, she answered, dressed in a uniform that matched mine, but hers clung to her figure. I'm too vain to wear anything like that. Her hair was pulled tightly into a bun and her makeup was basic. Without doubt, she was still the most attractive black female officer in the department. I always wondered why she was not already married.

"You load your gun?" she asked.

"Yup. Never know if we might need to shoot our way out of this party."

She opened a drawer in a table beside her sofa, pulled out a handful of loose nine-millimeter rounds, and pushed six into her revolver's cylinder. She spun it, and then holstered her piece. "Okay, let's go."

We climbed into my sedan and headed across town toward the Odd Fellows Hall in Schenectady. When we arrived, we saw the parking lot was empty. The hall was a three-story brick building with gargoyles and spires at each corner. The dark oak front doors were windowless and arched, standing at least ten feet tall, like a haunted mansion from an old B-rated black and white movie. I checked the tickets we purchased from Billy Travis.

"Oh, the party doesn't start until nine."

"You mean I could have had a nice dinner instead of shoving a peanut butter and jelly sandwich into my face because I thought we were gonna be late?"

"Looks that way," I sighed. We had an hour and a half to kill. "How about we go get a beer somewhere?"

"If you're buying."

I stopped and bought two tallboy Buds at a convenience store. The clerk gave me an inquisitive look, something like "What's a cop doing buying beer-to-go?"

"This is my Halloween costume," I said. "Going to a party."

He nodded and gave me my change.

I drove through Schenectady and found the entrance to Central Park, a woodsy place with tennis courts, ball fields, and various gardens. It was a nice place during daylight hours, but only a few brave souls ventured there at night. Count Helen and me among the brave, especially on a Halloween night. But, hey, we were cops, dressed up as cops, and our pistols were loaded.

I pulled into the parking area near a soccer field and killed the motor. Then I handed Helen a beer. We both opened them and sipped the foam off the aluminum lids.

"How are things with you and Rachel?" Helen asked.

"I haven't spoken to her since I moved out. Found a nice place on Mariaville Lake. It's old, but I can afford the utilities and it's pretty easy to keep clean."

"You gonna have to talk with her, you know. You

think she's still involved with Moretti?"

I really didn't want to talk about my personal life. But Helen was my closest friend and I needed someone I could confide in. "I know I need to talk with her," I said. "I would hope Moretti has backed off, especially since his daughter just died, but I don't really know."

"It's Friday night," Helen said. "Only one way to find out. Change seats with me."

We got out of the car and walked around to each other's side. Helen swatted my butt as we passed in front of the headlights. There is nothing better than friendship. We climbed back into the car, finished our beers, and dropped the cans onto the gravel parking lot.

"Somebody will pick those up and cash them in before noon tomorrow," Helen said.

She drove us back to Willow Falls and slowly cruised past my home. In the light from the streetlamp, I could see a burnt orange Ford pickup parked in my driveway. Helen went to the end of the block, turned the car around and cruised back, stopping across the street from my home. She killed the headlights and we idled for a few minutes, watching clusters of kids moving from house to house along the sidewalk.

"This is a better place to be a kid," Helen said. "It's safer than Albany or Schenectady."

"Yeah, that's why we settled here. But we never had any kids."

A group of six kids, mostly elementary schoolers and one toddler, rang the doorbell at my house. Rachel opened the door and passed out candy from my wooden popcorn bowl into each kid's bag. As she finished, Moretti came up behind her and smiled and pointed at the kids, as though he lived in my home and Rachel was his wife and not mine.

I could feel anger surging through my gut.

Helen must have sensed it because she reached over and squeezed my hand. "Well, now you know," she said. "It's probably time to move on."

I still felt Rachel was mine and I was not ready to share her with another man…or woman. Hell, we had been separated for only a week. But clearly, she had moved on. Maybe it was something I had to do, too, but I was nowhere near ready to move into another relationship. Instead of moving on, I opened the glove compartment and removed my emergency tactical knife. Then I opened the door and hopped out.

"Where you going, Jonesy?" Helen said. "Don't be doing something stupid. She isn't worth it."

"Keep the car running," I replied. I walked quickly to my driveway in the dark. I looked around for kids and nosy neighbors. It looked safe. So, I squatted down beside Moretti's right rear tire, opened the razor-sharp blade of my tactical knife, and slashed the sidewall. Instantly air began streaming out. Then I moved to the front right tire and did the same. Yeah, it was a juvenile thing to do, but it gave me a delinquent's sense of satisfaction. He would need two spares in order to drive home, and he would need two new tires because sidewalls are not repairable.

I walked back to my sedan and got into the passenger's side. "I thought if he was planning to stay, he might as well stay a little longer."

"You didn't leave your fingerprints, did you?" Helen asked.

"Hope not." I pointed straight ahead. "Let's go."

Chapter 12

The Odd Fellows Hall was hopping when we arrived at ten after nine. The windows on the ground floor were ablaze with yellow light and we could see shadows and figures of people moving across the drawn shades. The parking lot offered us two spaces, so we backed into a space closest to the exit just in case…well, you know.

Helen handed me the car keys and I locked the car. "Here goes nothing," she said.

We were greeted at the door by a guy dressed as a werewolf. "Tickets?" he asked.

"Yeah, here." I handed our two to him. "Is Billy here yet?"

"Billy?"

"Billy Travis…you know, from the Crystal Cantor."

"Yeah, I think so. He usually comes as a toad. We got a couple of them here tonight." The guy looked at our costumes. "You know, you're probably gonna scare quite a few people here tonight. They're gonna think you're really cops 'cause your costumes look so real."

"We always try to stand out," I said. "We thought these costumes might be arresting."

The werewolf wrote an X on the back of our hands with a UV ink marker and handed us two small tickets. "First drinks are complimentary."

"Thanks," I replied. Then I took Helen's hand and we melded into the crowd.

Inside, the hall had been decorated in a typical Halloween motif. Around the windows stood cornstalks, and each windowsill had its own carved pumpkin, glowing with a flickering artificial candle. Two life-sized witches rode their broomsticks on the ceiling above us and a full moon glowed down upon the merrymakers from one of the corners. The walls were plastered with cutout black cats, jack-o-lanterns, and cardboard scarecrows.

The guests were equally Halloween-esque: there were good and bad witches, the characters from the Wizard of Oz, cowboys, princesses, Superman and Batman, men with masks of Presidents George Bush, Bill Clinton, Barack Obama, Donald Trump, and want-to-be Hillary. Several slutty prostitutes and all the Power Rangers and Ninja Turtles strolled by. And, of course, Raggedy Ann and Andy. I felt like I was in elementary school again.

While Helen and I were standing back-to-back looking at the room and the crowd of costumed guests, a man in a ballerina costume approached her. "Hello. My name is Wesley. Is this your first time here?"

"Yes, it is. Did my costume a give me away?"

"That, and the fact no woman of color has ever attended."

"We sisters be getting around. You come every year, Wesley?"

"I missed the first one…was visiting my kid in Vegas…but I've been to all the rest. I think this makes five."

"You married?"

"Divorced just last year. She left me for a jockey she met at Saratoga."

He took a sip of a mixed drink which looked like vodka, except it was tinted red, probably with cherry juice. "She lives in Deerfield Beach, Florida now. Nice big place on the ocean with Cuban servants. Can you imagine her having sex with a guy who stands two feet shorter than she does?"

Helen shrugged. "Maybe she's got a thing for kids."

Wesley laughed. "Maybe he's hung like a horse." He reached for Helen's hand. "Want to dance?"

Helen looked at me.

I nodded. "Go ahead. It won't hurt my feelings any."

Wesley handed me his drink and escorted Helen onto the dance floor, where the song *I Put a Spell on You* was playing. I hoped he was not planning to dance with her all night.

Helen's connection with Wesley gave me a chance to approach one of the prostitutes who seemed as though she may have been interested in me when she brushed by earlier. She was wearing a very low-cut leopard print top and a short black skirt with a slit up its side, exposing the top of her black fishnet stockings. Her red heels must have been four inches high, but she stood no more than five foot ten, even with her bouffant of fake red hair.

"You planning to arrest me or are you looking for a freebie?" she asked when I walked up to her.

"I know nothing's free, sweetheart," I replied, looking her in the eye. "Do you mind wearing handcuffs."

"For the right price."

I liked this woman. Maybe her costume let her feel free to express hidden desires. I wondered if she was married. "Where's your pimp?"

"I came stag. Just looking for fun. Are you with the

other cop?"

"She's a friend. Didn't want to come here alone. I can't blame her, either. There's a few wolves and a lot of weirdos in the crowd."

The prostitute laughed and ran the back of her hand down my cheek. "My name's Trixie."

"Nice name for a hooker. What's your real name, Trixie?"

"Natalie."

"Hi, Natalie. My name's Bart. That's my real name. Can I buy you a drink?"

She smiled. "Sure."

I offered her my arm and we walked together to the bar. "What are you drinking?"

"Scotch on the rocks."

The bartender gave me the 'Can I help you?' look.

I don't know what got into me, but I pretended to be a big wig. "Give me two double scotches on the rocks. Make it good single malt stuff, not the blended crap."

The bartender checked around himself and then held up a bottle of fourteen-year-old Glenmorangie he plucked from somewhere under the table. "Will this do?"

I nodded.

"That will be thirty dollars."

I wanted to choke at the price, but I managed to maintain my cool. I handed him thirty-five dollars and kissed two months' worth of beer goodbye.

Natalie and I touched our plastic glasses together and toasted to "Christmas for the Druids."

We found a spot at a high patio table where we could stand and chat.

"This is my first time here," I said. "Billy at the Crystal Cantor told me about it. Looks like a fun group.

You come every year?"

"This is my third year. I'm just starting to get into the kinky stuff. I've never been a feeder or a host. I might try hosting this year. I mean, I like my steak medium well. I'm not sure I could lick blood off someone other than myself."

"When does all of that stuff start?"

"Closer to midnight, when the king and queen arrive."

"You mean they aren't even here yet?"

"Maybe they are, but I haven't seen them. They could be in different costumes until midnight. Have you heard anyone speaking in a British accent?"

I had only heard Natalie and Helen's dancing partner speak. Besides, the loud hum of the crowd and the blaring music made it hard to overhear anyone else speaking at all.

"What do you do?" I asked.

"I'm an elementary school teacher in Schenectady Schools. Fourth grade."

"Tough times to be a teacher. Do you get furloughed every year?"

"I did the first three years, but there've been enough retirements that I'm too high on the list for them to reach me anymore." Natalie sipped her scotch. "This is pretty good scotch once you get over the plastic taste of the cup."

I nodded. I should have asked for the cheaper stuff because of the plastic cups. It was a lesson learned.

"What do you do?" Natalie asked.

"I'm self-employed...private investigator."

"So, you're like really a cop, sort of...?"

"No, you wouldn't say that if you knew what my

current investigation entails. Cops give speeding tickets and direct traffic and play ball with kids. It's all upstanding stuff. I get to sit and watch for hours and occasionally take pictures and make reports to whomever is paying me. Nothing too dangerous or adventurous, but it's not always upstanding."

"Must be good money."

"I get paid by the hour…and, yes, it's good money."

"So, if I hired you, what would I ask you to do?"

"Probably spy on your boyfriend. See if he's being faithful. If he isn't, you'd want me to take pictures of him in compromising situations so you could show them to him after you burn his sportscar."

She laughed. "You want to dance?"

"Yeah, sure."

We left our drinks unattended and walked onto the dance floor, where a slow song was playing. Natalie put both of her arms around my neck and pressed against me as we danced to Eric Clapton's *Wonderful Tonight*. The sensation of her body against mine, the scent of her perfume and the touch of her flesh did things to me, like I was a high school kid.

She raised an eyebrow. "Are you getting aroused?"

"I'm embarrassed to admit it, but 'yeah,' Natalie. It's been a while since I danced with a woman, especially one who fits my body so nicely. I'm sorry if it offends you. Please don't take it the wrong way."

"I take it as a compliment, Bart." She kissed me on the lips, and then pressed her hand against my privates as she spun her tongue around mine. "Come on," she said.

Holding my hand, Natalie led me across the room, through a door, and into a dimly lit hallway. We passed several doors whose knobs had "occupied" signs on them. When we found one with no sign, Natalie opened the door and placed an "occupied" sign from the inside knob onto the outside knob. "There," she said, "we now have a reserved room."

"Are these for our use?" I asked.

"Yes, it's part of the ticket price. These rooms will get a lot of use after midnight, but right now it's ours alone."

I don't know why Natalie decided to treat me rather than trick me on a Halloween night. Maybe when we were talking and dancing she saw how desperately lonely I was. How much in need of affection I was. But I was grateful she took pity on me. Before midnight, the teacher in her had shown me a few things I had not been taught before. It was heated and passionate and I wanted to scream for joy when the moment came.

****

"Where you been?" Helen asked me. "Your uniform is all wrinkled."

"I was taking a little nap," I lied. "What have you learned?"

"It's almost midnight. That's when the serious stuff begins."

"Serious stuff?"

"Yeah."

As if on cue, the lights in the hall went out and we stood in the dark with all the other guests. Then without warning a loud fanfare burst from speakers which were mounted above the stage area. Lights slowly rose on the stage and the curtains parted. Standing behind them were two individuals, one presumably male and the other presumably female. I mean, you can never be sure these days. The male was dressed in a red cape with white fur trim. The female was dressed in a white cape with red fur trim. Their golden crowns identified them as the "king" and "queen."

The light from the stage shown on the audience. I looked for Natalie, hoping I had not disappointed her and I was not just a slam/bam or a notch on her belt. When I saw her, she was standing in front of a muscular man in a satanic mask whose tattooed arms were wrapped around her. She looked at me and smiled. Her right hand was behind her, fondling his privates. So much for fidelity and any hope of a long-term relationship.

The king's voice drew my attention to the stage. "Welcome to our humble castle," he said to the attendees. "The appointed hour is upon us."

A man dressed like an Arab muscle builder swung a wooden pole against a large brass gong. The sound shattered my ears. A maiden in a diaphanous gown appeared carrying a white pet-store rabbit. Accompanying her was another, carrying a small pitcher and a curved dagger. They stood center stage.

The queen was next to speak. "May the spirits of our Druid forefathers be with us tonight as we offer this sacrifice to the Guardian of the Dead."

The gong sounded again. I held my ears.

Quickly, the maiden holding the knife slit the rabbit's throat and held the pitcher beneath the rabbit's head. Its feet kicked wildly, but the maiden who held the poor creature hung it upside down over the pitcher as the blood flowed from its body.

Helen turned away, pressing her face into my chest.

When the rabbit gave up its life, it fell limp and the blood stopped flowing. The maiden offered the pitcher to the king. He drank from it, then wiped his mouth with a white cloth and showed it to the attendees, who erupted in cheers. The king then offered the pitcher to the queen. She drank from it and then wiped her own mouth. More cheers erupted from the crowd.

The maiden who had held the rabbit disappeared during the cheering and reappeared with a glass pitcher of sparkling liquid, perhaps seltzer or clear lemon soda. The queen poured the remainder of the blood into the clear liquid, turning it to a deep pink color. Then, as if in church, the attendees lined up and walked toward the front of the room, each taking a small clear plastic cup of liquid from the pitcher and drinking from it.

Helen and I--and maybe five other attendees--passed on the opportunity to share communion with those sick bastards. As we watched the communal procession, Helen asked, "Did you notice the queen spoke in a British accent? Didn't Miss Appleton…the old woman in the jail who drew hex signs all over the floor and walls…didn't she say she learned those hex signs from the Queen from England?"

"By god, you're right, Helen," I replied. "We've got to introduce ourselves to Her Majesty and see who she really is. She might be our first substantial lead."

The gong sounded again. I held my ears again.

"It's dinnertime," the king commanded. "Feeders to stage right and hosts to stage left."

The crowd separated, most guests standing toward the perimeter walls to observe the next activity. However, two lines of costumed men and women formed as directed by the king, approximately a dozen in the feeder line and approximately fifteen in the host line. Natalie was among the hosts, perhaps looking a little nervous or out of place.

The maidens appeared again, one carrying a plate full of razor blades and the other carrying a plate of bandages. They quickly passed out their wares, the feeders taking razors and the bandages finding their way into the hands of the hosts.

The gong attacked my ears again. The feeders approached the hosts. Using their razors, they made small incisions where directed by the hosts, some pointing at arms, others at shoulders or chests. Small amounts of blood flowed from the wound of each host. Feeders then sucked at the wounds, like vampires or wild beasts in the forest. As each feeder finished, the maidens sprayed the host's wound with an antiseptic and the host then bandaged it.

When all feeding had ended, the gong sounded again, and you know what I did with my ears. The feeders then kissed the hand of their respective hosts and said in unison, "It is through your sacrifice that I may live."

Natalie was one of three hosts who had not been selected by a feeder. As she passed by me, I reached out to her. "Better luck next year, Natalie."

"Yeah, thank you, Bart. And the name is Trixie."

Chapter 13

After the feeding ceremony, Helen and I had had enough. We stepped outside to get some fresh air and to get away from the clientele who were reveling inside. It was cold and damp outside, maybe in the upper twenties. I could see my breath and wished I had brought a coat.

We walked among the cars in the parking lot. Helen poked me in the ribs. "Where were you all that time? I was afraid something bad had happened to you."

I removed my cell phone from my duty rig, the belt which carries all my necessary equipment, and began snapping pictures of the license plates on the parked vehicles. "I met someone who I thought I had something in common with. Turns out she's probably going to do three or four people tonight."

"You had sex?" Helen asked with a look of annoyance. "You're supposed to be working, Jonesy. While you were getting your rocks off, I already did what you're doing now."

"You took pics of the license plates?"

She flashed a folded piece of paper at me. It was the party invitation with numbers and vehicle makes written all over the backside. "No, I did it the old-fashioned way. I wrote them down by hand. But I got them all anyway, so put your camera away before somebody sees you and figures out we aren't in disguise."

I slipped my cell phone back onto my duty rig.

"You're way ahead of me, Helen."

"Always have been," she said like she meant it. "Now how we gonna discover who the Queen from England and her king are?"

"Well, we can go back inside, or we can wait for them to come out."

"Now, I'm gonna ask you one more time. How are we really going to find out who they are?"

"I guess we're going to go back in and ask them, or we're going to begin interrogating the owners of every one of these cars until we get the same name a couple or three times."

"Let's go back inside and see what other disgusting things these peeps are gonna do, and then let's go home. It's already past my bedtime."

We walked back into the Odd Fellows Hall, and the party was still going strong. About a third of the crowd had disappeared. I noticed two fish tanks at the front of the stage, so I walked over to inspect them. Inside one tank were several dozen of those South American tree frogs I had purchased at the Crystal Cantor. Inside the other were fewer. On the table beside the tanks was an empty package of cigarette rolling papers. I was about to say something to Helen when one of the maidens appeared wearing yellow rubber cleaning gloves.

"It's too soon," she said. "The rooms are all occupied. If you can wait another ten minutes, I'm sure some of the guests will have finished and it can be your turn. I'll be sure you're next."

"We've never tried it before," Helen said. "Is it safe?"

"Once I wipe the frog's back, you eat the paper and go find an empty room. Before you take your clothes off, you'll experience the greatest high of your life."

"Does it last long? We've got to be heading home...the babysitter, you know."

"It lasts between fifteen and twenty minutes, depending upon how much kambo you get. But it'll be the best sex you've ever experienced...guaranteed."

"How much does it cost, again?" I asked like a typical male.

"Fifty dollars each."

I looked in my wallet. I had only eighty dollars left. "Would you take eighty?"

"Mr. Modern doesn't let us negotiate the price. It costs him a lot of money to breed and feed these little fellas. However, I do take credit cards," she replied.

"Are you a subcontractor?" I asked.

"No, I'm an employee. I work at Modern Scientific Supply. This is just an overtime job for me."

"Did you two ladies really kill the rabbit earlier," Helen asked, "or was it some kind of slight-of-hand trick?"

"Unfortunately, it was no trick. But we kill them regularly at work. Believe me, tonight was a faster and easier way to go. At work, we freeze them to death and then pack them in dry ice for shipping. It takes the rabbits almost an hour to die and another two hours to freeze solid."

"We're Helen and Bart Los Angeles," I said. "What's your name?"

"Angela. Please to meet you. Is your name like the city in California?"

"Yeah."

Angela looked up. "Okay, I guess it's your turn."

I turned and looked in the direction Angela had been

looking. The door Natalie and I had entered earlier was open and four people were exiting the back rooms. I opened my wallet and handed Angela my credit card. She swiped it through a mobile swiper which was inserted into her cell phone.

She returned my card without noticing that the last name on my card wasn't Los Angeles. "Here you go. All approved."

Angela lifted the lid on the cage with more frogs, reached in, and plucked one in her gloved hand. "Would you mind reaching into my pocket?" she asked. "I forgot to get out the papers."

Helen rolled her eyes and then pulled a new package of rolling papers from Angela's skirt pocket. Then she opened the package and handed Angela a single paper. Angela wiped the back of the frog with the paper then said, "Open wide."

"I'll take it in my hand," Helen said.

"I can't let you do that. If you wipe your eyes with your hand, you'll go blind."

Helen opened her mouth and bit down on the paper with her teeth.

When it was my turn, I did the same, trying not to let the paper touch my tongue. Then Helen and I waved goodbye to Angela and quickly walked to the doorway to ecstasy. Once inside the hallway, Helen removed my duty rig, opened an empty ammunition pocket, and spit the damp paper into it. She handed the duty rig to me, and I did the same.

"What are we gonna do now?" she asked.

"We're gonna hang around here for fifteen minutes and then go tell Angela how great the sex was."

"My lips are getting numb," Helen said.

Blood Bath

"Whatever you do, don't lick your eyes." I was trying to be funny.

I noticed my lips were getting numb, too. "Don't touch your lips, Helen. Maybe we can go to the bathroom and wipe them with a wet paper towel."

"Good idea. Best one you've had all night." Helen took my belt in her right hand and pulled me close to her. "Ever been with a sister? If you hadn't already done the deed tonight, you could have enjoyed the best sex of your life, Jonesy. But I ain't letting some guy do me who's already dirty from somebody else."

I pulled Helen's hand from my belt. "Listen, Helen, I think some of that frog slime has gone to your brain. Let's go rinse our mouths out and go home."

I led her down the hallway until I found a door marked LADIES. I opened it and gently pushed her in. "Wash your lips and tongue. Be sure to use soap."

Then I found the men's room and did the same.

****

The wind was blowing flurries out of the northwest the next morning. Nothing was sticking yet, but the whitecaps on the lake outside my camp reminded me of the Long Island Sound during a big blow. It was only the first of November and the investigation into the death of little Laura Moretti was progressing slowly. However, it was uncovering some shit. First, I had learned my wife had been having an affair with Laura Moretti's father. The result was that I had been forced to leave my home to give her some space. Could anyone blame me for not sticking around while she was sleeping with someone else? And second, I had discovered the neighboring city of Schenectady was home to a rather large group of Druids. Well, at least it was home to some twenty-five characters whose enjoy drinking each other's blood. And third, I suspected Helen might have a thing for me. It was something which piqued my interest, but it was also something I didn't want to act on. Amorous relationships, even friends-with-benefits relationships, in the workplace are almost always a road to disaster.

I made myself a cup of Deathwish coffee and sat down on my sofa to mull over the results of last night's investigation of the going's-on at the Odd Fellows Hall. The question was what to do next. I figured on Monday Helen would be handing over her list of license plate numbers to the traffic division so we could get IDs on last night's partygoers. And there was the growing issue of Horace Modern. His name kept popping up. Last night, it was his rabbit and frogs which drove the blood feeding and drugged-sex frenzies. Clearly, there was more to the guy than meets the eye. And what about the "Queen from England?" I needed to know who she was and what role she was playing in the blood drinking community. I also needed to know if this whole blood drinking thing was some rabbit hole that was taking me further and further away from Laura Moretti's killer.

When I finished my coffee, it was time to begin my private investigation duties. Cisneros was looking for information and I needed to find him some.

****

I was reading the paperwork that Cisneros had given me when the call came in. I put down the paperwork walked to the kitchen counter where my cell phone was ringing and charging at the same time.

I picked it up without unplugging it. "Jones here."

It was Helen. "Hey, Jonesy, I know it's your day off, but you may want to come down to the department."

"Why's that and what are you doing at work on a weekend?"

"Got a call from the desk sergeant. There was an accident last night involving one of the partygoers."

"DWI?"

"Probably. But he was DOA. Doc Foster is doing a work-up on the cadaver."

"It's my first real day on my parttime job, Helen. Can you go see what Doc Foster has to say and fill me in later?"

"Sure, I guess. I feel like you're standing me up, putting space between us, you know what I mean?"

"Honest, I'd be there, but I need the extra income, or I'll be hauled away to debtors' prison and never be able to take you out for dinner again. I'll make it up to you somehow."

"All right. But you're missing a chance to spend Saturday morning with the hottest sister in Willow Falls."

When Helen hung up, I went back to Cisneros' paperwork. The three guys in question were Juan Vasquez, Manuel Morales, and Julio Prognostico. The first two were from Mexico, which made sense to me. Both had served time in the Mexican Army but were now working for Cabrillo, a.k.a., Los Equis. Prognostico was different. Perhaps a distant relative or somebody's friend, he was Puerto Rican and did not fit the stereotype of a Los Equis foot soldier. So, I started with Morales and Vasquez, the two Mexicans. Hell, they lived at the same address, so finding them was going to be easy.

I dressed, donned my down vest, and drove into the Hispanic section of Willow Falls. It didn't look much different from the Black and Asian sections, except the back windows of many cars bore balled fringe and the windows closest to the doors of almost every house bore flag decals, proudly announcing the country of birth. Morales and Vasquez lived in a flat above a Mexican market. Their windowless front door opened beside the market onto a sidewalk on Oneida Street.

I parked across from the door and waited for something to happen. I didn't know what, but something was certain to happen. At least that is what private eyes do on television and something always happens. They sit on stake-out near a suspect's home and make note of everyone who comes and goes. So, I sat there until one in the afternoon, waiting. Nobody came or went from the door. Nobody passed in front of the window upstairs. I think nobody was home.

Then the mailman came by, a middle-aged black man dressed in the normal USPS uniform and wearing a lined raincoat. He stopped at the box mounted outside the door and slid a handful of letters into it. When he left, I climbed out of my car, stretched to promote blood circulation in my legs, and then crossed the street to the mailbox. I looked around, then pulled the mail out and began inspecting it. Eight letters in all, three from Laredo, Texas, and five from Tamaulipas, Mexico, and all the mail was addressed to four individuals. It was obvious at least four men lived at this address, so I jotted down the two unfamiliar names, Juaquin Obrador and Juan Lascano. Then I put the letters back into the mailbox and light-footed it across the street to my sedan. A few moments after getting behind the steering wheel, I noticed the proprietor of the Mexican market looking at me through his store window while he spoke into a cell phone. It was time to leave.

I started the motor and drove to the address of the third suspect, Julio Prognostico, who lived six blocks and a right hand turn away on Ontario Street. I pulled to a stop across the street from his place and started the waiting game again. Julio lived in a flat-roofed concrete block home, if you could call it a home. The front windows were floor to ceiling in height and the front door was recessed at least six feet, giving the place the look of a former storefront. A light was on in the rear of the main room, so somebody was probably home.

Again, I waited. And watched. And waited. Then, just like on TV, something miraculous happened. Who should show up but three of my old Mexican friends, pulling right up to the front of Lascano's residence on their black Harleys. I pulled up my camera and took half a dozen pictures. Then I took half a dozen more using the camera's automatic telephoto lens option.

As they set their kickstands and dismounted, I watched Prognostico come out of his place with a big smile and give Pedro "Mescal" Herrera a high five and a bear hug. Then he did the same to Miranda Goins' older brother "Gonzo" Goins and to the unknown third member of Mescal's gang. I had seen all I needed to see for the time being, but I couldn't leave until all the men were off the sidewalk. So, I sat for another fifteen minutes and watched patiently until Mescal and his sidekicks mounted and rode off toward whatever mischief they were making.

I started my car and accelerated to drive home. But then I remembered the homes and businesses on Ontario Street enjoyed a back alley where some would work, others would play, and all would park their cars and trucks. I turned onto McClellan Street and then turned again down the alley behind Ontario Street. Prognostico's back yard was easy enough to spot because a huge Mexican flag was painted onto the six-foot high wooden fence bordering it. I pulled up next to the flag, got out, and hopped onto the hood of my car so I could see over the fence and into his back yard. It was like somebody's farmyard. A couple of collared goats grazed on weeds along the left side fence. A fifteen-foot square pen held two brown and white spotted pigs. Chickens roamed freely. When a rooster crowed, I looked directly down and realized the back wall was home to eight or more cages with roosters, and I wondered why he penned them instead of letting them run loose, like the hens.

I was going to take a few more pictures, but two doors down a large man wearing sweatpants but no top walked out of his two-story clapboard house and saw me standing on the hood of my car. He plopped a bag of garbage into a dented steel trash can and slammed the lid down. I waved.

"You be gone, gringo," he shouted. "You don't belong here."

I waved again and got back into my car. I put the transmission into reverse and backed out of the alley so the guy would not get a closeup of my face. Then I drove home, where I downloaded the pics I had taken and drafted a few notes for Cisneros, including logging eight hours of investigative time. Before I went to see Cisneros, however, I wanted to spend a few minutes chatting with my old buddy Mescal.

Chapter 14

Sunday was a few degrees warmer than Saturday had been. The wind was calmer and, although the skies were gray, the clouds were not spewing flurries. I waited until respectable people were home from church before I went to see Mescal at his Mexican gang's clubhouse. I figured he was probably leading prayers for his buddies, or else sleeping off the alcohol and illegal substances he introduced into his body the night before.

At noon and dressed in an old Army-issued sweatsuit and tennis shoes, I drove to Mescal's address on Van Rensselaer Drive. It was a neighborhood which had been upper middle class back in the fifties, but which had slowly morphed into the slum it was today. The front door of his cinderblock clubhouse was the same as I remembered it, a piece of plywood which had been sawed to fit into the door frame. The chipped paint on the clubhouse window still advertised vacuum cleaner repair. I knocked and then stepped back onto the sidewalk.

A skinny guy whom I'd never met answered my knock.

"Wha' d'you wan?" he asked.

"I need to speak with Mescal."

"He ain't here."

"Go tell him the guy who he met in the park last spring needs his help again."

"I said he ain't here."

I pointed to a black Harley with a matching quarter-faring on it. "That's his ride. He's here. Go tell him what I said."

The guy shut the door. I heard voices inside. Eventually the door opened again, and Mescal stepped out. His eyes were bloodshot, and his fatigue trousers and sweatshirt looked like he had slept in them. Behind him came two young soldiers, there to defend him if I did anything stupid. They were dressed in the black jeans and black denim jackets I had come to know as the uniform of our local Mexican gang, the Banditos.

"It's you again," Mescal said. "I thought I tol' you I didn't wanna see you no more."

"I'm not a cop today, Mescal. I've got a part-time job as a private investigator. I'm hoping you can help me."

"It's gonna cost you."

I tilted my head. "How much you looking for?"

Mescal laughed. "Not money, hombre. Favors. That's all, jus' favors."

"No favors with the cops," I replied. "Only private dick stuff. I can't mix and match the two jobs."

Mescal put his hands into his pants pockets. "Wha' you wan' to know?"

"What's going on with Prognostico?"

"I don' know nobody named that."

"Yeah, you do. Yesterday I saw you at his place over on Ontario Street. You and Gonzo and some other member of your 'club.' You're doing some kind of business with him?"

"Oh, that guy. Wha'd you call him?"

"Prognostico."

"We call him 'Peckerhead.' He runs a business we got some interest in."

"Drugs? Prostitution?"

Mescal laughed. "Noooo, man. He's in the entertainment business. Runs a sports arena over near Albany."

"You playing soccer now?"

Mescal laughed again. "No. It's like this. This guy is from PR, you know? He's no Mexicano. What's the favorite sport in Puerto Rico?"

"Lemme guess." I thought of Bobby Munoz and Roberto Clemente... "baseball?"

"No, pendejo, it's cockfighting."

I was surprised. "Cockfighting? You gotta be kidding me."

"No, no joke. Peckerhead raises prize roosters for the pit. He's raising two for me right now. Next Friday night one of mine is gonna win his first fight. He's a big sumbitch, near fifteen pounds."

"Cockfighting in the Capital District? Where's the pit?"

"You telling the cops?"

"No," I said, "I already told you this is private detective stuff. There will be no cops."

"I guess I trust you, hombre. Besides, you owe me a favor now."

I got back on task. "So, Prognostico works at this cockfighting pit?"

Mescal took his hands from his pants pocket. "You don' listen too good, man. I jus' tol' you he *owns* the pit. Peckerhead came into some money about six weeks ago and bought hisself a urban renewal building near the railroad yard in Albany. He built the pit and the grandstands hisself with some help from some of my guys."

"So, if I want to go watch a cockfight, it's open to the public?"

"You the wrong ethnicity to go there alone. Somebody's goin' slice your throat for your wallet."

"So how can I go? Would you take me?"

"Take you? Like on a date?" Mescal and both the guys behind him were laughing now.

"No, you asshole," I replied, "like a couple of guys going to a football game."

"Hey, watch who you go calling names like that, man."

"Okay, sorry. You know I didn't mean anything by it. You've been having fun calling me names, so I thought maybe we were becoming friends."

"We're not friends, pendejo. But we got an arrangement, no?"

"Yeah, I guess we got an arrangement. I got no inroads into the Spanish community except through you. And you need me to help you with other things…except getting you out of any more trouble with the cops. I can't do that unless you got something else the cops might want, like last time."

"You meet me here next Friday, seven o'clock. You drive your own set of wheels, and you follow me to the new sports arena. You pay your own way in and buy your own beer. Be sure to bring lots of ones for the betting. And you be sure to bet on my cock 'cause you'll win back all your losings."

"See you at seven, Mescal. I'm looking forward to the experience."

"You guaranteed an experience, hombre."

****

On Sunday afternoon I did some internet research on the Mexican gang and the Los Equis Cartel. The Mexican Banditos, I learned, were a splinter group from the Mexican Mafia. The Mafia emerged in the 1950s in the California State Prison System, initially calling itself "la eMe," the M. Members usually have a black hand tattooed somewhere on their bodies, after the famous "Black Hand" syndicate of the nineteen twenties. I suspected that Mescal's gang might have its own special tattoo, but I had not seen one on Mescal. I was certain he had one somewhere on his body because of his position as gang leader.

On the other hand, the Los Equis Cartel, Spanish for "the X's," was formed by commanders of the Mexican Army who deserted their posts and began working as the enforcers for the Gulf Cartel in Mexico. Initially calling themselves Los Zetas, the "Z's," they were famous for beheadings and were once the largest cartel in Mexico. In 2015, a contingent broke away from Los Zetas and formed Los Equis, short for "ex" members of the Z's.

In the United States, Los Equis and the Mexican Banditos were bitter rivals until a formal truce was declared, less than a decade ago. Today, they tolerate each other, but are still considered rivals.

So, I astutely surmised Cisneros is an "X" and, if I was correct, his employee, Julio Prognostico, hangs with the rival "Banditos" on his own time. And if, as Mescal told me, Prognostico suddenly came into enough money to purchase a building and convert it into a cockfighting arena, it was a good bet he was the likely perpetrator in the heist of Cisneros' product. My case was essentially solved, well, at least based on circumstantial evidence.

Chapter 15

Monday morning was cold at Mariaville Lake. The sky was Carolina blue and the sun was bright, but the grass on the lake side of my cabin was white with crystalline frost. I checked the temperature on my cell phone. It was a crisp eighteen degrees in Willow Falls, which meant Mariaville was a degree or two colder.

I took a shower and then made myself a quick cup of coffee to clear the fatigue out of my head. Sunday Night Football had run into overtime as the Giants took more than four quarters to finally lose to my Redskins, now known as the Washington Football Team.

I pulled into my parking space at the Willow Falls PD at five minutes until eight, took the elevator to the third floor, and was at my desk when the day officially started. My desk phone rang as I sat down.

"Jones…"

"Morning, Jonesy." It was Helen. "You got time to go over the preliminary toxicology report on the DOA from Friday night?"

"Sure. You coming up or am I coming down?"

"You'd make a lovely young lady climb all the way upstairs just to see your ugly face first thing on a Monday morning? No wonder you're almost single."

"Okay, I guess I'll be down in a few. You want coffee?"

"Stopped and got some on the way in. You know I

can't stand the stuff from that vending machine"

"See you shortly."

I rummaged through my desk drawer until I found a lined notepad and a city-issued ballpoint pen. Then I headed to the elevator. On the way, I shoveled four quarters into the coffee vending machine and pushed the button for a cup of "French Roast—Black." I knew it would taste awful, but it would keep me going through the morning. I waited to take a sip until I was in the elevator, heading to the second floor. The coffee tasted worse than I remembered, and I emptied the thin cardboard cup into the drain of the drinking fountain two doors from Helen's office.

I stepped into Helen's office and dropped the empty cup into her trashcan. "Good morning, fair lady."

She had her back turned and was looking into her compact mirror. She smiled and then put her compact into her purse as she turned to greet me. Her lips were coated with a reddish orange lipstick, a spot of which had found its way to her top incisor. "Just fixing myself up in case some eligible gentleman might stop by to see me this morning. Did you see anyone looking for me when you were out in the hallway?"

"Enough with the cuteness. What does the coroner's preliminary report say?"

She pouted. "Aren't you the grouch this morning."

I shrugged my shoulders. "Sorry. I was up late last night. I'll be okay once the day gets started."

Helen pulled a report from under her desk blotter. "You can read it, but it says Warren Wilson—the DOA—was stewed and shouldn't have been driving. Combination of alcohol, amphetamines, and an unknown substance. I figure it had to be frog slime, but identification will come later from the State labs."

"How do we know he was at the Odd Fellows Hall?"

She waved the printed invitation at me. "I have his license plate number on my list of attendees."

"Good work, Helen. Anybody else in the vehicle?"

"Not at the scene. Maybe we should see if somebody checked into the hospital."

"Yeah, good idea. I'll do that." Helen always thinks of every stone to turn over.

****

I stepped out of the PD long enough to buy a good cup of coffee-to-go at Verrigni's Quick Sack and then hurried back to my desk to begin calling our four local hospitals. I tried Schenectady's first and scored a bullseye on my first try.

"This is police Detective Bart Jones of Willow Falls. I am investigating a possible crime and need information regarding patient admissions to your emergency room."

The switchboard operator connected me with the ER director.

"This is Dr. Morton. How can I help you?"

I explained the reason for my call.

"I assume you know today's code word?"

The local hospitals and the police departments of the capital region had established a protocol for identifying real calls from pranks. Without such a protocol, I would have had to drive to each hospital to ask the same couple of questions. The protocol also protected patient rights. This month, the code word for every day of the week was a different bird. Go figure. It was not my idea, but it worked for us.

"Blue Heron."

"Yes, Detective. How can I help you?"

"We're wondering if your intake people saw one or more people who had injuries which could have been sustained in an automobile accident, but who did not arrive via ambulance?"

"When would this have occurred?"

"Probably early Saturday morning, sometime after midnight on Friday."

I could hear Dr. Morton's fingers clicking on his computer keyboard. "Yes, we had one possibly fitting that description. A woman was dropped off at two forty-seven a.m. with bruises and contusions. She was concerned about damage to her chest and ribs, but x-rays showed nothing broken. She refused blood and breathalyzer tests. Her eyes were bloodshot, and she appeared possibly intoxicated. She was treated and released. Went home alone by cab."

"You got a name and address?"

"Yup. Natalie Pemberton. 657 Montclair. Willow Falls. You need a phone number?"

I took down Natalie's contact information and thanked the doctor. She was very likely the woman with whom I had enjoyed a brief tryst on Friday evening. I mean, from an investigative standpoint, "Natalie" is not exactly high on the list of popular first names.

I called Helen and told her what I had learned. "I'm going to go over to her house because I'll bet she's too sore from the accident to go to work today. Want to come along?"

"You gonna check out the other hospitals first?"

"Nope. This one is so close to the scene of the accident I don't think there's a need to check elsewhere."

"You go on ahead, then. I'll call the other hospitals while you're gone. Somebody's got to do the grunt work."

I heard Helen tapping her pencil on her desk. "Just one thing, Jonesy."

"What's that?"

"Don't let her trap you into some coital thing which will compromise this investigation, especially if she's guilty of something worth prosecuting."

"Yes, Momma," I replied. "I know you're always worried about my welfare."

"Yeah, and don't go catching some disease you might spread around to some other unsuspecting member of the fairer sex."

Helen was right about that. My tryst at the Halloween party had not been protected and I had no idea whether Natalie had regular medical examinations. I guess I had put myself at risk. I made a mental note to avoid unprotected encounters. I was going to have to buy some protection and keep it handy.

Dressed in plainclothes, I left the PD and drove to 657 Montclair. It was a cute gray bungalow with pink trim on the older side of Willow Falls, a neighborhood to the west of Binkley Avenue, where older residents had turned over their homes to younger folks who could not afford the more expensive homes on the east side of town. Her yard was neatly manicured, though the flower gardens had died away from the cold of the impending winter. Somebody had cut back the hydrangeas on both sides of the front door.

I rang the doorbell. Natalie answered. She was wearing a green and red plaid bathrobe and rabbit slippers. Her hair was disheveled, but it did not draw my attention away from her bruised cheekbone and black eye. I showed her my badge and she let me in. I was not sure she even remembered me.

"Miss Pemberton, my name is Bart Jones with the Willow Falls police department. I came to check on you."

"Don't emergency room doctors have some rule about patient confidentiality?" she asked.

"Not when the police are investigating an automobile accident."

"So, you know about the accident."

"Yeah. Can you tell me what happened?"

"Look, the guy was giving me a ride home. It was late and my girlfriend was busy with a guy she met at the party we attended. So, I bummed a ride off a stag who attended the same party."

"Might have been safer to take a cab, huh?"

"He seemed okay when I was talking with him, but we'd both had a lot to drink, so I don't know if my female radar was working like it should have been."

"What do you mean?""

"Well, right after we got into his car, he offered me a couple of tokes from a joint he had in his glove compartment. I shouldn't have said 'okay,' but I had been drinking and did. He lit it and we got a little higher." She looked at me a little closer, like maybe she was remembering me in some way. Maybe she was just worried about self-incrimination because I was a cop. "It was his stuff, not mine. I don't have anything like that in my house, if you need to search it, and I don't normally do reefer, especially when I don't even know the guy."

I nodded.

"Then he started the car and we headed back to Willow Falls. Along the way, he tells me how it would be nice if I'd give him a little something for the ride. I asked, 'What do you want?' So, he pointed to his crotch. I knew what he wanted, but I wasn't going there. He reached over to touch my breast. When he did, I grabbed his arm. He lost control of the car and hit a tree in somebody's big front yard. I guess I hit the dashboard and maybe the windshield. The seatbelt cut my chest."

"But you left the scene of an accident. That's against the law."

"Look, I don't need a lecture about what's legal and what's not. When I came to, the guy didn't look too good. I shook him to try to get him to come to, but he wouldn't. I wasn't sure what to do and I wasn't thinking clearly. I didn't want to be arrested for smoking dope. So, I got out of the car and walked back to the road. I was standing there when this black BMW stopped, and the driver offered me a ride to the hospital."

"Who was he?"

"The guy in the BMW?"

"Yeah."

"It was Mr. Modern. He's the guy who threw the party. Well, him and that real estate lady from England."

"Was she with him?"

"Nope. It was just him."

"Did he know you had been in an accident?"

"Yeah. I mean, look at me. Who wouldn't know?"

She was right about that. "So, did he say anything to you?"

"He said I should just tell the doctor I fell down my front porch chasing trick or treaters. He said, 'We wouldn't want the accident to cause the authorities to shut down future parties.'"

"He said that?"

"Yes. Those very words. 'We wouldn't want the

accident to cause the authorities to shut down future parties.'"

"And if you mentioned the party to the police at the scene of the accident, they'd have arrested the hosts for permitting their guests to drink too much and drive."

"So, how's the man who gave me the ride? Is he okay?"

"Sorry, but he was DOA."

"DOA?"

"Dead on arrival at the hospital."

Natalie's eyes fell to her lap and tears began streaming down her cheek. I took a couple of tissues from a box on her coffee table and handed them to her.

"Listen, it's not your fault," I told her. "But I may need you to come to the police department and fill out an accident report. I'll call you if it's necessary, okay?"

She nodded.

I let myself out.

Chapter 16

I arrived back at work at lunchtime. Helen had gone to get a salad with a couple of women from the computer center, so I couldn't debrief with her until she returned. I put a dollar into a vending machine and bought a package of peanut butter crackers, the orange kind I like. As I returned to my desk, I heard my desk phone ringing. I reached it after six rings.

It was the desk sergeant. "You got a visitor. Want me to send him up?"

I could not imagine who it might be, but maybe he would have some information about the Laura Moretti case. "Sure, send him up."

About two minutes later a guy in a wrinkled brown pinstriped suit and tennis shoes arrived at my desk. "Are you Bartholomew Jones?"

"Yeah. How can I help you?"

He plopped an eight by fourteen manilla envelope in front of me, right on top of my package of crackers.

"What's this?"

"Divorce papers." He turned and walked away, just like that.

"What the f—?" I stammered. "Divorce?"

I opened the envelope. Sure enough, Rachel was suing me for divorce, claiming desertion.

"I thought this was a no-fault state," I muttered. "I didn't desert her. She cheated on me. What the fugg?"

****

"What's the matter, sweet thing? You seem like you're really preoccupied."

Helen had come to my desk after receiving word I wanted to share details about my interview with the occupant in the DOA's car.

"Sorry, Helen. Rachel had me served with divorce papers this afternoon. I'm not going to be firing on all cylinders until I get this thing figured out."

"You saw it coming like your electric bill, didn't you? You shouldn't be shocked. And figuring it out ain't nothing you can do by yourself, Jonesy. You need to go hire yourself a crackerjack attorney. I don't mean some inexpensive guy who does house closings or chases ambulances. I mean a real live divorce lawyer who'll fight for you, 'cause if you don't, you're gonna get screwed."

I knew Helen was right, but how was I going to pay for a top-drawer attorney when I could barely make ends meet? In fact, I would still be sleeping in my city-owned sedan if Joey Astor hadn't loaned me his father-in-law's place free of charge. And the quality of my meals would be questionable by the end of the month if I had not launched a private detective business on the side. And that was something I had not cleared with the Chief, so I was in violation of some sort of labor clause. Worse than that, I was doing detective work for the Los Equis Cartel, which would be another cause for dismissal if anyone ever found out. I was on borrowed time.

"You know a good one?" I asked. "I mean a savage attorney who would be good in a divorce case?"

"I'll put out some feelers for you, Jonesy. Meanwhile, tell me what you found out from that woman who didn't die in the accident on Friday night."

"Saturday morning."

"Yeah, that's the one."

"She was inebriated at the very least and had been smoking pot in the car with the driver. He tried to cop a feel while driving, but she resisted, and he ran off the road. She left the scene and was picked up by a motorist who drove her to the hospital. She didn't know Wilson was DOA."

Helen always knew what to ask next. "Can we get corroboration from the driver who gave her a lift?"

"Yeah. You're going to love this: She was picked up and driven to the hospital by Horace Modern."

"My, my," Helen grinned, "doesn't his name always seem to pop up at the most convenient times."

"My thoughts exactly. I think it's time to go visit him again."

"I think I'll come along this time."

****

We arrived at Modern Scientific Supply at three in the afternoon. The sky looked snow-like, but nothing was coming down yet.

When we entered the building, the security guard at the front desk was not as cordial as the last one had been during our first visit. "Is Mr. Modern expecting you?" she asked curtly.

"No, but it's important he gives us a few minutes," I replied. "It's a matter of life and death."

While she buzzed Modern's cell phone, I took a hard look at her. She was probably in her fifties. Her hair was pulled back into a bun. It was brown, but her inch-long roots were gray. Her fingernails were not polished, and the first two on her right hand were stained orangish-brown, a sure sign she was a smoker. I wondered if she preferred the filtered or un-filtered coffin tacks.

"He'll be right down." She pointed at two plastic chairs against the wall to our left. "You can have a seat over there."

Helen and I walked toward the chairs, but neither of us sat. After ten minutes, the door to the office area opened and out strode Modern. "Oh, hello again, officers," he said with a forced smile. "I thought this was something direly important."

"Well, it is," Helen replied. "We heard you were out and about on Friday night."

"Yes, I had an engagement." He pointed toward the door to the inner sanctum. "Please, let's go speak in private."

We followed Modern into his office. He had not renovated it since our last visit. The walls were still khaki and the decorations were still African or South American tribal stuff.

"Mr. Middleton," I began, "we believe…"

"The name is 'Modern,'" he said. "Horace Modern."

"Yes," I said. "I guess we can explore that first. You graduated from Yale as 'Benjamin Middleton.' What caused you to change your name?"

Modern looked irritated. "Why are you investigating me? I've done nothing wrong."

"We never said you did anything wrong. We just like to know who we're dealing with, and we aren't sure who you are."

Modern huffed and crossed his arms.

"Aren't you a member of the Skull and Bones?" Helen asked.

Modern threw her a hateful look. "If I were, I

wouldn't admit to it or talk about it. Everybody knows that."

"George Bush, Sr did," Helen replied.

"He wasn't too bright. Maybe talking about the Bones cost him his second term."

"I guess you never know," I said. "So, I want to get back to your name. Why did you change it? You in trouble with somebody, like maybe the Mafia? You in a witness protection program?"

"Nothing so glamorous, Detective. I changed my name to something people would remember. Something which would stand out. Who'd give a rat's ass about a person named Benny Middleton? It's got no pizzazz."

"Horace isn't exactly Hollywood material," Helen said.

"It's got special meaning—at least to me. And people associate it with my business, Modern Scientific Supply."

"So, tell me about Friday night," I said. "What did you do?"

"I went to a private party over in Schenectady."

"The one at the Odd Fellows Hall?"

"Yeah. You know about that?"

"Yeah. I almost feel as if I was there. What were you dressed as?"

He waved his hands in opposite directions in front of his face. "I was Osiris, the Sun King."

"Was there a Sun Queen, too?"

"Yeah. The two of us sort of hosted the party."

"What's her name, the queen?" Helen asked.

"Roxanne Windsor of the Windsor family."

I looked at Helen. "Are we supposed to know something important about the Windsor family?"

Modern gave me a look of frustration, as though he thought I was totally ignorant. "The Windsor family is the royal family of England. Roxanne is fourth cousin to Princess Margaret."

"Doesn't that make her sort of unimportant as far as the Windsors are concerned? I don't even know my fourth cousins," I said. "My family doesn't much care beyond second cousins."

"Do a DNA analysis and you'll find you have plenty of fourth and fifth cousins, Detective," Modern said. "And Roxanne's name appears somewhere down the list of possible successors to the throne."

"So, is Roxanne Windsor known locally as 'the Queen from England'?" Helen asked.

"Only in a very small circle. It's sort of a standing joke."

"Is she a drug dealer?" I asked. "Specifically, of magic mushrooms?"

"Boy, you certainly get to the point, don't you?" Modern replied. "No, of course not. She's a real estate agent...only the prime properties, the ones over two million dollars."

"What company does she work for?" Helen asked.

"Royale Realty. It's her own firm. She doesn't need to advertise."

"How about after the party, Mr. Middleton?" I asked. "What did you do after the party?"

"He shot me a look of distain. "Listen, I went to court and legally changed my name to 'Horace Modern,' and I expect you to honor that change, or else you can leave."

"So, back to my question, Mr. Modern. What happened after the party?"

"I presume you're asking about the young woman I drove to the hospital?"

"Yes, although I wouldn't call her 'young.' She's at least approaching her late thirties."

"I'm approaching sixty. From my perspective, she's young, Detective."

He had a point. "Where did you encounter her?"

"She was walking along the road, weaving back and forth, about a mile from the Odd Fellows. When I slowed to ask if she needed a lift, I could see she was hurt. She wanted me to take her home, but I took her to the hospital."

"How long have you known her?" Helen asked. It was a good question.

"I don't know her at all."

Helen pressed him. "Yet she attended your party at the Odd Fellows Hall."

"I'm sure she was one of the dozen or so people who simply purchased a ticket at the Crystal Cantor, like everyone else did. The party caters to the Cantor's clientele."

"Natalie says she's attended three of your annual Halloween events. You're certain you don't know her?" I asked.

"Maybe I've seen her before, but I don't really recall."

Helen continued pressing, and I smiled at her as she did. "What happens to the proceeds of the ticket sales? Is it a charity event or a for-profit undertaking?"

Modern sighed again. "After expenses, and believe me there are plenty, the residuals go to help save the Amazonian rainforest. Did you know they're cutting down a million acres of rainforest every year just to expand cattle ranching? We donate the residuals to purchase land which cannot be cut down and burned."

"I'll bet it goes a long way toward saving the habitat for those psychedelic tree frogs, doesn't it?" Helen asked.

"How…?"

Helen anticipated his question. "Saw some at the Crystal Cantor when we bought our tickets for your party."

Modern's face took on a look of surprise. "You were there?"

I jumped in. "Yeah, and we saw your employees selling frog secretions to the crowd. There must be a law against that and when I find it, I may have to arrest you."

Modern looked shocked that I would even think of arresting him.

"And what about that yucky feeding ceremony? Isn't it against the law to drink somebody else's blood in New York?" Helen asked.

"No law was broken. The blood was freely given by volunteers," Modern replied.

"We'll see what the Health Department says about that," I said.

I could tell Modern was getting upset with our line of questioning. He squirmed every time Helen hit him with a good one. With me, however, he was a little confrontational and argumentative, so I hit him with another question: "And won't PETA take you to task over slicing a rabbit's throat and drinking its blood?"

Modern was about to say something, but I raised my hand and cut him off. "Most of all, I'm interested in what you can tell me about the blood drinkers of this community. Clearly, you and the queen are among them.

Who are the others? When and where do they meet?"

"You can't be serious," Modern protested. "There are no blood drinkers in this community. None."

"Then if not in this one, there's a group in the capital region. I want to know everything about them. Everything."

"You're out of your mind."

Helen stepped in. "We saw the minor leaguers at your party cutting each other and lapping a few drops of blood. They're probably in training, but you and the queen drank that rabbit's blood full strength. You both shared a cup of it before pouring the rest into the soda. You two are major leaguers."

Modern stood and opened the door to his office. "Unless you officers are bringing me up on some sort of trumped-up charges, I think we're done for the day. Please leave. And you can expect to hear from my attorney."

Chapter 17

"Well, he knows we're onto him," Helen said when we got back into my sedan. "From now on, he's gonna be more cautious and less visible with everything he does, especially the blood drinking and the frog licking."

"It's crystal clear there's more here than meets the eye."

"And I'll bet his parties won't be open to the cash paying public anymore, either."

Helen was right about that, too. We were going to have to find a better way to peel back the layers so we could discover the truth. Meanwhile, we were not any closer to finding out who killed little Laura Moretti, and Chief Comstock wanted the case solved quickly.

****

Back at the office, Helen found the website for Royale Realty and called Miss Roxanne Windsor at the number she had posted for inquiries.

"Roxanne here. Please leave your name and number and I'll get back to you shortly. It's a beautiful day to explore my listings, so I encourage you to do that until I return your call. Cheerio."

Damn recorded message, Helen thought. "Miss Windsor, my name is Helen Martin. I need to speak with you on a matter of some urgency. Would you please call me at the number from which I'm calling you? Thank you very much." *I hope her answering machine displays the number. Don't they all nowadays?*

Helen called my desk phone.

"Jones here."

"I called the queen and left a message, Jonesy." I recognized Helen's voice. "Her damn real estate website doesn't list an address. Her business must be entirely virtual."

"Well, I'm told the royals prefer anonymity. She's just trying to melt into the community like a 'common Joe.' Besides, Modern probably called her the moment we left his office. I'll bet she's gone into hiding."

"She can't sell any of those overpriced bungalows without answering her phone. Business is business and money talks."

Helen always had good ideas. "So, you're suggesting we get somebody to call her about buying one of her listings?"

"Yeah. How about you?"

"Give me the number."

"Better than that, I'll send you the website link so you can pick out your favorite fixer-upper and then call her about seeing it. Her number is posted on the website."

"You're always thinking, aren't you?"

"You gotta do some of the detecting on your own, Jonesy. Keeps your skills sharp."

Helen hung up. I turned on my desk computer, maneuvered out onto the internet, and keyed in the Royale Realty link. It came up instantly. The R on Royale wore a golden crown, tilted to the left. *Cute*, I thought. The background on the banner was, of course, royal blue and the lettering was snow white. Roxanne's face was pasted to the left side of the page, below the banner. She was dressed in a ball gown and was holding a scepter, much like Miss America holds a dozen roses when she is standing before the crowd after being crowned. In the photo, she appeared to be around twenty-two years old. I guessed the picture showed a much younger Roxanne than the woman I hoped to meet in the next day or two.

I clicked on the "View My Listings" link. A dozen homes appeared, not all in one community, but scattered around the entire capital region. They varied in price from two-point-two million to twenty-seven million dollars in price. I clicked on the least expensive, a four thousand square foot custom log home, located in a rural section of Saratoga County and overlooking Ballston Lake. I would not mind owning something like that, but it would never happen on a police detective's salary, especially one whose wife was suing him for divorce so she could run off with an ice cream salesman.

I called the number for Royale Realty and left a brief message. "My name is Henry Rockefeller. I'm interested in seeing the property on Ballston Lake, the one posted on your website. Please call me when you're available to show it to me. Thank you." I didn't leave my phone number because I knew Roxanne Windsor would have it on her cell phone.

When Ms. Windsor returned my call, it was late afternoon. I was sitting in Helen's office reviewing what we knew about the Laura Moretti case which, admittedly, was not much.

"Mr. Rockefeller?" she asked.

"Speaking."

"Are you certain I have the correct telephone number? Is this Henry Rockefeller?"

"Yes, speaking."

"It's interesting your number displays you as Bartholomew Jones."

"It's a friend's phone. Mine is in getting a new glass face. I broke it when I dropped it at a bar last night. The repair shop says it'll be ready by Saturday."

"Would you be able to see the home Friday morning, say ten o'clock? The sunlight on Ballston Lake is superb at that hour."

"Sure. Just give me the address and I'll meet you there at ten o'clock sharp."

"Excellent."

****

Helen and I left the police department at nine thirty on Friday for our drive to Ballston Lake. It was a sunny and warm Indian summer morning, almost sixty degrees with the high expected to approach seventy-five. How's that for November in the northeast?

The queen was not expecting Helen, so it would be interesting to see her reaction to a mixed racial couple having interest in one of her elitist properties. Of course, I never told her I was interested in buying the property. Instead, I had said I was interested in "seeing it." Also, I never said the reason I wanted to meet her—so I could jot down her license plate number and ask her a few questions about the existence of a blood drinkers' cult in the capital region. But I planned to do just that.

I had just turned onto Route 50, north of Burnt Hills, when Helen's cell phone rang. "Martin," she said officially. "Yes….yes…yeah, he's here with me now. Let me put you on speaker phone." Helen tapped some buttons on her phone. "You still there?"

"Yeah." It was Dr. Foster, the medical examiner.

"Can you hear me okay?"

"Yeah," Helen replied.

"How about you, Jones? Can you hear me okay?"

"Yeah," I replied. I put on my blinker and pulled off the road near a dairy farm with a big white barn. "I just pulled over so we can speak."

"Good. Listen, I got the toxicology report back from the State labs on that guy who died in the automobile accident last Friday night. They told me they were so stunned by their own results they had to send the sample to the university for verification."

This sounded interesting. Helen and I both leaned closer to her cell phone.

"The blood sample from Mr. Warren Wilson (deceased) arrived on…"

"Get to the good stuff, would you, Doc?" I said.

"Yeah, yeah," he replied. I could envision him waving his hand in annoyance.

"They found several stimulants and hallucinogens in his blood. He had been drinking alcohol…blood alcohol level .15 percent…twice the legal definition of intoxication."

"Yeah," Helen said.

A semi blew its horn as it passed by our parked car. The wind from its draft shook us violently.

Dr. Foster continued. "His blood also evidenced a medically significant amount of dermophin, a natural opioid which is forty times stronger than morphine. God only knows where he got ahold of that. I don't think it's sold on the black market, but maybe…" Dr. Foster paused. "I just got out my book on this stuff. The South Americans call it 'kambo.' It's a secretion of the giant monkey frog. It's used by Peruvians for religious and medical purposes."

Helen and I looked at each other. I still had our two sheets of rolling paper in a plastic sandwich bag in my desk drawer. Maybe I would give one sheet to Dr. Foster, along with the two tree frogs that were living in the aquarium on my desk.

"But there's more," Dr. Foster said.

"More?" Helen asked. "He was already stewed on two different mind-altering drugs."

"Yes, he was. And his bloodwork also evidenced Tetrahydrocannabinol, but not enough to declare him high."

"That's THC, right, Doc? The stuff in marijuana which gets you high," I said.

"Yes, that's right."

Helen shook her head in disbelief. "Wow, he was high on just about everything my mother warned me about when I was a kid."

"But there's more…"

"Really?" I wondered what else this guy had popped into his mouth. Obviously, he had been doing some hard partying.

"Yes. He was also nearing death."

"He died, Doc," I reminded him.

"No, I don't mean it that way, Jones," Dr. Foster replied. "He was probably going to die anyway. His blood also displayed high iron toxicity. I'm surprised he was able to find his car, much less drive."

"Iron toxicity?" Helen asked.

"Yes, he ingested a large amount of iron, more than the human body can tolerate."

"What did he do, eat nails?" I asked.

"The last time we spoke, it involved that little girl.

The one whose body was drained of blood."

"Yes, Laura Moretti," Helen said.

"I mentioned the wild possibility we could have a cult of people here in Willow Falls who drink human blood. Well, Mr. Wilson's iron toxicity is another symptom of that possibility. He could have been one of them."

"Why's that?" I asked.

"The ingestion of too much blood comes with the potential side effect of iron toxicity, a toxicity which leads to death." Doc Foster paused for a moment. I figured he was sipping coffee or soda. "But there's more."

"But wait, there's more," I said, mimicking the doctor. "You sound like that guy on the television."

"Yeah, I think I do. However, this may help you solve your case: His blood evidenced two other compounds—sodium heparin and adrenochrome. Sodium heparin is an edible anticoagulant which is used to keep blood a thin fluid so it can be transferred from one person to another. And if you remember, adrenochrome is the substance caused by elevated fear. Either he was very much afraid of something, or the blood he had ingested was from a creature that was frightened to death."

"Laura Moretti?" Helen asked perceptively.

"I can't be sure, but it's a very distinct possibility."

Chapter 18

Helen used the GPS function on her cell phone to guide us to the log home we were going to tour, supposedly as potential buyers. Following her phone's directions, we made a right turn off Route 50 about three miles south of Ballston Spa and followed a gravel road for about half a mile before it made a hard left turn. Through the trees we could see the morning sun reflecting off water. If it had been summer, the trees would have been full of rich green leaves and we would have had no clue a lake was hidden beyond.

We passed two large red brick homes and then turned right into the third driveway. It was layered with fine cut crushed gravel and lined with granite boulders on both sides. I guess if we had been driving drunk, the boulders would have kept us on the driveway as we bounced off them.

Ms. Roxanne Windsor was waiting for us when we arrived in front of the three-bay garage which adjoined the log home. Dressed in a brown tweed suit, she was standing beside a baby blue 2003 Bentley Azure convertible and waving her hand at the wrist, the way the British royals are prone to doing. I flashed my headlights twice, so she would be sure to see us. When I pulled to a stop beside her Bentley, she disappeared momentarily in the cloud of stone dust that followed us.

As the dust settled, Roxanne inspected my sedan

with a look of disgust and then broke into a big smile. "Welcome. Welcome," she said as we stepped out into the fresh air.

"You must be Miss Windsor," Helen said. "My name is Helen and the big galumph on the other side of our car is Henry Rockefeller, but you can call him Bart."

"Yes, yes. So happy to meet you. Are you new to the area? You seem somehow familiar."

Helen closed the car's door. "Been here awhile." She looked up at the log home. It was three stories high with massive round logs, all peeled of bark and polished to a high gloss. Its floor-to-ceiling windows exposed much of the interior to anyone standing outside, and its blue steel roof blocked the morning sun. "Seen places like this in magazines," Helen said. "I feel like this should be out west somewhere, you know, where the buffaloes roam and where antelopes play." She was putting it on thick.

"Helen may be a hard sell on this place, Ms. Windsor," I said. "I'm the one who's interested in seeing it."

"Please call me Roxanne. We're all soon to be good friends. In terms of touring the home, where would you like to begin?"

"How about the backyard?" I suggested. "I'd like to see the lake."

"Certainly. Please follow me."

Roxanne spun and walked through a breezeway which connected the main house to the three-bay garage. As we entered the sunshine on the east side of the home, the lake came into view. Yes, it was certainly magnificent, though narrower than Mariaville Lake at my cabin. The water also looked muddy. On the home's large back deck four ornate iron chairs hugged a round table with a Mexican tile surface. Grass swept fifty yards from the deck to the water's edge where a dock offered two boat slips, both empty due to the impending winter.

"Let's sit for a moment, shall we?" I said.

Roxanne felt the chair to see if the morning's dew had dissipated. It had, so she sat. "You were both at the festivities at the Odd Fellows Hall last weekend, weren't you? It took me this long to place you because you're out of uniform this morning." She pouted a bit. "I suppose coming here was all a ruse to speak with me, wasn't it? I could have used the sale, this being the off season for home buyers."

"Sorry about this," Helen said, "but you don't have an office and we had no other way to get to you. If we had told you who we were and why we wanted to speak with you, we assumed you probably would not have returned our call."

"You assumed correctly, Officer."

"Call me 'Helen' since we're soon going to be best friends."

Roxanne pursed her lips in a look of disgust. "So, why do you want to interrogate me?"

I jumped in. "We saw you drink chicken's blood at the Halloween party. Aren't you afraid of iron toxicity?

"No, not really. I avoid fortified foods, green leafy vegetables, and red meat for a week before I feed. That seems to do the trick."

"Are you a vampire?" I asked.

"No, not like Dracula. However, I know many people who wish they were."

Helen leaned forward. "Was Warren Wilson one of those people?"

Roxanne slumped a little in her chair. "Yes, he was a good friend. But I'm afraid he was more of an experimenter than he should have been -- you know, mixing alcohol and marijuana and similar things. It's what led to his demise, I believe."

"Yes, obviously he was into some illegal stuff," I said.

"I can't speak to his ingestion of anything other than blood. He drank a small amount of rabbit blood mixed with vodka and soda at the party. Nothing was illegal about it. It's simply part of the mystique of Halloween. People who are intrigued with the fictional concept of vampires taste a small amount of blood to feel a little naughty. And it's all perfectly safe."

"What about the frog slime?" Helen asked.

"Again, it's part of modern culture. Peruvian tree frogs are illegal to import into the USA, but it is not illegal to possess them if they have been cultivated here. And their secretions are not illegal to consume. Some doctors prescribe them to their patients for numerous medical conditions, including cancer, mental illness, and Alzheimer's."

"You used the term 'feed' to describe drinking blood," I said.

Roxanne showed me her teeth and hissed at me. I drew back. She laughed. "The use of that term is part of the Sanguinarian subculture. We use it all the time."

"Sanguinarian?" I asked.

"It loosely translates as 'blood drinkers.'"

"How many of you are there?"

"Across the nation, it's difficult to say," Roxanne replied. "The community likes to stay hidden because they fear ridicule from exposure."

"I mean, how many of you are there in the capital district?"

"I think, if you include the novices, we total around thirty, perhaps thirty-five."

"And how many if you exclude the novices? Like, how many fully active Sanguinarians can you count on your fingers and toes, here in the capital district?"

"Approximately eighteen, if you subtract Warren."

"And how many of those eighteen have drunk human blood?" Helen asked. She had a way of getting to the point.

"All of us," Roxanne answered as if the question were a no-brainer. "You witnessed a minor feeding ceremony at the Odd Fellows Hall."

Helen nodded.

"All us humans begin the journey by first tasting our own blood when we're children, sucking at a scrape or cut on our own bodies." She looked at Helen. "I'm sure you've done that yourself."

Helen nodded.

"We know we're truly Sanguinarians when we develop an appreciation for the taste. As adults, we migrate to tasting others' blood, always donated voluntarily by supporters who are most often novices."

"Is there an illegal trade in human blood?" I asked. "You know, like a black market for blood stolen from blood banks or hospitals?"

"Unfortunately, across the nation there is such a black market...especially in the deep south where voodoo culture demands it and on the west coast where the Hollywood elite crave it. But here in the Capital District we refrain from purchasing illegal blood. You never know what sorts of diseases it might carry."

"Is there any chance a few of your inner core of Sanguinarians might trade in illicit blood?"

"God, I hope not. It would hurt me deeply to discover that. If anyone might know the answer to your question, it would be Horry. I know you've spoken with him. Did you ask him that question?"

"Horace Modern? No. He was less forthcoming than you've been," Helen replied. "You've been very helpful."

"I will always be happy to answer your questions. As a hopeful American, I want to support this nation in any way I can."

"Hopeful?" I asked.

Roxanne placed her right hand across her heart, as though pledging allegiance to the flag. "Yes. I've finally applied for citizenship. I don't need an arrest or the suspicion of illegal activity to negatively affect my chances. I love it here. It's a bloody good place to live and do business."

****

When we returned to the department, I found a note to call Lester Brockbank, the attorney who had helped Judge Michael Agosta during his murder trial. I wondered whether he had new information about the case. From my posture, the investigation was completely over and the players were sitting in their respective penalty boxes.

"How can I help you?" I asked when he answered his phone. I thought I would have had to go through a secretary to get to him.

"I think the better question is, 'How can I help you?'" he replied. "I heard you've been served divorce papers. If you don't have an attorney yet, maybe I can be of assistance."

"How did you know?"

"That's not important. Let's just say a little birdie told me. At any rate, do you have an attorney to help you through the quagmire of a messy divorce?"

"Not yet," I replied honestly. Hell, I really had not given it much thought. I had just assumed I could not afford an attorney and Rachel's would simply bleed me and hang me out to dry.

"Well, bring me the paperwork from your wife's attorney and we'll see what we can do to make post-marital life easier on you."

I planned to leave work early so I could prepare for the cockfight. I was supposed to meet Mescal at his place at seven. "Will you be in your office around three-thirty?"

"Of course. As a self-employed man I don't enjoy the same short workweek and freedom to come and go as you city employees. I'll see you then."

After we hung up, I took the elevator down to Helen's office. "Want to do lunch?"

"Sure, Jonesy. We gotta talk about Queen Roxanne, anyway. Where you taking me?"

"Burger King is offering two for one this week. I think I can afford that."

"Sounds good. I want to try one of those new thingies they been advertising…the one with the onion rings, bacon, fries, and sauce all piled on top of the patty. Looks greasy good, like home cooking."

This time Helen drove, and I got to ride shotgun.

"Heard you got yourself a good divorce attorney," she said. "A real legal eagle."

"Did you sic him on me?"

"Must have been one of your friends, Jonesy. You got more than one, don't you?"

Helen was playing with me. I knew she had somehow gotten to Brockbank and asked him to help me. "So, did you have to do him a sexual favor to get him to call me?"

"What kind of question is that?" she asked. "Can't a friend help a friend? It just happened he was in Verrigni's getting coffee same time I was, so I told him about your situation...how you living in a shack and have to work a parttime job to make ends meet. That's all I did, 'cept give him your phone number."

"Well, I don't like telling people how financially strung out I am, but I suppose my attorney is going to find out anyway. I guess I owe you, Helen."

"No problem. You gonna pay up someday, anyway."

"I think I pay up every day."

Helen laughed. "You pretty smart for a white guy."

Chapter 19

I stopped by Lester Brockbank's office at three-thirty, as promised. His secretary told me he was on an unexpected long-distance call and would not be able to speak with me until Monday. She told me he would give me a call so we could meet, maybe over lunch.

I left the divorce paperwork with his secretary and headed to Mariaville, where I planned to catch a shower and change into my cockfighting uniform—blue jeans, one of several long-sleeved tee shirts, and hiking boots. For a gringo, I'd be dressed down.

The sky was already starting to change color as I pulled onto the gravel parking space in front of my cabin. The sun was kissing the horizon and the sheet of clouds above me was bright orange, striped with golden yellow sunbeams. If I could have, I would have waited and watched until dark, but time was of the essence.

I went inside and showered, and then threw a can of beef stew into a pot and put it on the back burner of the cabin's small stove. While waiting for the stew to come to a boil, I buttered a piece of wheat bread and popped a beer. When the stew was ready, I shoveled it into my mouth between bites of bread and mouthfuls of beer.

At six-thirty I locked the cabin and drove into Willow Falls. The sky was now full of flat-bottomed gray clouds, a signal that it might snow. At Albany Street, I turned left on Van Rensselaer Drive and, after a couple of blocks, pulled to a stop in front of the building whose windows advertised, "Vacuum Cleaner Repair." It was six-fifty-five, and I was right on time. I got out of my sedan and knocked on the plywood door, being sure to rap hardest on the death's head someone had painted there in black. I heard commotion inside and then the door opened. I was expecting some goon to greet me, but it was Mescal, himself. "Hola, gringo. You ready for the best night of your life?"

"Hola," I replied. "*Si, muchacho.*"

"Whoa, gringo. Watch your Spanish. You calling me a young man or your servant?"

"Sorry. What's 'friend' in Spanish, Mescal?"

"Amigo."

I think I knew that, and I felt a little foolish for asking.

"Don' you watch no Spanish television?" he asked.

"I guess it's time I do."

"We leaving your buggy here, gringo. You riding with me."

"Two wheels?"

"No. They sayin' snow mañana. We don' wanna be on no pony if it's snowing later on. I mean, I can manage two wheels in a little snow, but the other drivers go crazy, swervin' this way and that way and not stoppin' too good on snow. You lived here all your life, so you seen it all before. You and me, we'll take my winter wheels.

I looked around but didn't see anything but my sedan. Soon, however, loud rumbling broke the still of the cold evening air. It was coming from an approaching black Hummer, a 2008 four door, and one of the last models before General Motors stopped producing them in 2010. Mescal's was cherry—no dents, no scratches, and new tires. Its inspection sticker was out of date, but nobody would notice, especially at night.

"Here she is," Mescal said proudly. His gold eye tooth flashed in the light of his broad smile. "We ridin' in style tonight."

"I'll say. I've never ridden in one. Always wanted a Hummer but couldn't afford to buy one or operate it. They eat a lot of gas."

"You probably noticed this one needs a muffler. Can't get too many parts anymore. It's gotta be specially fabricated by a shop in Motown. S'posed to be shipped next week."

"How about a muffler from a wreck?" I asked.

"I'm getting' me one in solid chrome so it can't rust out no more. Gotta do thins right to keep me in style."

The guy who had driven the Hummer to the Mexican headquarters said something in private to Mescal. Mescal nodded and then gave him a special gangbangers' handshake. The guy then climbed the steps into the building and closed its plywood door.

"Time to mount up. gringo. We don' wanna be late."

I went to the passenger's side and hoisted myself onto the seat, using the running board as a lift platform. The black leather seat was hard and cold, but I felt like somebody special just by sitting in the cab. No doubt, people would stare at us as Mescal and I drove by them in our chariot of iron.

Then a chicken clucked. I turned and looked into the rear compartment. Mescal had brought a black rooster in a small wire cage.

"Dinner?" I asked.

"No. Tha's the main event. Tha's 'Diablo,' my prize

cock."

Mescal drove three blocks and then down the entrance ramp and onto the crosstown. After a couple of miles, he exited onto the New York State Thruway. Ten minutes later, we exited onto Route Ninety, which beelined across the north end of Albany. We got off just before crossing the Hudson River and made several turns into a dimly lit section of rundown warehouses. Then I saw it. A steel building sat in the middle of a giant paved parking lot. In front of it, more than a hundred cars were parked, not one of them a late model. Many showed evidence of bumps and bruises, rusty door frames, and Bondo. But some had been freshly painted and, like the photos we see of cars in Havana, were in a state of proud restoration.

"We're here, gringo. Contests begin in half an hour."

We jumped down onto the pavement. Mescal opened the back of his Hummer, donned leather gloves, and pulled Diablo's cage into the cold November air. The rooster kicked at the side of his wire cage.

"When we're inside later, you gonna hold Diablo while I strap on his spurs. Got it?"

I could not see myself holding a fighting cock, but I had to do my duty by helping Mescal prep his bird for the upcoming fight. I felt excitement, as though I was one of Mike Tyson's handlers just before a championship match.

I followed Mescal to a steel door lit by a single yellow lightbulb mounted above. He knocked three times, then paused, and then knocked twice. The door opened and my ears were greeted by the noise of a large crowd of men talking and shouting in Spanish in anticipation of the evening's sport. The air was hot and moist inside, and its aroma was heavy with the scents of body odor, beer, and tobacco.

A thin man with three days of whiskers stopped us as we stepped into the building. He said something unintelligible.

"Pay the hombre," Mescal said. "Three dollars each."

I pulled out my wallet and gave the guy a one and a five. He marked an X the backs of our hands with an orange dayglow marker.

"Wait here," Mescal said. He disappeared into the crowd with his cage in hand. A few minutes later he returned, minus the cage. "Diablo is in fight number four. We'll go prep him during the third fight." He looked around for a moment and motioned toward a man in the stands. "Follow me, gringo."

We pushed our way through the crowd and climbed over people as we ascended the grandstand. "You remember Gonzo?" Mescal asked.

It was Miranda Goins' brother. Miranda was a young woman whose ring had been stolen by a guy called, "Big Wax." When Big Wax turned up dead, Miranda was high on the list of possible suspects. It turned out he had died of a drug overdose, and she had cut a finger off the cadaver in order to reclaim a ring which rightfully belonged to her. *Small world*, I thought.

"Nice to see you again," I said to Gonzo.

He knew I was a cop and was surprised to see me in the cockfighting arena, especially since cockfighting is against the law in the U.S. of A. He looked at Mescal, who nodded to him.

"Hola, hombre," he said.

"How've you been?" I asked. "Haven't seen you since we chatted in the park last year. That conversation helped Miranda get her ring back from Big Wax."

Gonzo just nodded nervously, still unsure of my presence.

I turned toward around and examined the ring below. It was approximately twenty feet in diameter with wooden walls, the boards mounted vertically to create a circle more precisely than if the planks had been layered sideways. The floor was covered with a thick layer of sawdust. Outside the ring and pressing into its sides stood fifty or more men and women, all hoping to see the impending fight up close.

A loudspeaker was mounted on a panel of floodlights high above the center of the ring. Energetic Hispanic music was blasting from the loudspeaker, causing everyone to shout in order to be heard above it. As I was taking in the scene, the music suddenly stopped, and a man's voice spoke Spanish over the loudspeaker so rapidly I'm not sure I would have been able to follow it, even if I spoke Spanish.

"What'd he say?" I asked.

"He welcomed us here and reminded the spectators cervezas are cold and available at the concession stand."

I knew cervezas were beer. "You and Gonzo want a cerveza...my treat?"

"After Diablo fights."

The music came back on while the announcer paused for a few minutes. Then it stopped again, and the announcer came back on. A short man with a pot belly and a crew cut entered the ring carrying a white rooster under his arm. Many in the crowd cheered. The announcer said something else. Another man, this one

151

thin and with a short moustache, entered the ring carrying a red rooster in both hands. More people cheered than before.

"I gather the red rooster is the crowd's favorite."

Mescal tilted his head. "Yeah, but they don' know nothin'."

A tall man wearing a referee's shirt stepped forward with an equilibrium scale. Hanging from it were two burlap bags. Each bird was stuffed into a bag and the man with the scale held it high. The red rooster was a little heavier than the white. The crowd became more excited. Four scantily clad women entered the ring and began taking money and returning red or white slips of paper to those who were making bets.

This looked like a sure thing to me. "I'll bet the red one wins," I said.

"Save your money, gringo, until Diablo fights. You need to see how it's done before you go wasting your paycheck on loser cocks."

I turned back toward the ring. The two men were holding their roosters in both hands and poking them back and forth at each other, taunting them into fighting.

The man in the referee shirt re-entered the ring and separated the two men. Then he lifted his arm and quickly brought his hand to his waist. The two men dropped their roosters and hopped over the walls of the ring to stand among the cheering spectators.

The cocks charged each other, flapping their wings and pecking savagely at each other's heads. As they charged and charged again, with wings flapping they rose three, sometimes four feet in the air at the moment of impact. Their legs swung at each other violently. I saw silver-colored steel spurs had been strapped to each bird's ankles.

As they fought, blood streamed from each bird's head, most noticeably from the white rooster because of the contrast in color between his feathers and his blood. After ten minutes and no clear victor, the referee blew a whistle. Each bird's owner entered the ring, picked up his bird, and used a wet cloth to clean its eyes and head.

After a three-minute break, the referee called the birds into the ring again. At his whistle, their owners dropped the birds to the sawdust floor and the fight started again. This time the birds stalked each other, moving in circles around the ring before charging forward again. At the point of impact, the spur on the red rooster's right leg entered the white rooster's chest. The white one knelt to the ground. The red one struggled violently to free its spur. As it twisted and turned, I could envision the damage being done to the internal muscles and organs of the white rooster. Finally, the red rooster broke free. He pecked twice at the white rooster, who lay still on his chest, beathing heavily. The red rooster then strutted proudly around the wounded white one.

I leaned over to Mescal. "I told you so. Weight makes a big difference."

"Maybe, gringo. Maybe not."

I turned back to watch the birds. Why hadn't the referee called the match? The red rooster approached the white one to peck at his head again. Without warning, the white rooster sprung up and swung wildly with his spurs, driving one into the eye of the red. The red crashed down to the floor, and the white strutted around, his spur tearing at the brain of the red as his full body weight kept the head of the red pinned to the sawdust.

A towel flew into the ring, thrown by the red

rooster's owner. A cheer erupted from the crowd, and both owners entered the ring. The owner of the white lifted his champion and removed its spur from the red's eye. The red sat still on the sawdust floor, while the owner of the white held his bird high in the air and paraded around the ring. The owner of the red then retrieved the towel he had thrown into the ring and gently placed it over his prized bird. Then he lifted it into his arms and left the ring.

The four young women reappeared in the ring and began handing money to members of the audience who excitedly waved their white pieces of paper in the air.

The voice on the loudspeaker announced a ten-minute break, while the owners of the next pair of cocks prepped them for combat. Attendees were encouraged, once again, to purchase cervezas at the concession stand.

"So, wha' did you think, gringo?" Mescal asked.

"It was exciting, but a little gory. What's going to happen to the red cock that lost?"

"Depends. If he gets better and can still see good enough to fight, he might be back in a month. If not, he's gonna be baked, fried, or boiled. Too expensive to feed and train a cock that's useless. You know wha' I mean?"

I nodded.

"These matches are 'to death' or surrender," Mescal continued. "Tha's why the owner threw in the towel. If he waited any longer, his cock would be a goner. At least now he can decide if his cock lives or dies instead of letting the other cock make the decision for him."

"How do they make the cocks so aggressive?" I asked.

"Nature makes them tha' way. You ever see two women living with one guy? Sure you do, all the time.

You ever see two men living with one woman? No, you don'. Same way you never see two cocks in a barnyard. The king cock always kills his competition. It's like tha' with some people, too."

I nodded again.

"And you train them to bring out their nature. You put them alone in a cage to keep them away from women. You poke them with a stick and rap on the cage until they get pissed. Just like being in jail. They come out pissed at the world."

"So, you never let Diablo hang with the hens?"

"Only if he wins tonight, and then only for a day or two. Then it's back to training with me and my stick. He gotta be horny and angry. He gotta be mean."

****

Before the end of the third bout, Mescal and I went behind the concession stand and into a private room where eighteen roosters were waiting in separate cages for their turn in the ring. I calculated quickly and figured tonight's entertainment was a twelve-bout card. Not bad for a three-dollar admission fee. Mescal handed a five-dollar bill to a large man who was seated in an aluminum folding chair. "Gracias, Miguel."

"De nada, señor."

"Miguel makes sure nobody messes with cocks before their fights. Don' want no bird doped up and killed 'cause he ain't got no chance."

He handed me a pair of leather gloves. "Here, put these on. Save you some pain."

I did as Mescal directed. Inside his cage, Diablo looked like any other barnyard rooster, only maybe more sinister. His black feathers were shiny and perfectly groomed. His comb was not the red I expected. It, too, was black, as was his beak, except for white trim around its sharp point.

"I gonna poke at Diablo on the other side of his cage. When he turns, you grab him with two hands like a football. Hold onto him and bring him outside the cage. ¿comprendes?"

I was not sure what he meant.

"You understand?" Mescal snapped in English.

"Yes. I'll grab him like a football and hold him while you put his spurs on. Right?"

Mescal realized he had snapped at me. "Si, gringo. Didn't mean nothing to upset you."

He did as he said he would. Mescal stood opposite the door end of the cage and slapped his hand against it several times. Diablo turned and pecked violently at him. I gently opened Diablo's cage, grasped his body and pulled him out. It was no big deal. But I imagine if I had grasped him the wrong way barehanded, he would have pecked my fingers and they would have become a bloody mess.

"Hold him higher and tilt his feet at me," Mescal said.

I did as directed. Mescal clipped on the shiny steel spurs.

A loud cheer drew my attention to the ring in the other room. "Somebody win?"

"Probably." Mescal finished attaching the last spur. "Be careful now, gringo. Those espuelas is razor sharp."

"Do you want me to put him back in the cage?"

"No."

Mescal said something to Miguel. Miguel brought him a terrycloth dish towel. He placed it carefully around Diablo's back. "Gimme him. It's almost time."

Soon I could hear the loudspeaker announcing the beer break and I knew Diablo was going to be in the next bout.

Another man appeared in the room and, like Mescal, he tipped Miguel for ensuring the birds had not been tampered with. Then he opened a cage and with his bare hands pulled out Diablo's opponent, a very large white rooster named, "El Chupacabra." The feathers on his head were yellow, and a brown cape of thin feathers descended from the back of his head to his shoulders. His beak was multicolored, but basically red.

I motioned with my head toward El Chupacabra. "Interesting color combo."

"Tha' hombre is holding tomorrow's dinner, but he don' know it," Mescal said.

When it was our turn to enter the ring, we were paged by one of the young ladies. I followed Mescal to the ring. The other gentleman followed us. The announcer called Diablo's name. Mescal held him high for all to see. Maybe half the crowd cheered. When El Chupacabra's name was announced, the cheering was louder. The birds were placed into the gunny sacks on the scale. Diablo's opponent outweighed him significantly.

The girls entered the ring and began taking money and handing out red and white pieces of paper. I placed a ten-dollar bet on Diablo. How could I possibly bet against him when Mescal was both my mentor and my ride home? The girl who took my money wrote a "10" on my piece of red paper and handed it to me.

"Aren't you betting?" I asked Mescal.

"My bet was part of the entry fee. Besides, Señor Esplada and I have a side bet of two hundred dollars.

Tha' white chicken shit is his."

"Oh." Now I really hoped Diablo could handle this much larger cock.

The birds were retrieved from the gunny sacks by Esplada and Mescal, who poked their contenders at each other. Then the referee motioned for both men to go to opposite sides of the ring. He raised his hand and forcefully dropped it. The men dropped their cocks to the sawdust and hopped over the ring's wooden walls.

El Chubacabra and Diablo charged at each other. Diablo tripped and fell. El Chubacabra stood over him and pecked twice at the back of his head. Diablo stood and ran from his opponent. El Chubacabra gave chase, twice around the ring. Then suddenly, Diablo turned and kicked, driving his right spur into El Chubacabra's neck, just below his skull. El Chubacabra's head went to the sawdust and, as Diablo walked back and forth in a semicircle, blood gushed onto El Chubacabra's white feathers.

Señor Esplada threw in his towel. Mescal ran to Diablo and pulled him from his injured opponent. The entire match had not lasted a full minute. Beaming from ear to ear, Mescal paraded around the ring, holding Diablo high in the air. The crowd cheered wildly.

Señor Esplada entered the ring solemnly. El Chubacabra lay dead, his carotid artery severed by Diablo's spur.

I collected my eighteen-dollar winnings and then followed Mescal to the back room. He placed Diablo back into his cage. Señor Esplada entered behind us. He handed Mescal two one-hundred-dollar bills and said something in Spanish I could not understand. Mescal waved a twenty-dollar bill at him. Esplada growled something and waved his hand angrily at Mescal.

When Esplada was gone from the room, I asked Mescal what had transpired.

"He said it was a lucky kick for a cowardly bird. I offered him twenty dollars, which is twice what it costs for a dead chicken in the grocery store. He didn' like wha' I said."

Chapter 20

Mescal dropped me off at his clubhouse at two in the morning. It was cold, and snow was beginning to come down, already sticking to the concrete sidewalk. I thanked him for teaching me about cockfighting and for showing me the location of the sports arena. "Maybe we're becoming friends," I said.

He made a face that told me maybe we were not really becoming friends. Given that I'm still a cop, I should not have been surprised. "Don' try goin' there by yourself, gringo. Tha's not a place you can go without no protector. They gonna cut you to ribbons and feed you to the cocks."

I thanked him again, started my car, and drove toward Mariaville. The road was starting to get slick, so I drove slowly and braked softly long before reaching stop signs. By the time I was a mile from my cabin, the snow was already over an inch deep, and the lane markers were no longer visible. There were no tire tracks ahead of me, so I was certain the roads were safe because I was the only idiot out at this hour of the night. When I finally turned into my driveway, a doe leaped from the boxwoods beside my front door. She had probably bedded down there to be out of the wind, which almost always comes from the west.

****

I woke at eleven in the morning, surprised I had slept

so late. I took a quick shower and then called Cabrillo Construction to see if Cisneros would be in during the afternoon. His secretary answered and directed my call to his office.

"I've got a little information to share with you. I think you'll find it interesting. You gonna be in this afternoon?"

"Yeah, but only until one. Then I'm going to go watch the Gators play Arkansas."

"Thought it was a night game."

"It is. Seven p.m. Gotta catch a nap before it starts. You be here before one."

It was already twelve fifteen. I looked out my kitchen window. The roof of my car was supporting three inches of snow, so I knew at least four inches had come down overnight. But the sun was out, so getting to Cabrillo Construction was not going to be too difficult.

I dressed in jeans and a denim work shirt, slipped on my boots and coat, and carried my broom outside to sweep the snow from my car. When it was all off, I started the motor to warm the cab, and went back inside to get my official private investigator's notebook.

The drive to Cabrillo Constriction took twenty minutes. I checked my watch, and it was only twelve forty-five, so Cisneros would still be inside. I got out of my car and tramped through the wet snow to the door. When I opened it, Cisneros' secretary Laverne greeted me. "Good. You made it. He's been waiting for you."

"Thanks. I know where to go."

I opened the door to the work area and found Cisneros inside his office talking with one of his men. I stood outside the door and waited until they were finished. I heard Cisneros say something about making a delivery "before five o'clock so the merchandise can get out onto the streets for the evening." I assumed he was discussing drugs, but I was not sure because he never used the name of a drug. I suppose the guy could have been delivering rock salt for the icy sidewalks.

"Hola," Cisneros said. He was dressed down, wearing blue jeans and a pinstriped golf shirt under a leather jacket. "Whadya you got for me?"

"So far, I've only focused on one of the names you gave me: Julio Prognostico, the Puerto Rican. It seems he came into a small fortune a few months ago and has gone into business for himself in Albany."

"What's he selling? Is it some of my merchandise?"

"I think he already sold your merchandise in order to get the funds to purchase a sports arena."

"Arena football?"

"No, not football. What's the number one sport in Puerto Rico?" I asked.

"Baseball?"

"That was my answer when somebody asked me that question. Guess again."

"Enough of your bullshit. Where's my merchandise?"

"If I'm correct, it's already in the hands of consumers. However, the profits he made went into purchasing a building and outfitting it as a cockfighting arena."

"No shit? I didn't know we had one in this region. I've seen them in Texas and Florida, but you're saying young Julio got himself one going up here?"

"Yeah, in northern Albany. I went there last night. There were over a hundred paying customers. He sells beer and cigarettes, probably all untaxed. You ought to go check it out."

"I think I will." Cisneros gave me a strange look and then asked, "You don't speak Spanish and you don't look Spanish. How come you're not cut up or bruised?"

"I went with a friend who's fluent. He raises fighting cocks, and I went as his guest."

"Interesting. You got more balls than I thought."

"So, I got a little more info: I drove over to the alley behind Ontario Street and looked into Julio's back yard. He's got a regular barnyard back there, including a bunch of roosters he's got penned up. I figure he's raising them as fighters."

"I guess I'm going to check that out, too."

"How do you deal with men who steal from you?" I asked. I was pretty sure I already knew the answer. The newspapers are full of stories about the butchered and headless bodies of men and women who try to cheat the cartels.

"Normally, very harshly. But Julio is my sister's godchild, so I must exercise some restraint. I think, perhaps, he is going to have a new business partner."

I handed Cisneros a photocopy of my hours thus far. "I'm going to check out the two other men this week. But I think you already know where your merchandise went."

"Go ahead and be thorough, Mr. Jones. I can easily pay you for your investigator's time. But I think you already solved this case. You'll get a call later this week telling you where to go to get your paycheck."

I smiled when Cisneros did not balk at the ten hours I was asking him to pay me. Half of it was research, and half of that was spent at the cockfight arena. The remainder was stake-out time in front of the two houses the three men occupied. I felt bad I had not snapped any pictures of Prognostico's back yard to share with Cisneros. But I didn't feel bad about failing to take pictures of him doing business with my new friend Mescal. I was certain that because Julio was a member of Los Equis, he should not be collaborating on a business venture with the local Mexican gang unless his boss had given him the nod to do so. If Julio was not aware of that protocol, I was certain he soon would be.

****

I watched football all day Sunday, two afternoon games and one at night. In that timeframe I managed to drink an entire six-pack of Budweiser tallboys and consume a party-size bag of Fritos. On Monday morning I felt sluggish, and my mouth was pasty. I always feel guilty when I waste a day like that. But I rationalized I had drunk only two beers per game, which was way less than I would have consumed if I had attended a pro game at a stadium.

On my way into work, I stopped at Verrigni's for a large coffee and a sausage biscuit. Lester Brockbank was there. He recognized me at once, though I had to think for a minute before I realized who he was.

"I got your materials late Friday and perused them over the weekend," he said. "You got a minute to talk here, or would you rather make an appointment?"

"I've got a few minutes."

We looked around and saw an empty booth. Les pointed me at it, so I led and he followed. Once we had squeezed into the booth, he gave me the good news. "I wish you hadn't moved out of your home. The court usually sees that as desertion."

"What was I to do? She cheated on me, and I didn't

have the heart to kick her out. I tried to be a gentleman."

"In a divorce case you can't be a gentleman, or she'll take everything you own and send you to debtor's prison. But I think we can work things out so you don't get hurt too badly." He took a sip of his coffee. "Any chance you two might reconcile?"

"I might have thought so, but then on Halloween her married lover spent the night at my home instead of his own and she followed it up with this divorce suit. She's probably broken up his marriage, too. I'm done with her."

"Okay, so I guess we shall proceed. I'll let her attorney know I'll be handling your side and that reconciliation is out of the question."

"What about all the stuff she's asking for?"

"New York is a joint ownership state, so we should be able to get stuff divided up equally. It may not be fifty-fifty. You two don't have many assets to divide. Where you'll run into issues with the court is you've been the principal breadwinner for the family. She's asked for some sort of financial maintenance and probably will get it."

"She's been working part-time."

"Good. The judge will take that into account. We'll work on reducing the amount she's to receive from you, though you may have to pay support until she gets formal training in an occupation which permits her to earn a comfortable income."

"What if she marries somebody else?"

"Let's hope she does, because that will free you from any further financial burden."

Les and I chatted a little about yesterday's game between the Giants and the Eagles—thus far this season, the Giants had lost every game. Then we shook hands and went our separate ways, Les to call Rachel's attorney, and I to meet with Helen to determine our next steps in solving the Laura Moretti case before the trail got any colder.

Chapter 21

Helen was sitting in the green metal armchair beside my desk when I arrived at work. She was dressed in her uniform, including her gun belt, as though she were headed to a formal ceremony of some kind. Her makeup was basic, and her curly black hair was pulled into a tight bun at the back of her head.

"Wondered if you decided to take the day off," she said.

I set my paper coffee cup on my desk blotter. "I ran into Les Brockbank at Verrigni's. He invited me to sit for a few minutes to discuss my divorce."

"How's it going?"

"He tried to reassure me a little, but he said because I moved out of my own home, it's considered desertion."

"Thought she stepped out on you."

"Yeah, me too. I guess I should have contacted a lawyer before I packed my stuff and moved out. When Rachel and I agreed I would move out, I set myself up for being the bad guy in all this."

"The law's crazy sometimes, isn't it, Jonesy?"

"Yeah it is." I removed the lid from my coffee cup and took a sip. "So, you're here to decide what to do next about finding Laura Moretti's killer?"

"Oh, I already decided that. I was just waiting for you so we could go together."

"You could have left me a note to tell me where you

were going and given me an alternate assignment. Then we could have met up at noon at Ruby's and shared what we learned."

"Thought about that, but my plan didn't include Ruby's." Helen tapped her pen on my desk. "You and me, we're going to go visit Warren Wilson's next of kin. Got her name from the funeral home web site. She buried him yesterday."

"Who is she?"

"His sister, Madelyn, with a "y." They have the same address. She's probably like me, an old maid."

"What about his parents or other siblings?"

"Parents are deceased. She's his only sibling. He was forty-six, so she's probably around three years older or younger."

I finished my coffee and then we took the elevator to the ground floor and walked outside to my car. It was a blustery day, gray skies and a damp cold. Helen pulled her neck into her coat as a shield against the wind.

"Good we takin' your car," she said when she got in. "Still has some residual heat."

"Residual?" I asked. "You sound like some kind of scientist."

"I am a scientist…a 'weatherologist.' I determine whether you telling me the truth or lying. I also determine whether you drunk driving or whether you the bank robber we're looking for."

"I see," I said. "So, tell me whether I'm headed in the right direction or not," I said as I backed out of my parking space.

"If you drivin' away from the Department, you headed the right way, Jonesy."

"You got an address?"

"Yeah. She lives at forty-three Plott Road in Marshfield."

"We probably ought to check in with Chief Parillo."

"Already done that. If she's a suspect, he wants us to do our interviewing at his place. But if we're just looking for information about her deceased brother, he says to go ahead. Just let him know if we run into something illegal."

Helen plugged Madelyn Wilson's address into her cell phone and gave me directions as we drove from Willow Falls into the uppity community of Marshfield. When the pothole-filled roads gave way to smooth asphalt, I knew we had crossed the city line.

"Haven't been to Marshfield since BabyX," Helen said. "Wonderin' how that family's doin'. You keep in touch with them?"

"Margo and Henry Lumpas? No reason to bother them anymore. Last I knew, Margo was still giving lectures to youth groups, counseling them against premarital sex. Don't know how Henry is handling it. My guess is he's probably over his anger and has forgiven her for lying to him. He seems the type."

"Turn here. This should be Plott Road," Helen blurted.

I looked at the street sign. Yup, we had reached Plott Road, a one lane strip of asphalt which followed the curvy contour of the Mohawk River as it meandered to the Hudson River, a few miles north of Albany. On our left, a few homes perched along the cliffs above the river, but most were on our right, where there was enough land to enjoy a back yard with a vegetable garden. Rural route mailboxes were planted at the end of every driveway, so finding number forty-three was not difficult. I made a right-hand turn onto the gravel and pulled to a stop behind an orange Volkswagen camper, probably from the late nineteen-seventies.

We got out of my car and studied the camper. "Old hippies," Helen said. "Wonder if they bought this new?"

"If they did or didn't, they've kept it pristine. Looks like it just came off the showroom floor."

"It was our father's," said a woman's voice from behind the screen door of the mint green bungalow which must have been Warren Wilson's home until last week.

"It's really nice," I replied. "You must be Madelyn."

"Yes. You must be Detective Martin," Madelyn said to Helen.

"Yes. And this is Detective Bart Jones."

We climbed the concrete steps to the concrete landing. Madelyn pushed the screen door open. "Come in, come in. It's really chilly outside. Can I offer either of you a cup of coffee or Red Zinger?"

Helen and I both waved off her offer. "That is kind of you, Miss Wilson," Helen said, "but we just finished our morning coffee a few minutes ago."

Madelyn showed us to her sofa. We sank a good six inches into its cushions such that the small glass-topped coffee table was higher than my belt buckle. The room was painted light blue and was pleasantly bright, in spite of the gray skies outside. Flower-print curtains were tied back at the base of the room's four windows. The floor was lightly polished oak. To the right, we could see a small Queen Anne dining room table with its four matching chairs, and we could see the doorway to the kitchen, which opened into the dining room.

"Now, how can I help you two officers this

morning?" she asked.

I let Helen take the lead, especially since she had made the call and arranged the interview.

"First, let me say we're sorry about your brother's passing. It was a terrible accident and certainly a tragedy. He was too young to be moving on."

"Yes, thank you. I'm getting over it now. I've just begun rummaging through his closet so I can donate his clothes to the City Mission in Schenectady. With winter already here, I'm sure the homeless can make good use of his things."

Helen got down to business. "What can you tell us about Warren's private life?"

"Well, he was a bachelor. He dated every now and then, but he never dated anyone long enough to get serious. I don't think it was their fault—the women he dated. I think he just wasn't the kind of man who any woman would see as a good catch."

"Can you explain what you mean by that?"

"Well, he had a steady job at the glove factory, but during his private time he was usually an escapist. I mean he was intoxicated or high on something almost all the time, except at work. That's why I came here to live with him. If he took too many pills or smoked too much of his home-grown hallucinogens, I was here to feed him orange juice, talk him down, or get him to the hospital."

"Sounds like you loved him very much to do that for him," I said. "I don't know too many sisters who would have done that for their older brothers."

"Younger. He was five years younger than I am."

I inspected her appearance. Other than a few gray streaks in her brown hair, Madelyn did not look like she was fifty-one years old. Her face bore no wrinkles or age spots. Her eyes were sharp and clear. Protruding from her brown A-line skirt, her legs were still shapely and well cared for. And her hands seemed to be those of a twenty-year-old. She was too old for me, but a lot of guys would consider her attractive.

"So, he never married?" Helen asked.

"No. Like I said, he wasn't really the kind of man a nice woman would marry. One of those crazies he hung around with might have hooked up with him, but it never happened. Like me, he remained unattached all his life."

"Did he have any hobbies or was he a member of any organizations?" Helen asked.

"His primary hobby was dabbling in anything that would get him high. Out back he would grow various species of marijuana. There are several bunches of it hanging to dry in the garage if you'd like to see it. In the basement he experimented with growing hallucinogenic mushrooms. You can see them, too. He grew them in horse manure which he dried in our oven. His bookshelves are full of books that delve into the religious and ceremonial sides of taking hallucinogens. He always said he was trying to find God."

"I guess he finally did," I said.

"Are you trying to be cruel, Detective?" Madelyn asked.

"I apologize, Madelyn. I guess I should keep my thoughts to myself."

"What about friends, Madelyn?" Helen asked. "Did he have any friends?"

"Yes, a few. He went to weekly meetings with a group who shared his interests. Sometimes he would host them here. The meetings were usually held on Saturday afternoons and led into the late evening. Most often, he would come home around midnight. Sometimes later. That's why I wasn't too concerned when he wasn't home at midnight on Halloween. I knew he'd be home before dawn. I went to bed at nine. The phone call from the police woke me about three."

"Can you give us any names and contact information for his friends?" I asked.

"Why, yes I can. He kept a Rolodex on his nightstand."

Madelyn got up and walked out of the room. She returned in less than a minute carrying an old Rolodex. "You can keep this if you think it might be helpful. I would have just thrown it away." She held up an iPhone. "My friends are all in my cell phone. Warren didn't carry a cell phone. He was worried about magnetic fields damaging his brain."

I flipped through the Rolodex quickly. Most of the cards were empty, but maybe fifty of them had something scribbled on them. I'd have to take a closer look later. "Can you remember the names of his closest friends?"

She held out her hand and I gave her the Rolodex. "This one, Timothy, called often. And so did Earl."

I handed her a red pen. "Would you mind putting a red "X" on the cards with his closest friends."

"I'll try. I don't know exactly who were his closest, but I can mark those who called and left messages for him."

"That would be great," Helen said.

Madelyn flipped through the round file and marked cards. Then she hopped up and went to the kitchen. "Here," she said as she came back into the living room. She handed Helen a folded piece of pink paper. "I found this in his top dresser drawer."

When Helen unfolded it, her eyes opened wide. She handed it to me.

"What is it?" I asked.

"Just read it, Jonesy."

I unfolded the pink paper. Printed in red ink was this:

Sanguinarian Celebration of the Blood Moon

9:00pm, October 3

Biological Auditorium

Regrets Only

" 'Biological Auditorium' could only mean one place," I said.

"That's what I think, too," Helen replied. "Got to be Modern's place."

"You two know what this notice means?" Madelyn asked.

"We think so," Helen replied. "We're gonna go find out if we're right."

Madelyn handed the Rolodex back to me. "I've starred half a dozen names, but they may lead you to more people."

"I hope so," I replied. "Is there anything else you can remember?"

"I remember Warren couldn't go to that event—the one on the pink paper—because he had a stomach thing going on. Maybe a virus or maybe something weird that he ate. I think really he was afraid of exposure to COVID-19 at the party. He called somebody and I overheard a little of what he said. I wasn't really eavesdropping, but some of the things he said worried me."

"I understand," I said. "What can you remember

from that phone call?"

"He was talking about getting something from the man on the phone. It came in a six-ounce container and had to be refrigerated. I remember the guy saying he would hold it for Warren in a refrigerator. "

"Did somebody deliver it here?"

"No. Warren said he'd pick it up at the Halloween party at the Odd Fellows."

"Do you remember the name of the person he called?"

"No, sorry."

"Can we have your permission to check your call records with the phone company?"

"Sure."

We didn't need Madelyn's permission to check her phone records, especially since we were investigating a murder. But it was nice to let her know we would be doing so. It was nicer, yet, that she didn't mind our checking her records.

We said farewell to Madelyn Wilson, took the Rolodex and the folded pink announcement, and headed back to the department. We needed to crosscheck the names in the Rolodex with the names of the people who had attended the Halloween party at the Odd Fellows Hall. We also needed to contact the phone company and get Madelyn's outgoing phone calls for the month of October.

Helen had the names and addresses of the owners of the cars which had been parked outside the Odd Fellows Hall on Halloween night, so she spent the next hour checking the names in Warren Wilson's Rolodex against the names in her list. Meanwhile, I contacted the phone company and had them email me the chronological list of calls made from the Wilson's home phone during the month of October. The phone was in Madelyn's name and not Warren's, which I found strange. I wondered if maybe the house was in her name as well. The list the phone company sent me gave me the numbers called but did not include the names of the businesses or individuals who Warren and Madelyn called. I found that to be frustrating.

I took the elevator down to Helen's. "Are you finished with the Rolodex yet? I sure could use it."

"Better than that, I took all the name cards out and put them alphabetically on the glass of the photocopier. Five seconds later: Bingo, I've got three copies of every name. One for me. One for you, and one for whomever else might need it."

Helen handed me a single sheet of paper with twenty or more names, addresses, and phone numbers, all hand-scrawled by Warren Wilson. The one at the top of the list already had a red star beside it. "Who's this?" I asked. "Adrenochrome?"

"Check the number."

Helen handed me the list of names and phone numbers she had received from Motor Vehicles. "You'll find it."

"Come on, Helen, do we really have time for games?"

"You'll find it," she repeated.

I rolled my eyes and then began matching the phone numbers from Helen's list against the Rolodex phone number for Adrenochrome. Then I saw it. "You're shitting me," I exclaimed.

"Did Wilson list Horace Modern as his adrenochrome supplier?"

"I wondered the same thing at first. But last night I was reading an article in the *New York Times* about anagrams. You know, it's how you can make up a different word or maybe a couple of words by rearranging the letters in another word. Like, 'dog' can become 'god' by rearranging the letters."

"Yeah, I get what you mean. So. what's your point?"

"The article said in the past secret societies used anagrams all the time."

I nodded.

"So, my point is this: Write the word 'adrenochrome' on a piece of paper."

I followed Helen's instructions.

"Now, cross out all the letters that spell 'Horace.'"

I did it.

"What you got left?"

"D-R-E-N-O-M," I said.

"So…?"

I looked at the letters for a few moments and then it hit me. I spelled it aloud: "H-O R-A-C-E M-O-D-E-R-N." I slapped my forehead. You must think I'm a dunderhead for not seeing that sooner. You've just pegged our guy!"

"Thank the *Times,* Jonesy. I never would have figured it out by myself, either. Just must have been luck or my feminine intuition that caused me to read that article."

So now, Helen and I were convinced Modern was connected to Laura Moretti's abduction and murder. Of course, all our evidence was circumstantial. We were relatively certain he was the person taking photos from a distance at Laura's funeral, but from our observation point, the person we had seen behind the wheel looked like a woman. We knew he regularly sold South American tree frogs to the Crystal Cantor Shoppe, but there was nothing overtly illegal about that. We knew he drank rabbit blood at the Halloween party, but, again, there was nothing illegal about that. We knew his professional name is an anagram for "adrenochrome," but the law doesn't prohibit that, either. So how were we going to squeeze him to get him to spill the beans about his knowledge of Laura Moretti's death? I wasn't sure.

Chapter 22

Modern was not happy when he was picked up by two uniformed policemen and hauled down to the Willow Falls Police Department for questioning. In fact, when he arrived he was livid.

"Why was I handcuffed? I didn't need to be handcuffed like some common criminal."

One of the officers looked at the desk sergeant. "I don't know who he thinks he is, but I've told this guy half a dozen times we are required to handcuff everyone who goes for a ride in a squad car."

"I demand you remove these handcuffs immediately."

"You got the best," the desk sergeant told Modern. "They put you in Smith and Wesson one-hundreds. If they had used Model three-hundreds, you would have had far less freedom of movement."

"Do I get a phone call?"

The Desk Sergeant smiled and handed Modern a universal mobile phone. "Sure. You calling mommy?"

Modern wrenched the phone out of the Desk Sergeant's hand and punched in a number. A moment later he started talking to someone on the other end. "Sal, it's me, Horace Modern. They've brought me in for questioning... I'm at the police department... Willow Falls... I'm not sure of the charges." He looked at the two officers who had brought him from his office.

The taller of the two shrugged his shoulders. "We told you, you've been brought in for questioning. That's all we know."

Modern gave them a look of exasperation and pressed the receiver against his ear again. "They said I've just been brought in for questioning. But they handcuffed me...Yes, they told me handcuffing is standard practice...Well, are you coming down, or what?...okay."

Modern handed the phone back to the Desk Sergeant. "My attorney will be right down. I'm not answering any questions until he gets here."

"Would you care for a cup of coffee?" the desk sergeant asked.

"I just told you I'm not answering any questions."

"Suit yourself." The Desk Sergeant turned to the two patrolmen. "Don't book him. Just escort him down to Interrogation Room C. Remove his cuffs only if he's a good boy. I'll call Martin and Jones to let them know he's here."

Five minutes after hearing from the Desk Sergeant, I took the elevator down to the second floor and walked to Helen's office. "Hey gorgeous. He's here."

Helen was dressed to kill in a tight-fitting heather-blue pants suit and, with her hair brushed straight down below her ears, she looked a lot like Claire Underwood in *House of Cards*. "I know," she said. "Got a call from downstairs. Sarge says Modern called his attorney."

My hopes for a hard-press interrogation dimmed. "Bummer. Well, I guess this will be interesting."

Helen picked up a notepad. "You ready?"

"Yeah. Let's go see who his attorney is and find out if he'll let us ask any probing questions."

We took the elevator to the basement, walked past the medical examiner's small complex, and entered the room where Modern was waiting at a steel table with four chairs. As we entered, an officer was removing Modern's handcuffs. Modern looked up as we came in. He was wearing a distinctly feminine tangerine-colored jump suit with a green and yellow pineapple embroidered over his left breast. I could not resist a little dig as Helen and I sat in our chairs across from him. "It was so nice of you to come in this morning, Mr. Modern."

"You didn't have to drag me in like some common criminal," he replied. "If you had called, I would have gladly come on my own."

"Sure. You threw us out the last time we spoke, so we assumed you would be hostile if we visited again."

The officer who had uncuffed him turned to me. "We have some of his stuff in our squad car. What do you want me to do with it?"

"How much stuff are we talking about?" I asked.

"A woman's wide brimmed hat and a blonde wig. He was getting ready to drive away when we pulled up. Found the hat and wig under the driver's seat of his Beemer. Charlie thinks he stuffed it there when we stopped him. Saw his right shoulder drop lower than his left for a moment."

"Charlie?"

"Yeah, my partner, Officer Pullman."

"Yeah, thanks. Would you please bring that stuff here. We wouldn't want Mr. Modern's valuables to be misplaced."

The officer left the room, and Helen got down to business. "Mr. Modern, we are conducting an unnecessarily prolonged inquiry into the kidnapping and murder of a little girl. We believe you are involved in her disappearance and demise. You can be upfront and helpful to us, or you can continue to be hostile. Either way, we are going to solve this case. It will go easier on you if you decide to be helpful."

There was a knock on the door, and then it opened. In walked Lance Freeborn, dressed in a gray three-piece suit with fine white pinstripes. Helen rolled her eyes at me. Freeborn had been the defense attorney in the Margo Lumpas case. Margo was the mother of BabyX, a stillborn baby whose skeleton was discovered in the basement of an abandoned house during an urban renewal project a little more than a year ago. Freeborn had not been the easiest defense attorney we had ever dealt with. In fact, I found him to be obnoxious and prone to walking out of investigative inquiries, always taking his clients with him when he departed.

Freeborn got right down to business, speaking to his client first. "They haven't asked you any pertinent questions without your attorney present, have they?"

"No, not yet," Modern answered truthfully. "But they did try to bribe me."

Freeborn looked at Helen and me suspiciously.

Helen pursed her lips in annoyance. "I merely suggested things will go easier on him if he cooperates with us as we pursue this investigation. That's hardly a bribe."

Modern smiled at her.

Freeborn handed each of us one of his business cards. I already had one from the Lumpas case, but I took another, just in case his phone number or office location had changed.

"So, what sort of information are you seeking from Mr. Modern?" Freeborn asked.

I placed my digital tape recorder on the table. "Mr. Modern, is it true you sell South American tree frogs to retail businesses to resell to their customers?"

"No."

"We have testimony from a retail merchant who claims you do."

"I assume you are referring to the proprietor of the Crystal Cantor. I don't sell him South American tree frogs. He advertises them as tree frogs, but they're really Colorado River toads."

Helen jumped in. "Are you admitting to a federal offense?"

Freeborn pulled Modern aside and conferred with him for a moment. Then he turned to us. "My client acknowledges it is illegal to remove those toads from the Colorado River Basin and sell them for a profit. However, under current federal legislation, it is not illegal to purchase those toads."

Modern raised his hand. I nodded at him.

"Four years ago, I was approached by a man who offered me a mated pair of Colorado River toads. I purchased them for a one-hundred-dollar bill and placed them into a heated aquarium which simulated their natural environment. They seemed to like their new home and began reproducing at a prolific rate. Yes, I sell the offspring of those two toads, but, no, I did not remove them from the Colorado River Basin, and I have not sold the original mated pair. I sell only toads which have been born and raised in New York State."

"Why do people purchase those toads?" Helen asked.

"You already know the answer to that question, Officer," Modern replied. "You attended the Halloween party at the Odd Fellows Hall."

"I'd like to hear your answer," Helen said. She was pressing him to get his answer recorded in case we ever needed it in a courtroom.

"Certain people like to ingest a small amount of the liquid the toads secrete from their glands. They get a short high from the bufotenine it contains. It's a sexual stimulant, among other things."

I had been doing some research on the topic, too. "Is there more than just that?" I asked. "Do some people do other things with it?"

"Some people kill the toads and dry their skins."

"Why?"

Modern knew I already knew the answer, so he obliged. "They smoke the skins for a prolonged high."

"And you sell the toads for those purposes?" Helen asked.

"No, I sell the toads to retail outlets for commercial profit. They sell the toads to their customers without asking why the customer wishes to purchase them. Frankly, it's none of their business what a customer does with a commodity he purchases. Does a farm supply store ask you what you plan to do with the bags of fertilizer you bought from them?"

Helen looked baffled at his response.

"Let me make it simpler for you, Detective. Do they ask you if you plan to put it in your garden or if you plan to manufacture methamphetamine in your bathtub? Hell no, they don't."

Helen stood. "I take offense to your insinuation, buck-o. Do you think I'm stupid or something?"

Modern raised his hand. "I apologize, Officer Martin. I meant no offense. I was simply trying to make a point. The retailer sells the toads for a profit without really caring if the customer wishes to lick them, smoke them, or feed them to his pet cat."

Helen sat back down with her arms folded across her chest.

"Let's please be respectful of each other," I said. "There's no reason to cross the line of propriety."

Modern snorted. "Like the way you were respectful of me when you had me hauled in for questioning in handcuffs."

Freeborn raised his hands at both sides of the table. "Do you have any more questions for my client?"

"A few…"

"Well, get on with it. He pays me by the hour and the meter is running."

"Do you sell toad skins, as well as live toads?" I asked.

"No, with a few exceptions, I only sell live toads." Modern could see from the look on my face I had a follow-up question which was based on his answer. "The exceptions are a few Native American organizations in Arizona, Nevada, and New Mexico, which have permits to smoke toad skins as part of their indigenous religious ceremonies. They hold federal permits for those ceremonies based upon court-recognized religious freedoms."

Helen jotted a few notes and then looked up. "Tell us about your relationship with the Sanguinarians in the capital region." She had a way of making a softball question hit like a hardball.

Modern looked surprised by her question.

"Relationship?"

"Yes, you were one of the two gods on the stage at the Odd Fellows Hall, weren't you? You drank real rabbit blood and your staff sold toad slime like it was candy."

Modern leaned over to confer with Freeborn again. Freeborn answered for him. "My client refuses to acknowledge the term 'Sanguinarians.' He acknowledges he enjoys a fraternal relationship with a private group of wealthy individuals who wish to remain anonymous. Some of them drink small quantities of blood at fraternal ceremonies, such as the one you witnessed at the Odd Fellows Hall."

Helen looked directly at Modern. "Do you mean the one where some people cut the others with razors and licked the blood off their skin?"

Freeborn looked shocked at Helen's description. He turned to Modern. "You don't need to answer that question, Horace. She's goading you."

Modern turned to Helen. "On counsel's advice, I refuse to answer that question."

It was my turn. "Do you keep a supply of sodium heparin in your business?"

"Yes," Modern replied. "It is an anticoagulant used when we ship blood samples to college science laboratories. Sometimes we use it with small animals -- cats, rats, and piglets -- that we need to preserve for lab experiments."

"Did you use sodium heparin to preserve the blood you gave to Warren Wilson the night of the Halloween party?"

"I don't know anyone named Warren Wilson," Modern replied.

"Do you know the names of any of the Sanguinarians, or do they all use fake names, like yours?"

"I refuse to speak about that group. They are all powerful and influential members of the local community and do not wish to be party to any form of negative publicity."

"Warren Wilson died that night when his car ran off the road and hit a tree. You already know that. You picked up his single passenger and took her to the hospital. Do you know *her* name?"

Modern just stared at me silently, his face stone cold and unemotional.

"Warren Wilson had your name and phone number in his Rolodex. If you didn't know him, he certainly knew you. Can you explain why your name appears in his Rolodex?"

Lance Freeborn smacked his hand on the tabletop and rose to his feet. "Your questions are becoming less inquisitive and more accusatory. This is becoming a witch hunt, Officer Jones."

"Before you leave, Mr. Freeborn, I have one more question," I said.

Freeborn tugged at Modern's sleeve. "Come on Horace, it's time to go."

"Just a minute," Modern said. "I'd like to hear this last question."

"Wilson listed your phone number under the name 'Adrenochrome.' Were you his adrenochrome supplier?"

"Preposterous," Modern replied smugly.

Freeborn tugged at Modern's sleeve again.

As Modern rose, I shot him one last question. "If

you unscramble the letters in adrenochrome, do you know what it spells? It spells 'Horace Modern.' Why is your name an anagram for adrenochrome, Mr. Middleton?"

Lance Freeborn shot me a questioning look which told me he did not know his client very well.

"That's right, Mr. Freeborn. Your client's birth name was Benjamin Middleton. He uses a pseudonym so his friends and clients can list it under the term 'adrenochrome' in their address books. He's a supplier and a user and when we have all the details together, we're going to nail him for the murder of Laura Moretti."

Modern started to lunge at me, but he tripped over Freeborn's feet and crashed down to the floor.

The door burst open and two uniformed officers stepped into the room. "You okay in here?"

I pointed in the direction of Freeborn, who was helping Modern to his feet. "Please show these two gentlemen out."

Chapter 23

Officer Pullman handed me the blond wig and woman's wide-brimmed felt hat which he had removed from under the front seat of Horace Modern's BMW sedan. I thanked him, stuffed them into my desk drawer, and headed down to Helen's office.

"Got the search warrant?" I asked when I knocked on her door.

Helen was dressed in her uniform, her hair pulled back into the tight little bun which she always wore when the occasion called for a brimmed cap. On her hip was her department-issued nine-millimeter Glock semiautomatic, a set of handcuffs, and a can of mace. "Yeah," she replied. "Also got a couple of officers to come along, just in case he gives us any trouble."

We were going back to the Crystal Cantor Shoppe to see what we could learn about the group of influential people in the capital region who regularly drink blood. More than anything else, we needed names or information about the date, time, and location of their next meeting, so we could swarm in from all sides, like cops did back in the days of speakeasies. We hoped the proprietor of the Crystal Cantor, Billy Travis, would willingly give us that information. If he refused, we would use the court order to confiscate his books and computers so we could dig through all his records until we found what we needed.

Helen threw on her insulated waist-length jacket and black leather gloves and motioned for me to follow her down to the department's motor pool. When she was on point like this, I never questioned, but simply followed. Any suggestion opposite of hers would be taken as argumentation, and I didn't want her feeling that way. We took the elevator to the ground floor and turned right out of the elevator, away from the medical examiner's rooms and toward the motor pool. Officers Bergen and Feinstein were waiting for us in the hallway outside the door to the motor pool.

Feinstein looked nervous. He touched the black rubber grip of his Glock. "Never been on one of these unannounced visits. Should we expect resistance?"

"I'm not expecting any," I replied. "The guy is basically a wuss. If he doesn't give us the info we need, we're going to impound his computers and any handwritten logs we can find."

Bergen opened the door for Helen and then followed her into the motor pool. Feinstein caught the closing door and held it for me. Maybe he felt like we were on a date or something.

When I walked through, he caught my sleeve. "Give them a few feet of distance. Bergen wants to ask your partner out on a date."

"Can't he do that in her office or over the phone?"

"He's got her undivided attention right now. That's all he wants."

Not wanting to interfere with Helen's opportunity to find love, I stopped and watched the door close behind us. I slid my Sig out of my shoulder holster, popped the clip and examined it. Feinstein followed my lead and did the same thing. In the distance, I could see Bergen chatting with Helen as she stood beside the front passenger side door of our city-issued sedan. He smiled and then opened the door for her. She climbed in, and he closed it. He turned toward us and gave Feinstein the thumbs-up sign. I guessed Helen had accepted his advance.

Bergen was younger than Helen by maybe two years, but in today's world, that is nothing. He had been with the department for eight years and was a respected officer who had never been the subject of an internal affairs investigation, which meant he generally operated by the book. I could not say that. My record was blemished by two investigations: one was the killing of a burglary suspect who fired twice at me before I put a round into his forehead. He was a minority, and I was a white officer, so the hearing probed potential racial bias. I was acquitted of any wrongdoing. The other was an accusation by a hooker that I demanded free sexual favors in trade for not arresting her. She said after she performed oral sex with me, I arrested her anyway. The charges never stuck because the details of her story kept changing. I never did what she accused me of doing, but I'll admit several times over the years I have thought about it when the situation presented itself.

Bergen took the driver's seat and Helen rode beside him in the front seat. I sat behind Helen, and Feinstein was to my left. Bergen drove us through town and found a parking space half a block from the Crystal Cantor Shoppe. We exited the squad car at the same time, like a hit team on a mission. I guess that's what we were. When we got to the door, Helen and I asked Bergen and Feinstein to wait outside until one of us signaled for them to come in. Their very presence outside would deter customers from entering while Helen and I interrogated Travis.

Billy Travis seemed surprised to see Helen was still wearing her Halloween costume. When she flashed her badge, he knew she was not pretending. "Mr. Travis, we're here hoping you'll voluntarily offer us your assistance with a murder case we're investigating."

Her words did not seem to diminish the surprise Helen was, indeed, a police officer. "Ugh, I didn't murder anybody," he replied nervously.

I jumped in. "Detective Martin and I are seeking your help with a murder investigation."

"Oh, yeah," he said. "I'm not the accused?"

"No," Helen said, "but we have some questions you may be able to help us answer."

"Shoot," he said. Then he caught himself. "Well, don't really shoot, if you know what I mean."

"Let's begin with the two tree frogs you sold us," Helen said. "They weren't what you advertised them to be."

"They weren't?"

"No, they were Colorado River toads. There's a difference."

Travis just nodded.

"So, you know you knowingly have been selling river toads as tree frogs. And nobody has called you to task on it?"

"Well, either they don't know or they don't mind. You get the same kind of high from the secretions of both species. And the toads live longer than the frogs, so you get more for your money."

"Did Modern sell them to you as tree frogs or as river toads?" I asked.

"River toads," he admitted.

"Do you keep any sort of list of the people who have purchased river toads from you?" Helen asked.

With both of us asking probing questions, Travis could see we meant business. "I can generate such a list if you need one."

Helen was not buying it. If we let him generate the list, he would have the power to eliminate certain names, especially of those in influential positions in the community. "Don't bother," she replied. "We'll do it ourselves."

Travis cocked his head as though he didn't understand what she was suggesting.

"Has anyone ever asked you for information about the black-market sale of human blood?" I asked.

"That's not the sort of question I usually get."

"But you haven't really answered my question. I assume you've been asked that several times?"

Travis stepped backwards. He knew the sale of human blood for ingestion or for use in rituals is against the law. "Yes. One or two people have asked me about that, but it's been a long time."

I pulled out a pen and a small spiral notebook. "Specifically, who has asked you about such sales?"

"I'd rather not say. I'm not really at liberty to divulge that information."

"Okay," Helen said, "I guess we'll have to find that for ourselves, too."

"Have you ever sold human blood in any quantity to an individual in the capital region?" I asked.

"Of course not."

"Was Mr. Warren Wilson a customer of yours?"

"Oh, wasn't that terrible…the way he died. Yes, he

was one of the people who purchased river toads from me. They say he was high on kambo when he crashed."

"Was he one of the secret group of blood drinkers you told us about?" I asked.

A muscle beneath Travis' right eye was twitching. "Possibly."

"Can you give us the names of any other members of the group?" Helen asked.

"That would divulge names of the rich and powerful. If I told you who they are, my life wouldn't be worth spit. Besides, I'm not certain the names I have are their real names. If you were a member of the group, wouldn't you use a pseudonym or an anagram?"

"I guess that's something we'll have to find on our own, too," Helen said.

Travis gave her a quizzical look.

Helen turned toward the store's door and waved Bergen and Feinstein inside.

Travis turned at the jingling sound of his old-fashioned doorbell, and he gasped when he saw the two officers enter in uniform. "What's wrong? Why are they here?"

Helen handed Travis the search warrant which she had concealed in her jacket. "Mr. Travis, in compliance with City and State laws, we are ordering you to turn over your business computers and any handwritten lists and logs with information related to our search for the capital region's blood cult and the killer of Laura Moretti." She pointed at Feinstein and Bergen. "These officers are here to confiscate those items, which will be returned to you within the next six weeks, unless they are held as material witness to any crimes committed by the individuals in question."

"Six weeks?" Travis stammered. "You can't do that. You'll ruin my business."

"Indeed, we can and we will. You can still buy and sell goods to customers. Just keep written logs which can be transferred to your computers when they are returned."

"But..."

Helen directed Bergen and Feinstein to remove Travis' computer, rolodex (if he had one), and any logs which appeared to hold information that could be pertinent to the Laura Moretti murder case.

Travis pulled at Bergen's arm. "You have no right..."

Bergan slammed him up against the sales counter. "Keep your mitts off me or I'll arrest you for interfering with a police investigation."

Fear shot from Travis' eyes, and he backed down immediately.

"There now, Mr. Travis," Helen said, "we just need information and when we can't get it willingly from a person, we are often forced to get it legally. You aren't the first and won't be the last."

Travis looked at me. I shrugged and walked into the back room where Bergen and Feinstein had already dismantled Travis' desktop computer. I pulled open and rummaged through his desk drawers, except for the bottom right drawer, which was locked. "Helen," I called out, "would you send Mr. Travis in here with the key to open his bottom desk drawer."

Moments later, Travis appeared in the doorway. I held out my hand, and he reluctantly handed me a ring of keys. I inspected the ten keys. The drawer key had to be the smallest. I was right. The drawer unlocked easily, and

I opened it, only to discover a leatherbound ledger. Inside, the sections were all labeled by hand in red ink, and included such headings as Halloween ticket purchasers, Frog Sales, and Sanguinarians. I was certain we had hit the jackpot.

Chapter 24

It was Friday night, and the weekend was upon us. Helen had the department's computer techs download all of Travis' computer files onto a flash drive, which she took home to explore over the weekend. I took the handwritten log with the intent of looking at it to see if anything juicy popped out of it under casual scrutiny. I planned give it a hard inspection on Monday. For now, though, I was an off-duty cop and an on-duty private eye.

Thanksgiving was arriving next Thursday, and I wanted another payday from Cisneros so I could buy a bottle of Gentleman Jack to sip on during the holiday football games. The only way to see money flowing my way was to investigate the two other hombres in Cisneros' employ to see if they might be involved in the disappearance of his product. So, I changed into street clothes and drove back into Willow Falls after a quick bite to eat at home. I cruised down Oneida Street until I spotted the Mexican market. Juan Vasquez and Manuel Morales, both former members of the Mexican gang and both now members of Los Equis, supposedly lived above the Mexican market. I parked half a block away on the opposite side of the street where I could watch people flowing into and out of the market and, if I was lucky, I could see something—anything—which might implicate Vasquez or Morales in the theft of Cisneros' product.

At nine o'clock, the Mexican market closed, and I

was beginning to think I would have to find a better way to learn what Vasquez and Morales did in their spare time. But then the door beside the market opened and both men stepped out. With them were two women, scantily clad, especially for a chilly November evening. Morales kissed one of the women and then both men went back through the door to their second floor apartment. The women began pacing back and forth seductively in front of the Mexican market. Occasionally a car would pull up and a driver would chat with one or both of the ladies. Then it struck me: they were hookers, and this was the corner they worked.

I checked my wallet. I had forty dollars, which was hardly enough for a hooker, even in a minority neighborhood. But I started my car anyway, drove up to the corner and asked the girls if they both wanted to come for a ride.

"You want two of us, gringo?" the one in a red miniskirt and matching lipstick asked.

"Si, mamasita," I said. Other than taco, burrito, and cerveza, I had just used every Spanish word I knew.

"Tha's gonna cost you," the other said. She was wearing black leotards and a leopard print blouse.

"Where do we go?" I asked.

"Central Park," the one in red said.

"Get in."

The one in red hopped into the front seat and the other elected the back. As soon as they shut their doors, I drove quickly across town to Central Park. It is not a place I generally visit at night because of frequent muggings and, well, hookers getting it on with their johns.

They directed me through Central Park to the spot

where they conducted their business. It was a small, paved area behind one of the dugouts at a ballfield used by Little Leaguers in spring and summer. Anyone passing by would never expect a car to be parked there afterhours, so it appeared safe.

"What do you want? And show us the money, gringo," the one in red said.

"Sure," I replied. I reached for my wallet and pulled out my two twenties.

"You better start your motor and drive to an ATM," she said. "You don't got enough for me to show you my boob."

I removed my badge from my belt and flashed it at them both.

"Mother of God, we got us a cop," the one in red said to the one in leotards.

The one in leotards shrieked and tried to get out of my car, but the child locks were on and she was stuck inside.

"Listen, ladies," I said, "I'm not going to arrest you and I'm not looking for free sexual favors. All I want is some information and you can each go home with a twenty-dollar bill."

"You're wasting our best working hours, hombre," the one in red said. "No twenty dollars is going to make up for the loss in income you're causing."

I thought about it, and she was right. Their johns were going to expect much more, and I was cutting into their business hours. "Okay, maybe there's more, but only if I get straight answers."

"Like what do you want to know?"

"First, are you citizens of the United States?"

"Is that important?" the one in leotards asked.

"So, I assume you aren't. How long have you lived in the USA?"

"You writing a book or something?" the one in red asked.

"You got an answer?" I asked.

The one in leotards began talking. "Me and her, we came here through Renosa into McAllen."

"Good," I said. "Thank you. How long ago?"

The one in red answered. "We been here almost a year. Stayed in McAllen for three months working the trade to get the money to come to Willow Falls."

"Why here? What is so special about Willow Falls?"

The one in red pointed to the back seat. "Her brother lives here."

"Who's your brother?"

"Juan Vasquez."

"What's your name?"

"Carlita"

"How old are you, Carlita?"

"Eighteen."

I looked at the one in red. "You?"

She looked down at her hands. "Twenty-two."

"And what's your name?"

"Rosalee Baez."

"Who's your pimp?" I asked.

"Got no pimp," Carlita said. "We're not in the business fulltime."

"I don't understand."

Rosalee spoke up. "It is like this. We wanted to come to the USA. There's no work in Mexico. No jobs pay nothing. We had to sell our bodies to save enough money to pay the coyotes to show us the way across the border."

"Then we worked in McAllen for a while," Carlita said, "and saved bus fare to come here, like she already told you."

"You turned tricks there, too?" I asked.

Rosalee nodded. "We got more family down there near Los Cabos. "It's a dangerous place. We work like this to earn money to send to our family down there. Someday we will have enough to bring them here."

I nodded in understanding of Rosalee's self-sacrifice. "You kissed one of the men who brought you downstairs this evening. Who is he?"

"That was my husband, Manuel."

"Manuel Morales?"

"Si. You know him?

"You told me your last name is 'Baez.'"

"I do not use our married name when I work like this. It would bring him dishonor."

Suddenly I felt compassion for these women, especially for Rosalee who was performing sexual acts with strange men and for her husband who was permitting her to do so in order to bring more family members to the USA. It was nothing I would have let Rachel do, no matter how little money we had. At least I don't think I would ever have let it reach that level of sacrifice.

I started the motor and put my car in drive.

"You taking us back now?" Carlita asked.

"One more stop."

I stopped at my bank, ran my card through the ATM, and withdrew four hundred dollars. I gave each woman two-hundred dollars in twenties."

"Wha's this for?" Carlita asked.

"For giving me what I wanted."

"You don't want sex?" Rosalee asked.

"No. Go home and be with your husband."

I dropped Carlita and Rosalee off at the Mexican market and then stopped at a sports bar across town. After putting two draft Blues into my belly, I drove past the Mexican market again. It was eleven p.m. and the ladies were still working, walking up to cars and chatting with their occupants. I watched Carlita climb into the front seat of a rusty Ford pickup with some fat slob who drove off in the direction of Central Park. I wanted to follow them and arrest the guy for patronizing a person for prostitution. But if I did that, then I would have to arrest Carlita, too, and I just didn't have the heart. She was sending money to her family back home and hoping to save enough to bring them here.

****

On my way to work on Monday, I stopped off to see Cisneros. "You always come so early," Laverne said. She picked up the phone and mumbled something in Spanish. Then she smiled at me. "He's happy you're here. Go on back."

I walked through the doorway to the work area and found Cisneros sitting behind his desk, dressed in a collarless Nehru jacket, black, with a holiday tie. *Christmas must be coming*, I thought.

Cisneros' face lit when he saw me. "Ola, amigo," he said as though we were old compadres. "You got something good for me?"

"Nothing you'll find to challenge your leadership or undercut your profit margins."

"That's good. So, fill me in."

"I spent some more time watching Juan Vasquez and Manuel Morales, as you asked. You should know they're engaged in a small prostitution ring, but nothing to truly impact your profit margins. In fact, with a little help, they might be coaxed out of the business."

Cisneros sat down in his chair. "'Explain what you mean, please."

"Look, those two guys are trying to raise enough money to bring their families to the States. You know how they're raising the money?"

Cisneros leaned back in his chair. "Enlighten me."

"So, Vasquez has a sister named Carlita and Morales has a wife named Rosalee. Both women are turning tricks in order to earn the money they need."

Cisneros frowned. "So, Morales…that cabron is letting his wife be a puta so he can bring family here? What must she think of him?"

"Maybe it's unconditional love," I suggested. "Maybe she'll do anything because she loves him."

"You're a romantic, amigo. My wife would cut my throat if I made her do that."

"I think that's the only skill these women have. They crossed the border at Renosa and turned tricks in McAllen, Texas, in order to raise enough money to come to Willow Falls. For all I know, they slept with every coyote who helped them along the way. Somebody needs to teach them a trade so they can earn a respectable wage somewhere."

Cisneros leaned his chair back on two legs. "You thinking that someone ought to be me?"

"Look, I gave them each two hundred dollars because I felt sorry for them. But I can't really afford that. You've got the cash. The question is 'Do you have the inclination?' You could probably pay to have both families brought to Willow Falls and gain all sorts of respect from the men who work for you."

"Every one of them probably has the same problem—family members who were left behind and who could benefit by living here in the land of free health care and food stamps. I couldn't afford to pay the freight for all the family members of all my employees."

I drummed my fingers on the edge of his desk. "Don't you Mexican Americans have any organizations which sponsor immigrants? A gift in the right hand at the right moment might help certain immigrants arrive sooner than otherwise expected."

"I don't know. I never thought about it. How do you say?...ah, yes...it is out of my pay grade." Cisneros plopped his chair back onto all four legs. "I don't think like a gringo, you know. I could use an hombre like you in my organization...somebody to teach me how to think like an Americano."

"In my day job, I'm a cop. I can't be in your organization because I'll get fired or go to jail."

"Can I put you on retainer for a while as my personal private eye? We could see how things work out."

"I already have a full-time job, but I wouldn't mind continuing to work for you when you need something investigated or you need support with something which doesn't expose me to prosecution."

Cisneros reached across his desk and offered his hand. "Then it is done."

I shook his hand and then rose to leave. "I'm going to bill you for my latest investigation into Morales and Vasquez. I'll drop it by tomorrow."

"Just email it to my secretary."

I shook my head. "No. No trail of breadcrumbs which leads to me."

Cisneros smiled at me. "Hey, gringo, be sure to include the four-hundred-dollar gift you gave to those two putas."

Putas? Just when I was beginning to think Cisneros had a heart, he destroyed the image for me.

"By the way, am I permitted to ask you questions about the aftermath of the investigations I conduct?"

"Only if you recognize I can't always give you a direct answer. Never know if you might be wearing a wire."

"You can trust me on that issue. Search me every time we meet if you want."

"I might." Cisneros leaned back in his chair again. "You got a question about this case?"

"Yeah. I'm wondering what you did about your wife's godson, Prognostico. Is he still in business?"

"Yeah. Nice place he's running if you don't mind feathers and blood. Have you been back there lately? He's upped the admission fee to five dollars per person. The extra two dollars are for me, and I get ten percent of his concession receipts."

"So, the price of cerveza has gone up, too?"

"Not too much. I'm a generous business partner. Besides, we don't want the customers to think he's fleecing them."

Chapter 25

I pulled into my parking space at the department later than usual. It was almost nine o'clock, and the note on my chair told me Helen had already been looking for me. I set my Styrofoam cup of coffee on my desk, took off my coat, and opened the ledger I had taken from Billy Travis' locked desk drawer. The list of names under the "Sanguinarians" heading read like a who's-who of regional leaders and businessmen. It included two family physicians; the CEOs of an insurance firm, a medical insurance group, and a major international manufacturing industry; three attorneys from two different firms; a college president; the president of a bank; two past presidents of the Albany chapter of Rotary International; a surgeon; a psychiatrist; and, of course, the owner of a mortuary group.

I photocopied the handwritten list and called Helen to tell her I was finally in and ready for her to come up to my desk.

"Where you been?" she asked in her African American vernacular. "I be looking for you all morning, Jonesy."

"Had to stop and debrief with my client. Sorry I'm a little late. If you promise not to rat me out to the chief, I'll skip lunch to make up my time."

"You got anything interesting in that ledger you found?"

"I'll show you when you come up. Don't want to say the names over the phone. You never know if the Department's lines have been tapped or if we're being recorded."

"You going Serpico on me?"

"Nope. Nothing like that. You're just going to be interested in what I've uncovered." I took a sip of my coffee thru the little hole in the cup's plastic lid. It burned my tongue. Styrofoam always seems to keep the coffee hotter longer. "You find anything interesting on Travis' computer?"

"This reminds me of playing, 'I'll show you mine if you'll show me yours' when I was a little girl. You sure you don't want to go over to my place so we can show each other what we got?"

"My desk will do. Did you print anything worth sharing?"

"Yeah. The next blood moon comes soon after Christmas, and then again in May. The next one after that is a year later. He's even kept a record of all the invitations he's mailed out."

"If he's the one doing the invitations, do you think he's the leader of the group?"

"Naw, Jonesy. Travis is a small fry. Maybe he's like secretary of the group, or maybe he's employed to do the grunt work. The leader of the group is somebody we wouldn't expect. And I don't think it's Modern."

"You coming up?" I prodded.

"Been up twice. How about you come down, so I don't build too many varicose veins in these delicate little legs of mine?"

"Okay. I'll be down in a few." We hung up.

I checked my computer calendar to see if anyone

had scheduled me for any meetings. It was as clean as a baby's butt. So, I stuffed the photocopies I had made into the ledger, picked up my coffee, and headed to the elevator.

When I walked into Helen's office, she was sitting at her desk examining stuff on her computer screen. She was in casual clothes today, a green and orange flowery blouse, burnt orange slacks, and black flats.

"'Bout time you showed your ugly face around here," she said without looking up. "People beginning to notice you're never in the office."

"Got places to go and things to do if we're ever going to solve the Moretti case."

"We getting close, Jonesy." She motioned for me to walk behind her desk. "Looky here."

I walked behind her desk and bent over to look at her computer screen. Helen moved her right hand to her throat, pressing her blouse against her collarbone. I thought maybe she didn't want me looking down at her breasts. I would not have done so intentionally, but sometimes my eyes drift away from where I'm supposed to look.

With her left hand, she pointed at her computer screen. "I've been developing my own list of people who Travis interacts with around the dates of the blood moons. The invitations go out electronically, so we don't need to go looking at post office records. It's all right here in his email files under messages sent."

I squinted to see the screen better. "Show me, would you? I'm not sure I understand."

"Pull up a chair, would you? I'm already tired of you looming over me trying to take a look at what I got."

I set my coffee on the edge of her desktop and pulled

the visitor's chair around to her side of her desk. When I sat down, she released her grip on her blouse. Its neckline plunged forward, and I realized if I had looked down from above her, I could have seen all the way down to her navel. "So, show me what you've found out."

She had a series of tabs open on her screen. "Look at this. It's a list of all the blood moons for the past five years, including months and dates. The next one is December 31. That's New Year's Eve. Then there's one on May 26 called the 'Total Super Blood Flower Moon Eclipse.' The one after that is a year later, on May 16."

"Would you print me a copy of those dates? I want to run them by Eric Petronis at the Schenectady PD. He's got two unsolved murders where the victims' bodies were drained of blood. If they happened around the dates of blood moons, then we can expect a similar victim will turn up a day or two after New Year's Eve."

"You mean here in Willow Falls?"

"Not necessarily here, but somewhere in the capital district."

Helen sent a copy of the list to her printer. "Looky what else I have." She moved her cursor to the next tab and tapped it. The screen switched to another list. "This is a list I complied of all the people who Travis invited to an event at the 'Great Hall' over the past three years. It's mostly the same people, but there's always one or two new ones added each time."

None of the names matched the list I had photocopied from Travis' ledger. "Where's the 'Great Hall'?"

"The invitations don't give its location. All the invitees must know where it is."

"Looks like it's time for us to pay a few visits.

Maybe somebody will sing."

"Yeah, but we've got to figure out who they are."

"We could always begin with the list of bigwigs Travis kept in his ledger." I handed Helen the list I had photocopied, and she began reading them aloud, "Simone Rutledge, Michael Lofton, Robert Upton, James Carter, Arthur Easter, Edwina Faraday, Roxanne Windsor…These are some important dudes, aren't they? Do you think they'll mind if we start asking them questions about the Sanguinarian folks?"

I smiled and shrugged my shoulders. "Who knows? But it may create some activity which we can monitor."

"We gonna have to visit some of these folks in the evening. Can't interfere with their workday."

"Let's start by dropping in on Natalie again."

Helen leaned back in her chair and looked at me. "Why?"

"Maybe she knows who some of the people on the invitee lists are."

"Good luck. She's only a minor player at best. When you wanna go see her?"

"Right after lunch."

"You drive."

****

Helen met me at noon at my assigned parking space behind the department. She opened the door to my sedan and slid in quickly. "Brrr, it's cold," she said. "Thanks for heating up your car before I got here."

"Always thinking of you and your needs, my dear." I started the motor and backed out.

"Where we going, anyway?"

I put the car into drive and drifted out of the parking lot. "Lenny's Rib Shack. They've got a BOGO special all this week."

"BOGO?"

"Yeah. It stands for 'buy one, get one.'"

Helen raised the right side of her upper lip. "Their meat's probably going bad and that's one way of getting rid of it."

"No, no, it's not like that. They run a special like this every year during the week before Christmas. Everybody's too busy shopping to eat anywhere except fast food, so Lenny runs this special to draw in customers. I promise you it'll be good."

"Lenny's is a redneck joint if I ever saw one. You sure they gonna let a sister share a table with a white guy?"

"No problem. I fixed a speeding ticket for Lenny a couple of years ago. He likes me."

"How'd you do that? You're not in the traffic division."

"A guy in the traffic division owed me a favor. That's how I got him to repay me."

"You know, you're almost crooked."

After a quick trip across town, I pulled into Lenny's. There were four cars in a parking lot which could easily hold sixteen.

Helen pointed to the empty lot. "Nobody's here 'cause they all died of ptomaine poisoning."

I climbed out and stretched. "Last one in the door will be the coldest."

Helen beat me to the red and green foil-covered door and opened it before I could. "Looks like Lenny's in the holiday spirit," she said, pointing to a hand-cut white snowflake which had been taped to the inside of the door's window.

We sat on vinyl seats in an empty booth with a Formica tabletop. Inside, Lenny had hung multi-colored Christmas lights along the top of each wall. A small Christmas tree was standing near the jukebox which was playing Gene Autry's *Santa Claus is Coming to Town*. Mounted above the bar, a wild boar's head was decorated with a red nose.

"This is a family place," I said.

"Oh yeah, looks like it," Helen lied. Then she laughed. "You know, Jonesy, you take a girl to the nicest places."

The waitress brought us two waters and took our order: a plate of baby back ribs each, with collards, black eyed peas, and corn bread. When she returned a few minutes later, she was carrying two plates and set them down in front of us.

As we ate, Helen asked, "How are things going with Rachel and your divorce?"

"It's uncontested and we've already divvied up our stuff, so Brockbank says it should be final within a month."

"You took an expressway, Jonesy. Some of those things drag on for years."

"Well, Rachel wants out quickly. I guess Moretti is doing the same thing to his wife. I think he's already moved out of his house and in with Rachel."

"Wouldn't want to be his wife. She lost her daughter in early October and her husband in December. I'll bet he doesn't even care that he's driven a knife through her heart."

"My heart is ripped apart, too. But Rachel just seems so happy when I see her. Maybe it's for the best."

"Sorry, Jonesy."

When we finished eating, I paid by credit card and left the waitress a forty percent tip. Hell, it was the holidays, and she was not going to earn bug bucks today with only five tables to serve.

The seats were cold when we got back into the car. And our hot breath fogged up the windshield, so I had to run the defroster for a few minutes before we could drive over to Natalie's. While we waited, Helen got back on task. "We probably need to go see Horace Modern again, too, just to ask him about the people on our lists. We need to see if he starts sweating when sees what we have."

"Yeah, only this time I want to bring a team to do a search of his place."

"We might need a dozen officers. His place is big. Lots of places to hide stuff."

"I'll get a search warrant. Maybe we can go tomorrow afternoon."

It was a five-minute drive to Natalie's on Montclair Avenue. I got out of my car and knocked on her door.

"Oh, it's you," Natalie said when she saw me standing outside in the cold. "Come on in."

I waved to Helen, who opened the car door and hurried against the cold wind into Natalie's. Unlike me, she wiped her feet on the doormat before she walked in. I shut the door behind Helen. "Natalie, this is my partner, Detective Martin."

"I know you. You were at the Halloween party with another guy who was dressed like a cop." She paused for a moment and then looked at me. "Was it you? Were you at the party with..." She obviously had forgotten Helen's name.

"Detective Martin? Yes, I was."

"Did we...?"

"Yes, we did. And thank you. I mean it, really. Thank you."

Natalie put her hands on her cheeks. "Oh god, I'm so embarrassed."

"It's okay," Helen said. "I'd be embarrassed, too, if I'd wrestled a round with this guy."

"Natalie, we're working on a murder case," I said. "It possibly involves some members of the sanguinarian community. The problem is we have names which aren't identifiable. We're hoping you can help us identify who they are, so we can interview those people and possibly find the killer and the motive."

"It all sounds so terrible. I'll try to help you, but I'm probably not the best person. I mean, I don't know if I know enough to be helpful."

"Can we sit down to go over this list of people?" Helen asked.

"Oh sure. I'm sorry I didn't ask you to sit. My mother always said I have bad manners."

We sat on Natalie's sofa, Helen to her left and I to her right. Helen pulled out her list of Billy Travis' contacts and they began going over them while I watched.

Natalie read the names aloud. "Palatine...Regimented Soul...Porno Butter...Halftime Colon...Ramjet Races...Thruster Area...Fadeaway Drain...Nonwaxed Norris. These names are so bizarre."

"Does any of them mean anything to you?" Helen asked.

"No. They're meaningless."

I handed her my list of names.

Natalie nodded. "I know who some of these people are. Like it says here, Simone Rutledge is President of

Willow Falls National Bank, and Michael Lofton is the head Priest—"

I cut her off before she read anything else off the paper. "Have you ever seen any of these people at any of the events where people feed on blood—you know, like the Halloween party at the Odd Fellows?"

"No, but I know who they are. Everybody in the capital region does. But I don't know any of them personally. The only possible sanguinarian I know is Roxanne Windsor."

"You know Roxanne?" I asked excitedly.

"Yeah. I met her the first time I went to a Halloween party, three years ago."

"Can you tell us where she lives?"

"Sure." Natalie took her address book from a bookshelf and wrote Roxanne's address on a three by five card.

Helen took it from her with a smile. "How did you get her address?"

"She sent me a Christmas card three years ago. Since then we exchange cards every year."

I extended my hand to Natalie. "Natalie, I think you've made our day."

Chapter 26

When we returned to the department that afternoon, I put a call in to Eric Petronis at the Schenectady PD. "Petronis here," he said when he picked up his desk phone.

"Eric, it's Bart Jones. Got a minute?"

"Sure, Bart. Nothing happening here, except a few burglaries because Christmas is a couple of days away and some people don't shop in the store. What's up?"

"When I called you a couple of months ago, you told me you had two unsolved murders where the victims' blood had been drained from them."

"Yeah, that's right. You were looking for the perp of a similar case, right?"

"Yeah. Listen, I'm interested in knowing the dates your two bodies were discovered, and where they were found. Is it possible to get that for me?"

"Sure. You gotta give me a couple of hours. I'll have to pull the case files. They've never been solved."

"Great. No big rush on that info, but maybe in a couple of days?"

"Maybe tomorrow. I'm taking off after that. Gotta spend some time wrapping presents. This business of staying up until three in the morning on Christmas Eve wrapping and putting stuff together for the kids has gotten old. I plan to spend a couple of hours in the attic each night between now and Christmas getting it done.

Pauline will keep the kids occupied decorating cookies for the Great Bearded Fat Man."

"Santa?"

"Yeah."

"How old are they?

"Shannon is eight and Eric Jr. is five."

"I envy you, Eric. We never had kids."

"Well, don't envy me too much. I've got to pay for two college educations and a wedding. I'll be in the poorhouse before I retire."

"Well, as my mother used to say, 'If you didn't love the first one, you'd never have had the second.'"

"Yeah, you're right." Somebody interrupted Eric and I could hear his muffled conversation, though I couldn't make out what he was saying. "Gotta go. Expect to hear from me tomorrow on those two vampire cases."

"Thanks, Eric."

It was nearly time to punch out for the day. On my way down to the rear exit, I stopped by Helen's. "What's up?" I asked as I entered her office unannounced.

Helen's shoes were off, and she was dabbing some sort of cream on her big toe. She looked up from her business and pulled the collar of her blouse closed. "What you want, Jonesy?"

"Heading home. Just thought I'd stop by. I touched base with Eric Petronis in Schenectady. He's getting us the dates and investigative details about their two unsolved cases which are similar to Laura Moretti's. How about you?"

"We're all set for tomorrow. I called Roxanne Windsor and set up a meeting with her at her home at nine in the morning. Then, exactly at noon, when his employees are at lunch, we're going to drop in on Horace

Modern and do a search of his premises. Chief is letting us have two squad cars of support.

"That's nice of him."

"He's getting anxious. Doesn't want the Moretti girl's death hanging out there when the department begins budget negotiations with the County after Christmas."

I motioned toward her foot. "Did you go dancing with Bergen Saturday night?"

She squeezed some gunk out of a tube of triple antibiotic ointment and rubbed it on her big toe. "I wish. Turns out Chaquille just wanted two things: an inexpensive meal and a quickie. He got the first one at the Hunan House—chow mein and three beers. He was on his way to the second one when he bit my big toe. What a turn off. But he didn't want to stop, even though I was complaining about the hurt he put on my toe. I had to kick him you know where and then throw him out of my house before ten-thirty." She held her toe up for me to see. It was red with the impressions of two teeth in the fleshy pad. And it looked infected. "Don't know what else he gave me. Hope he isn't spreading herpes."

"Too bad. I thought you might have had an enjoyable evening with him."

"What is it with men, Jonesy? Do I look like a girl who's just interested in one-night stands?"

"You're asking me for advice? The guy who hopped into the sack with Natalie, a woman I had known for all of three minutes?"

"Yeah, you're right about that. I got to get me a new social advisor."

I walked Helen to her car, if only to send the message to onlookers that I was her protection from any unwanted advances by Chaquille Bergen if he was lurking around work afterhours. She was my partner, and we detectives do those sorts of things for each other.

****

I arrived at my cabin after dark. It was only five o'clock in the afternoon, but the moon was up and shining its light on the frozen lake behind the cabin. I could hear the season's last remaining Canadian geese honking as they flew overhead to settle in the north end of Mariaville Lake, where a warm spring bubbles up, creating a thirty-foot circle of never-frozen water.

Inside, I took a shower and then popped a beer and ate two pieces of pepperoni pizza left over from Sunday afternoon's football binge. I had watched three games, although during the early afternoon time slot, I switched back and forth between the Bills and the Giants—so make that four games. The NFL should know better than to schedule two New York teams at the same time slot. Which team is a die-hard fan of both going to watch?

I tried to stay up to watch Monday Night Football, but it was two loser teams vying for who was going to be at the absolute bottom of the ladder. I gave it up and went to bed when my chin hit my chest at ten o'clock. The life of a bachelor can get that bad. I don't recommend it to anyone.

****

The next morning, I arrived at work at seven-forty-five. Helen pulled in right behind me.

"How's your toe?" I asked when I saw her in tennis shoes.

"Went to the emergency room last night. They put me on a doxycycline pit drip until two in the morning. I'm loaded with antibiotics. Wait until I see Bergen today. I'm going to hand him my bill and demand payment."

Helen had bags under her eyes from lack of sleep, and we had two important engagements today: Roxanne Windsor and Horace Modern. The paperwork afterwards was going to take hours.

At eight-forty-five we pulled out of the department, and because of Helen's foot, I drove us to Roxanne's home in Marshfield, a three-story brick with a tudor roof. I was impressed a real estate agent could own a place which looked like it belonged to a millionaire. I figured she bought it for a song from some poor sap who lost his fortune in the last stock market plunge.

I pulled into Roxanne's circular driveway. "Think we should have contacted Chief Parillo before we came into his jurisdiction?" Helen asked. "We did that when we interviewed Margo what's-her-name."

Helen was referring to Margo Lumpas, the principal suspect in the murder of BabyX, a case we investigated a year ago. "If she becomes a major suspect, then I think we probably should. But for the moment, we're just asking her a few questions related to a crime in our jurisdiction."

We exited the car and pushed the doorbell button. Deep throated chimes echoed inside. Almost a minute elapsed before Roxanne greeted us, still in her pink silk pajamas and wrapped in a red bathrobe. Her chestnut brown hair was impeccable, as though she had just finished at the stylist's. "Come in," she said. "I forgot you were coming this morning."

Helen rolled her eyes. "I called you only yesterday to make this appointment."

"Yes, but I was up late watching an old movie and

forgot. It was Cary Grant and Joan Fontaine…*Suspicion*. Have you ever watched it?"

"No, I don't think so," I said.

Roxanne led us into her living room, a space as large as my entire cabin. Its floor-to-ceiling windows looked out onto a football field of new white snow, probably covering a well- manicured lawn of dandelion-free grass. Roxanne's taste in furniture left little to the imagination. She liked rich woods and plush red velours. Her walls were covered with paintings which could have been done by the old masters, though they probably were works completed by their understudies. And her pink and white marble floors were covered here and there by wool carpets, most appearing the be Persian.

"Sit." Roxanne pointed to her sofa. "I'll bring coffee." She left the room.

Helen and I sat on Roxanne's sofa. I could feel the end of a spring prodding at my gluteus and wiggled until it seemed to go away.

"This is all for show," Helen whispered. "Lot of old stuff in here. I think everything came with the house when she bought it."

Two minutes later, Roxanne reappeared with three mugs of coffee on a bamboo tray. She offered us cream and sugar. Helen took a little of each, but I prefer my joe black, so I politely declined her offer.

Roxanne sat opposite us in a large wing chair. Once we were all settled, she asked, "How may I help you?"

"Thanks for making time to see us this morning," Helen began. "We're still chasing down information about the sanguinarians in the region and have a list of people who we may need to chat with, but we need your help in deciphering the list."

Roxanne leaned back in her chair and crossed her legs. "What you ask holds some amount of risk for me. Many of the sanguinarians are among the wealthy and elite of their communities. They prefer anonymity and frown heavily upon those who disclose their proclivities."

"Can we begin by simply looking at the list we've discovered and, perhaps, you can help us to understand it?"

"I'll give it a try, but no guarantees."

Helen handed her the list of names which Natalie had called "bizarre." Roxanne read it briefly and smiled. "What you have is a list of pseudonyms for individuals who wish to remain anonymous. Deciphering it is not difficult, but it would take most people a long time to accomplish."

"Can you help us to understand?" I asked.

"Certainly, Detective Jones. These are anagrams, most likely developed with the assistance of a computer program, although a skilled linguist could accomplish them by hand."

"Anagrams?"

"Yes. Look at the first name, Palatine. If you unscramble and rearrange the letters you will see a woman with whom you had conjugal relations at the Halloween party."

"How would you know my private affairs?"

"I watched you leave the main room with her and enter the hallway where the rooms with conjugal beds were waiting ready for customers. When you returned twenty minutes later, the satisfaction on your face told me everything I needed to know."

"Weren't you with that Natalie woman for a while,

Jonesy?" Helen asked.

I looked at the name Palatine again. I wrote it down on my note pad and then began crossing out letters until I deciphered the name "Natalie P."

"The 'P' must stand for her last name: Pemberton," I said.

"Exactly," Roxanne said. "Now, who else do you have on your list?" She picked up my list again and began to study it. "Okay, let's try this one: Porno Butter."

I wrote the letters on a clean page in my notebook.

Helen looked over my shoulder and began to suggest letters, "R, U, P, E, R, T...That doesn't work because you have TOBON or BONOT or BOONT remaining. We have to try something else."

"This is where a computer becomes useful," Roxanne said. "Do you have a list of people whom you suspect might be sanguinarians?"

I shook my head and took a sip of the coffee she had made for us. I didn't want her to know everything we had because she could be feeding information to the membership.

"I've already figured it out, and you're very close," Roxanne said. "What if you change the first vowel in the first name?"

"The only vowel we have left is 'O'," Helen said. "That would be ROPERT." She thought for a moment. "We've got to change the P to B. That give us ROBERT."

"That leaves TNOPU," I said. "Maybe it's POUNT or PUNTO..."

"How about UPTON?" Helen suggested. "Isn't Robert Upton the priest at St. Bartholomew's in Willow Falls?"

"Bingo," I said. "Way to go, girl."

Roxanne smiled. "Now you've got it. You just need to do the same thing with the other names."

"It would be a whole lot easier if you'd just tell us who they are," I said.

"Then I would be guilty of tattling on people I know. If you do your homework, you'll figure out the puzzle on your own, and I truthfully will be able to tell the others I did not give you any of their names."

I wanted to threaten her with a court order or perhaps with deportation if she did not provide us with the names on my list, but so far she was cooperating and pleasant, so I changed the subject. "Okay, then, do you know the location of a place called the 'Great Hall'?"

"It's on the third floor of the Odd Fellows Hall. It has no windows. The Odd Fellows were, well…odd about that. I believe it was the room they used for their secret ceremonies. You're the police, so you can probably get a warrant to search it."

"And who manages the Odd Fellows Hall?" Helen asked.

"Why, I believe that would be Horace."

"Horace Modern?" I asked.

"Yes. He is the Druids' procurer."

"Procurer?" Helen asked.

"Yes. Whenever the group has special needs, he procures whatever it is. I believe he procured the Odd Fellows Hall for the Druids when the hall went on the auction block."

"That's twice you used the term 'Druids.' Are you a member of the Druids?"

"You must already suspect I am. We are not witches, if that's what you think. We worship Mother Earth as a conscious being. Oh, and we are recognized as a religious organization by the State of New York."

"Who's your leader?"

"I am not at liberty to say, but I'm sure you can find out. We took a blood oath not to reveal the names of our members. I've tried to live up to that oath by the manner in which I've answered your questions today."

"How often do you Druids meet?" Helen asked.

"We gather on the nights of the full moon each month. So, we gather once per month, unless there is a blue moon. In that case, we gather twice that month. The gatherings are held from ten until midnight."

"So, you go to meetings every month?"

"Yes, except for the months of the blood moons. I'm only a Fledgling and am forbidden to attend blood moon gatherings. When I achieve full Sanguinarian status, I'll be able to attend those, also."

"Would you mind clarifying the differences for me?" I asked.

"Certainly, Detective. When one first joins the Druids, he joins as an Initiate. You saw some of those who are hopeful of achieving Initiate status at the Halloween party."

"You mean the ones who were cutting people and licking their blood?" Helen asked.

"Yes, it begins there. When one has demonstrated a proclivity toward the Sanguine life by participating in the ritual seven times, he receives an invitation to pledge the Druid Society. The invitation does not guarantee acceptance into the Society, but it opens the door to conversations and interviews with full members. Pledges are then voted on by the entire group during a special meeting called a 'Moot.' The vote is conducted by secret ballot, where members drop a white or black ball into a clay urn. If an individual receives even a single black ball, his candidacy is terminated, and he can go no further. Those who are unanimously selected are invited to a ceremony where they drink an ounce of chicken or pig blood and become Initiates."

"It sounds a lot like joining a fraternity," I said.

Roxanne sighed and sat back in her chair. "Yes, I suppose it does."

"Go on, please," Helen prompted. "Tell us more."

"Once one has achieved Initiate status, there are classes to attend, where one learns the history of the Druid Society and its seven ranks. And one also learns certain rituals, much like going to Sunday School, except it is only for adults, and only for those who express a desire to learn more. In that sense, it's much like the Masons."

"So, what are the ranks?" I asked.

Roxanne held up her hands and counted on her fingers as she recited the ranks. "Pledge, then Initiate, then Neophyte, then Fledgling, then Bard, then Sylvan, followed by Sanguinarian, in that exact order. I suppose there is one more step, but only a few aspire to the last level. It's called the Archdruid, or priest."

"So, you're at the halfway point in terms of rank?" I asked.

Roxanne nodded. "Yes, there are three ranks below mine and three above. An individual must serve at least three years in each rank before he may qualify to be a candidate for the next rank."

"And who is your Archdruid?" I asked.

"You already asked me that question, Detective. You know I'm not at liberty to tell you or I will be excommunicated." Roxanne looked annoyed. "It's a religious thing. I've told you as much as I'm going to. I assume as good detectives you'll be able to take it from here."

Helen spoke up. "That's fine, Roxanne. You've given us a lot of interesting information. We may uncover more confusing things and come to you for clarification. You've been very helpful and, if you ever need us to, we'll testify regarding your assistance at a deportation hearing."

Roxanne's jaw dropped. "You mean someone wants to see me deported?"

"No, I mean if that ever happens, we'll come to your defense."

"Oh, thank God. You gave me quite a start."

Chapter 27

"I wish we hadn't scheduled the search and seizure procedure for today," I said to Helen. "I think we first should have tried to gather more information from the Sanguinarians on Travis' list. Besides, I think the reasons we gave to obtain the warrant were flimsy."

"Yeah, well, the judge signed the search warrant, and we have two squad cars of men scheduled to help us search Modern Scientific Supply at noon."

"Is Bergen…?"

"Nope. I made sure he isn't involved. Don't want no pigs messing up our investigation."

I couldn't blame Helen for her feelings about Patrolman Bergen. We put on our cold weather jackets, met eight officers downstairs at the motor pool, and led them in their two squad cars to Modern Scientific Supply. We arrived at five minutes after twelve, when most of Modern's forty employees were eating lunch in the cafeteria.

Modern must have been alerted to our arrival by his security guard because he met us at the front door and held his hand up, directing us to stop. I showed him our search warrant.

"My attorney is on his way," Modern announced. "You can come into the building only after he reviews your warrant and lets me know my rights."

"Fine." Modern was within his rights to keep us

standing out in the freezing cold until Lance Freeborn arrived. I guess if I were in his shoes, I would have done the same thing.

Helen and I conferred for a minute and then I motioned for four of the officers to come over to us. "Please encircle the building," I said, "and watch for anyone who might try to remove or throw anything from the building while we're waiting out front."

They climbed into their squad car and drove around to the loading dock area at the rear of the building. Shortly after they disappeared around the building, Helen's radio went off.

"Yeah?" she asked.

"We're stationed," was the reply. "Loading dock is quiet."

"Ten-four."

Fifteen minutes later, Lance Freeborn squealed into the parking lot in a steel gray Range Rover with mag wheels and a white top. I had a feeling he wouldn't be driving an American car which runs on regular gas, though I figured him more as the BMW type.

Lance pulled to a stop in handicapped parking and walked quickly up the sidewalk in a thin herringbone coat, the kind which looks nice but doesn't keep you warm. Because of the chilly westerly wind, he held his fedora on his head with his left hand. When he saw Helen and me, he frowned. "Let me see your search warrant."

I handed him the same paper I had held up for Modern to see. Freeborn examined it.

"It's kosher," I said.

Freeborn grunted, "Wait here," and walked into the building. Through the glass doors I could see his hands moving in all directions as he was talking with Modern.

Finally, he opened the door. "You may now come inside. My client is very upset you dropped in without prior notice."

Helen waved the other four officers forward and then walked through the door. "That's the idea, Mr. Freeborn," she said. "We're seeking evidence on several possible charges, and if your client knew we were coming, he would have disposed of it."

Freeborn nodded at me. "Good afternoon, Detective Jones. You always seem to be engaged in frivolous investigations involving my clients."

"Maybe you should consider raising the caliber of the clients you serve, Mr. Freeborn."

Helen spoke directly to Horace Modern. "Mr. Modern, we're going to search your premises from top to bottom. You may not interfere with our search. We may confiscate certain items we believe will serve as material witness to several charges pending against you. Your employees are not to return to their workstations unless accompanied by one of the officers. This search may take several hours, and since tomorrow is Christmas Eve, you might consider sending your employees home early for the Christmas holiday."

Modern was escorted by one of the officers to the lunchroom, where he sent everyone home. "Call in on Monday morning after Christmas," he told them. "I'll leave a voicemail telling you when we will reopen. We'll have lots of packing and mailing to do before the spring semester begins. Happy holidays, everyone."

Within fifteen minutes, the building was empty, except for the pickup truck driven by Modern's janitor, Jesse Swann, who had just arrived and would not finish his work until nine at night.

"He's only going to do the restrooms and floors," Modern protested. "Certainly, he can stay and complete his work, can't he?"

I looked at Helen and she shrugged her shoulders.

"Yeah, I guess so," I replied.

We told Modern to wait in the entry foyer with his security guard while we conducted our search of the building. Helen radioed the four officers who were guarding the rear. "One of you stay in the rear to prevent anyone from entering or leaving. The other three meet us in the cafeteria, where we'll go over search details."

When all of us had assembled in the cafeteria, Helen and I handed out a brief and discussed the Laura Moretti case, especially the bizarre state of her body when it was examined by the ME. I gave the marching orders. "We're looking for anything which can link Modern to the killing, including anything linking him to cults whose members drink raw blood. That means memos, emails, ceremonial clothing, containers of blood or blood-letting equipment. Also, we want to confiscate any illegal drugs and any live animals on the endangered species list, such as Colorado River toads or Amazonian tree frogs. Questions?"

"Is this guy for real?" one of the officers asked.

"We think so, but we need each and every one of you to consider everything you see for its potential to link him to the crime."

The men dispersed, all seven going to the fourth floor to conduct a room-by-room search. From there, they would go to the third floor and repeat the process before descending to the second floor. Anything they confiscated was to be placed into a plastic bag and labeled as to exact location and date. Well, except for living creatures, which would need to be photographed and then relocated to the loading docks for removal into the trunks of the squad cars.

Helen and I began on the first floor with Modern's office. We checked his desk, his desktop computer, filing cabinets, shelves, and closets. Modern got angry when we asked for the password into his computer, but Lance Freeborn suggested he give it freely so we would not confiscate his computer and accidentally corrupt his files when they were opened by our department's computer experts. In that sense, perhaps Freeborn was helpful.

Finding nothing in Modern's office, Helen and I found our way to the attic, hoping something incriminating would be waiting for us. It was a large empty space, encased in dust and probably haunted by schoolchildren who died before they matured.

Helen looked disgusted. "Looks like we might strike out, Jonesy."

"I think we're going to have to go explore the third floor of the Odd Fellows Hall, Helen. Maybe there'll be something there."

At the end of the long afternoon, we had collected several jars of dried mushrooms which we suspected were the illegal variety, four aquariums full of croakers labeled as *Colorado River toads* and *Amazonian tree frogs*, a dozen plants we suspected were varieties of marijuana, and ten four-ounce vials containing liquid blood. The mushrooms, plants, and the blood would have to be analyzed for identification by the State Labs.

Helen and I met with the officers at the loading dock, where they had made duplicate lists of the items we were confiscating. They officers drove to the front of the building to wait for Helen and me to debrief with

Modern and Freeborn. As we were walking toward the main foyer, Helen and I passed the janitor, Jesse Swann, who was washing windows with a rag and then drying them with a squeegee. We smiled and nodded at him as we passed. Halfway down the hallway I stopped. Helen kept walking and, when she realized I was not beside her, turned and asked, "What's wrong, Jonesy?"

"Come on," I said, hustling back to Jesse Swann.

"Mr. Swann," I called out. "Can I see that cloth?"

He scratched his head and handed it to me when I arrived beside him.

Breathless from sudden exertion, Helen joined us.

I opened the wet cloth. It was a section of printed cloth, originally white with a penguin print. "Where did you get this?" I asked.

"It's just an old cloth," he replied.

"Yes, but where did you get it?"

"I found it in a trashcan down in the basement, near the incinerator"

"Are you sure?"

"Yes, sir."

Helen realized what we had found—possibly a piece of the top that Laura Moretti had been wearing on the day she was kidnapped. "When did you find it?"

"Please don't tell Mr. Modern I've been using it. He gets upset if I don't use paper products, but they don't work as well as cotton on glass and furniture."

"When did you find it?" Helen asked again.

Around the second week of October, just after there was some kind of late-night party here."

"Where's the rest of it?" I asked.

"I threw it away as I used it. That there is the last square of it."

"Does Mr. Modern host a lot of parties here?" Helen asked.

"Mr. Modern holds them a couple of time per year. Next one is scheduled for the middle of... let me think...Oh yes, next week. December 31. Isn't that New Year's Eve?"

"Yes. It is," Helen replied.

"I'm sorry, but we're going to have to confiscate this rag," I said. "We won't tell Mr. Modern we have it. Is that okay?"

"Like I said, he don't like me using anything but paper products."

I stuffed the wet rag into my coat pocket and walked with Helen to the main foyer.

We opened the door into the foyer. Lance Freeborn sprang to his feet. "Did you find anything which would cause you to arrest my client today?"

I handed him a list, then I asked for it back. I wrote another item at the bottom of the list and handed it to him again.

"What's this?" Freeborn asked.

"It's a list of everything the department has confiscated for analysis by the New York State Labs. All except for the thing I scribbled down at the bottom."

"Piece of cloth?" Freeborn asked.

"Yes." I pulled it from my pocket, squeezed the liquid from it, and opened it up for Freeborn and Modern to see. "It's just a rag."

Freeborn looked puzzled, but Modern's eyes grew large with the realization he might have been discovered.

"Don't leave town without my permission for the next two weeks, Mr. Modern," I said.

His eyes met mine, and I knew he knew I had him.

Chapter 28

On Christmas Eve, Chief Comstock announced the department would shut down at noon for all but essential staff. Jews, Hindus, Muslims, and other staff whose religions did not celebrate Christmas would man all operations until the return of Christian officers the day after Christmas. That sort of balanced Yom Kippur, Diwali, and Eid Al-Fitr, which were holy days when officers of other faiths were given a day off and Christian officers worked in their stead.

Helen and I spent an hour unscrambling the names on Billy Travis' list, the way we were taught by Roxanne Windsor, the Queen from England. We already knew "Porno Butter" was Fr. Robert Upton of St. Bartholomew's Catholic Church. By slow determination we identified "Regimental Soul" was Simone Rutledge, current president of the Willow Falls National Bank; "Ramjet Races" was James Carter, an attorney with Pitman, Freeborn, and Carter, LLC; "Thruster Area" was Arthur Easter, President of Albany College of Liberal Arts; and "Fadeaway Drain" was Edwina Faraday, business owner and current president of the Marshfield Rotary Club. There were probably more Sanguinarians to be uncloaked, but we did not have their names yet. Maybe we would learn more in our upcoming interviews, but the Christmas holiday was upon us.

Helen boxed up the stuff we had confiscated at

Modern Scientific Supply and marked it for shipment to the state labs in Albany. There was not much left to do except wait for the results to see if we could hang something illegal on Modern. We still had not identified Laura Moretti's killer, but Helen and I both thought Modern was our guy, especially since we had found the penguin-printed cloth in his place of business.

On my way home, I wanted to drop by Imogene Moretti's to see if she could identify the cloth we found at Modern's, but Helen suggested Christmas Eve just was not the day to send Mrs. Moretti's emotions into a spiral. I think she probably was right about that. So, I decided to wait a few days before bothering Mrs. Moretti. Then I thought about dropping in on Wayne Moretti, who was now living in my house and sleeping with my soon-to-be-ex-wife Rachel. Just the thought of ruining his Christmas holiday gave me pleasure, but my conscience would not let me act on my thoughts. What would Rachel think of me if I did that. Did it matter? Probably not.

I arrived at my cabin on Mariaville Lake at one in the afternoon. The weatherman had forecast a line of snow squalls would pass over Willow Falls in the late afternoon, but they were already hurling large snowflakes against my cabin's westerly-facing sliding glass doors. I could hear a few geese honking from the warm spring across the lake. I'll bet they wished they had traveled south with the flocks.

I popped a beer, flopped down on my sofa, and thought about the Sanguinarians we had recently identified. Then it hit me: *If Billy Travis' list is accurate, right here in Willow Falls we have a goddamn Catholic priest who drinks human blood.* There was just something about that revelation which didn't sit right with me. I had heard of priests who knocked up a parishioner and had been forced to leave the clergy and priests who were pedophiles, but I had never heard of priests who were actually practicing Druids. Could a person truly be both? Which belief system was Fr. Upton scamming—Catholicism or Druidism? Could he be scamming both? It was time to visit him again, but my visit would have to wait until after Christmas. Besides, he would be too busy celebrating masses and drinking wine and sharing after-dinner cordials with parishioners to have any time for me now. Maybe I would go see him in a couple of days.

****

On Christmas morning Helen called me right after breakfast. "How 'bout you come over for Christmas dinner, Jonesy. We're eating at two."

I felt a little awkward eating Christmas dinner with Helen and her family because she was my partner and she was probably offering me a meal out of pity, like you would do for a homeless person or someone with an incurable but non-communicable disease. "I don't know, Helen. I've got lots of things to do out here today…"

"Quit with the cheap excuses, Jonesy. You got a better invitation? I don't think so. You be here about one-thirty and dress in something nice. My momma has standards for dress when we're fine dining. And besides, my family thinks most white folks need all the charity we can give them." Helen hung up her phone.

"Great," I muttered. I was certain she was inviting me to dinner because she saw me as a charity case.

I opened a loaf of wheat bread, tore half of it into small cubes, then threw them out onto the snow in the back yard for the birds. I envisioned cardinals, blue jays, finches and possibly a mouse pigging out on the Christmas feast I had given them. Then I closed the door, took a shower, and ironed a shirt to wear to Helen's family dinner.

At one, I drove from Mariaville to Schenectady, where I stopped at a twenty-four-hour liquor store owned by a Sikh and bought a bottle of Bailey's Irish Cream liqueur to give to Helen for after dinner. Then it was a five-minute drive to Helen's home in Glen Cove, a two-family she had purchased from a department retiree. The rent she receives each month from the long-time tenant pays her taxes and the home's upkeep, like the new roof she had to have added last year and the cost of the removal of asbestos-wrapped piping when her boiler gave out in October. Eventually, once all the important systems in her home have been replaced, Helen will enjoy a nice annual income to supplement her retirement pension. I, on the other hand, will probably be on the street corner selling pencils to supplement what little of my pension I get to keep until Rachel re-marries. I hope she gets on with it.

When I arrived at Helen's, the curbside parking was full, so I did a U-turn and parked across the street. I grabbed the Bailey's, crossed the quiet street, and knocked on Helen's door. There was much laughter coming from inside her home. The door opened, and a short chunky woman in her seventies greeted me. She grabbed my head in both hands, pulled my face toward hers, and planted a kiss on my cheek. "You must be the famous Detective Bart Jonesy," she cried. "I'm Helen's mama. Just call me Gracie."

I nodded. "Yeah, I guess so."

She took the bottle of Bailey's from me, pulled me in the door, put her arm around my back and in a loud voice announced, "Everyone, this is Helen's detective partner, Bart Jonesy."

"Jones," I said, but it was already too late. I was "Detective Jonesy" to everyone I met, all of Helen's cousins, aunts, and uncles. I was the token white guy in a crowd of a dozen people of color who were in festive holiday spirit. It was a nice surprise, because I had been expecting to eat only with Helen and her mom.

"What do you want?" her cousin Nadine asked, pointing at the small bar which had been arranged on a side table. She was a thin woman in a red and green checked dress. Her hair was in a short afro. Her eyes were bright, and her teeth bleached white.

"You got enough Jack Daniels?" I asked.

"New bottle, never opened," she replied.

"On the rocks, please."

She poured four fingers of Jack into a glass and plopped a single ice cube in it. When she handed it to me, she gave me a peck on the cheek. She pointed above my head. "You're under the mistletoe."

I laughed and lifted my glass to thank her for the holiday kiss and then excused myself to find Helen in the kitchen.

"Hey, Jonesy. Mama told me you were here." Helen was busy checking the temperature of a ham in her oven. A full-front apron was covering her black skirt and red top. Her jet black short afro sparkled in the kitchen's fluorescent lighting.

"What can I do to help?"

"Nothing. Just go chat with my cousins. They've all heard of you 'cause we're partners. Your being here

239

helps make my profession seem real to them. Otherwise, they can't believe a woman of my good looks would want to be a cop when she could be a Vogue model."

I laughed. "Maybe a 'vague' model."

"Go on, now," she said, pointing toward the living room.

I walked back into the living room and eavesdropped for a while before being dragged into a conversation about "defund the police." This crowd was clearly against it.

Helen's mom was especially vocal. "They unemploy Helen, who's gonna come help us when somebody's tryin' to steal our car or break into our home?"

"Un-huh," Nadine and cousin Rowanda said, almost in unison. "It's plain foolishness," Nadine added.

"What you think, Jonesy?" Mama Gracie asked.

I didn't want to find myself on the wrong side of the discussion, but I answered truthfully. "People depend on police for a lot of services beyond capturing bad guys. We deliver babies in cars, we stop traffic so funerals can go by, we help settle arguments between family members before they get violent, we try to reduce addiction among youth. If the number of police officers is reduced, I don't know who will attend to those things, unless neighbors get together to protect themselves and their property."

"See? I told you so," Gracie said in a loud voice. "Just 'cause he's white don't make him no fool. He and Helen is partners. He learns from her about black folks and their situations. He's a good one."

The heads in the conversation all nodded at Gracie's remarks, including Uncle Raymond's. Helen once told me he was a Vietnam War veteran who had earned a purple heart and silver star by saving his company from certain death at the hands of a Viet Cong machine gun nest. Back in the US after the war, he had difficulty finding work because he had only one good eye. The other had been damaged by shrapnel when the two hand grenades he lobbed into the machine gun nest went off. He was a proud man, living off whatever menial work he could find most of his adult life, and refusing welfare and VA benefits for his disability. I admired him for his inner strength and commitment to independence.

When Helen called us for dinner, we left her living room en masse and squeezed shoulder-to-shoulder around her dining room table. I sat between Mama Gracie and Uncle Raymond. Helen sat across from me, where she could get up to go into the kitchen if anyone asked for something which was not on the table.

Dinner looked delicious—a spiral cut ham, scalloped potatoes, black-eyed peas, homemade biscuits, sweet potato pie, fried apples, and pitchers of iced tea and water for those who were not carrying mixed drinks or beer.

We all joined hands and then Mama Gracie led us in prayer. "Lord, we ask you bless this family as we celebrate the birth of your only begotten son, Jesus Christ our Lord. May our blessings continue throughout the coming year and may you grant us world peace, especially between BLM and the Christian Coalition. Amen."

"And may you be with those who have lost children and loved ones in the peaceful protests throughout this nation," Cousin Nadine added.

"And we ask you be with the many businessmen

whose livelihood was lost to the fires set by those peaceful protestors," Uncle Raymond said.

"And bless us all, regardless of our political persuasions, Amen," Helen said. "Time to eat, now."

We ate for almost a full hour, though the time spent eating was interrupted and extended by calls of "please pass this or that." It seemed like every time I put a forkful of something in my mouth, I had to pass two or three platters of food to someone else. It was an endurance event. There was a lot of laughter about family members and friends, and many comments about how good the food was. I truly enjoyed being included in this family celebration.

Later in the day, we enjoyed apple and blueberry pie a la mode and everyone received a glass of Bailey's to wash down the pie. Then the family dispersed into various rooms where low-level conversations ensued. Mama Gracie sat beside me on a chair in the dining room with a cup of coffee. "You like my little girl?"

"Yeah, she's the best partner a detective could ever ask for."

"I don't mean it that way, you goofball," she said, hitting my arm with the back of her hand. "You seem to fit in nicely with our family. I mean, they all seem to like you and they aren't offended a white man is here in a private party with a family of color."

"Thank you," I replied. "You have a really nice family, Gracie. I've enjoyed being here and sharing the day with you."

"You know, it could be like this every holiday if you and my little girl became closer."

I knew where she was going. "Do you mean Nadine?"

"Now I know you're pulling my leg. I mean Helen. She's something special, isn't she?"

"Yeah, she's something special all right. But I'm still married for a while and I'm not sure jumping into another relationship so soon would be a good thing for either one of us. I'm carrying some emotional baggage."

"Oh, Helen could help you work through that, sure enough."

I looked down at the floor and nodded.

Gracie patted my thigh. "I know she's got a thing for you, the way she talks about you and all. Give it some thought. Nobody in this crowd is going to be upset if Helen hooks up with some white guy, at least not if it's you."

She got up and walked into the kitchen, leaving me to contemplate what she had said to me. Almost on cue, Helen came into the dining room and sat beside me. "You having a good time, Jonesy?"

"Yeah, you have a really nice family."

"Oh, we got our differences, but we love each other and respect our varying opinions about things."

"I got a real sense of that during grace."

She smiled. "Yeah, I was afraid everyone was going to jump in with something different to ask God. You know She can't answer everyone's prayers when they are so opposite in viewpoint."

"She?"

"Yeah, of course. You don't think some man had the vision to build this entire interrelated network of plants, animals, and environments, do you? Everything is too interrelated to have been created by a male."

"You're sounding way too philosophical for me, Helen. I've never given that sort of thing much thought."

"Yeah, I know. Sometimes you're so wrapped up in what's going on inside you that you don't see what's going on right beside you."

I knew what she was trying to tell me, and it frightened me. I mean, I've kidded around with her at work about having some sort of emotional relationship, but I never thought she'd give it serious thought.

I stretched my arms over my head. "This has been nice, but I have things to do in the morning, so I've got to be going." I stood up. "Helen, thanks so much for inviting me today. I guess I'll see you on Monday so we can strategize who we're going to interview next...I mean after we go back to visit Fr. Upton."

"I didn't mean to chase you off, Jonesy. You can stay a little longer, can't you? It's just six-fifteen."

Helen's mom came back into the dining room. "How you two children getting along?"

"Just fine, mama," Helen answered. "Jonesy here has to go home now. We were just saying goodbye."

Mama Gracie took us both by the arms and pulled us under the mistletoe. "Nobody's going anywhere until you give Jonesy a holiday kiss."

The room quieted as all eyes were on Helen and me. I didn't know what else to do, so I bent over and gave Helen a polite kiss on her lips. She reached behind my head and pulled me closer. Then she gave me a passionate kiss. "Merry Christmas, Jonesy."

"Woohoo!" Nadine shouted. The room exploded into cheers and applause.

Helen leaned close to me and whispered, "I guess we got that over with, didn't we?"

I raised my hand like Santa Claus. "Merry Christmas to all, and to all a good night!"

I opened the front door and stepped outside into the still cold of early evening. My breath formed a white cloud of steam in the air. I reached my car, opened it, and started the motor. Before driving away, I stared back at Helen's home. Today's events were something I had not expected, and they frightened me. Workplace relationships are dangerous things because if they don't work out, somebody has to leave or both people live in Hell. Besides, for me, a multiracial relationship carries a burden of its own: How would my family members react if I brought Helen home for dinner? I was sure they would not be as welcoming as Helen's family had been to me.

****

When I got home, it was almost seven-thirty. Before removing my coat, I turned on the deck lights and opened the sliding glass doors to my back yard to give the birds the remainder of the loaf of bread I had sprinkled on the snow for them in the morning. Instead of seeing tiny tracks of the little birds that hang out around the lake, I saw deep imprints in the snow, and the usually pristine white was covered with large piles of black and yellow goose poop. I brought the bag of torn bread back into the cabin and sat on my sofa in frustration. *So, go the best laid plans of mice and men.*

Chapter 29

Monday morning arrived. I drove into town feeling a little tentative about seeing Helen again, especially after we had kissed in front of her family on Christmas day. I stopped at Verrigni's for coffee and a cinnamon bun to go and then parked in my assigned space and made my way to my desk. People in the department—the officers, clerks, and secretaries—all seemed a little quieter than normal. I guess it was the usual letdown after a holiday, something that is especially symptomatic after Christmas.

After finishing my pastry and half my coffee, I called Helen and asked if I could come down so we could determine who we would interview next.

"Yeah, I s'pose," she replied. She sounded like she was in a funk.

I took the elevator to the second floor and knocked on the edge of her open door.

"It's open, Jonesy," she said.

"You down or something?"

"Not sure I wanted to see you today."

"Why's that? The kiss? Was my breath bad or something?"

"No. I'm embarrassed my mama would tell you what she told me she did. Does that make any sense?"

"You mean when she told me I ought to marry you?"

"Did she really say that?"

"Not quite in those words."

"Darn her hide. She's always trying to set me up with this one and that one. Wish she'd butt out of my personal life. You know, every time she sees some guy who she thinks would be a good match, she tells them I have a thing for them when I don't. She figures I'll get interested in them if they show interest in me."

"So, there's no hard feelings about the kiss in front of your family?"

"None whatsoever. They all know what Mama is like."

I felt Helen wasn't telling me the truth about that kiss. I mean, I gave her a gentle peck, then she pulled me toward her and gave me tongue. That didn't seem like casual disinterest. Maybe she was embarrassed she had crossed the line between police partners who should never have sexual relations because sex muddies the waters in critical situations. But her kiss certainly let me know if I wanted to ignite our relationship, she was willing to go there.

I changed the subject. "We've got to go visit that Catholic priest again, especially since he's on Billy Travis' list of Sanguinarians. Got anybody else in mind?"

"Yeah. Edwina Faraday. So far, she's the least powerful person on our list. We may be able to squeeze her for more information than the others."

So, I called Fr. Upton and made an appointment for after lunch. And Helen called Edwina Faraday and made an appointment for ten o'clock the next morning. Things were moving again.

I took Helen to Ruby's Red Hots, where we both ate two hotdogs with onions and hot sauce. I laughingly told

Helen, "Maybe the fires emanating from our mouths will scare the beejeesus out of Upton and he'll tell us everything we want to know."

"Probably not," she replied. Helen was a realist.

We arrived at Saint Bartholomew's Roman Catholic Church at one o'clock sharp. The front doors were locked, so we got back into my city-issued sedan and drove around the church until we found the entrance to the church offices. An older woman was unlocking the door. We watched her enter, and then we parked and got out.

After a brisk hike up the sidewalk, we rang the doorbell and were buzzed in.

The lady who had unlocked the church door was seated behind a glass window. I could see her puffy pink winter parka slung across the table behind her. She was probably between sixty and seventy years of age, though her head of completely gray hair could have belonged to a fifty-year-old who grayed early. She wore a cotton sweatsuit of matching green color and black padded snow boots.

"We have an appointment with Fr. Upton," I said.

"Is he expecting you?"

"Yes, I made the appointment this morning."

"Well, I don't think he's back from lunch yet. But you can wait if you'd like." She pointed to two metal chairs with green plastic cushioned seats.

Helen and I sat down and played with our cell phones. I deleted old text messages. Helen read a romance novel she had downloaded.

Half an hour later, Fr. Upton came into the office. "Oh," he said, "I thought we settled on one-thirty as our meeting time."

I knew better because I had clarified it with him twice over the phone. His late arrival was just his way of busting our chops.

He disappeared through an inner door. Two minutes later the lady's office phone rang. She looked up. "He's ready for you now." She pointed at the door he had entered. "Through there."

When we entered Fr. Upton's private office, he was sitting behind a dark oak desk checking his weekly planner. Other than a few notations here and there across the paper grid, from a distance it did not appear he had many appointments this month. That made sense because we had just ended the busiest season for a priest. Things would not heat up again until we approached Easter.

Upton was wearing the black trousers and shirt which are the normal uniform of the clergy. He had removed his white collar and his shirt was open, exposing a small patch of protruding gray chest hairs. "I'm interested in what you've found," Upton said. "Have you solved the little Moretti girl's murder?"

"We're close," Helen replied. "We're hoping you'll help us piece together a few missing pieces."

"I'll do what I can. My parish doesn't need this kind of tragedy, you know. We've already had two other parishioners die this year, one from AIDS and one from COVID."

"We're working on this case as quickly as we can, Father," Helen replied. "There is precious little to go on and certainly no witnesses to her kidnapping."

Upton cracked the knuckle on his ring finger. "Frankly, I'm concerned the police don't have a good record when it comes to solving murders in this city, at least over the six years since I've served here as parish priest."

"Our record is better than those of any neighboring city," Helen said in defense.

Upton looked at me and smiled. "I wonder if a good private detective should be brought in on the Moretti case. Would the police object if the church paid for one and offered a reward for information leading to the arrest and conviction of the murderer?"

His smiling stare made me wonder if he knew I was moonlighting as a private eye for Cisneros. From the small shrine Cisneros kept on the shelf behind his desk, I surmised he was a Catholic, and the Catholic Church has not been free from corruption over the ages, not at the local or the international levels. Maybe Upton and Cisneros were golfing buddies, or maybe they were doing some business together. Maybe he knew something or maybe he was only fishing. I decided to get down to business.

"When we were here last time, we asked you if you were aware of any blood-drinking cults in the capital region."

"Yes. I was astonished at the question."

"What I should have asked is how you, as an individual, can practice Catholicism and, at the same time, be a practicing Druid?"

"Preposterous," Upton cried.

"Your name appears on two separate lists which have come into our possession. Are you a member of the local Druids or the Sanguinarians?"

"How could such a fabrication come into existence? Who would give you such a list? Clearly it would be someone trying to throw you off his own trail."

"He's telling you the truth, Fr. Upton," Helen said. "We have witnesses who will testify you are a practicing member of the local Sanguinarians, and you drink human blood."

Upton stood, grabbed his Bible, and held it in the air like an old-time revivalist. "Bring them before me. I have the right to face my accusers."

"All in due time," I said. "But we need to know more about the Druids and—"

My question was interrupted by the loud ringing of Helen's personal cell phone. She pulled it out of her purse and checked to see who was calling.

"Excuse me, but I have to take this." Helen lifted the pink phone to her ear. "Helen Martin."

Upton returned to his chair, his face and neck splotchy red.

"Yes. Yes," Helen said. "Yes, I can be. Yes, I've eaten lunch. Okay."

This was the first time I had ever seen Helen use her personal cell phone. In fact, I didn't even know she had one. I wondered if perhaps her mother had taken ill.

Helen pushed a button to end the call and then put the phone back in her purse.

"Jonesy, I hate to do this, but we have to go."

"Is your mom okay?"

"Yes. It has nothing to do with her. It's just that I'm a blood donor, and the hospital needs a pint of my blood immediately."

"They just had a blood drive a few days before Christmas to replenish their stockpile for the New Year's," Upton said. "They should have plenty on hand."

"Not like mine. I'm '0-negative.' It's very rare. About twice each year a baby is born with an immune deficiency and needs an immediate transfusion. Since I'm what they call a 'universal red cell donor,' the hospital calls me in, and I go immediately to help save the child's life."

"What a great act of Christian charity," Upton said. He looked toward the ceiling and raised his right hand into the air. "Lord, bless this woman for what she does for her fellow man."

"We'll be back to see you soon, Father," Helen said. "This donation is just more important right now."

"I understand," Upton replied. "Go with haste and do the Lord's work."

Helen and I left the church and hurried to my sedan. As I started the motor, Helen let out a sigh of frustration. "That guy is a regular two-bit charlatan."

"Yeah, I thought the same thing. He reminds me of one of those televangelists."

"Let's get to the hospital asap, Jonesy."

****

I waited at the hospital while Helen donated her blood, a process which took about ninety minutes. An hour after Helen was hooked up with tubes, I learned the hospital's blood bank was in the next room, so I stepped into the hallway and knocked on its door.

A woman with a nose ring, colorful neck tattoos, and blue hair answered. "May I help you?"

She did not look clean to me, but I did my best to get by her appearance. "Yeah, I'm Detective Bart Jones from the police department. I have some questions about blood and blood storage."

She opened the door and let me in. "Glad to meet you, Detective Jones. I'm Dr Pratt."

I could not believe a doctor would decorate herself

as she had, but it's a new world. I mean, if I were looking for a new family physician and saw her picture as someone accepting new patients, I would run the other way.

Dr. Pratt pointed to a stool and motioned for me to sit. She sat on a stool a few feet away. "Doctor, are your facilities secure?"

"Certainly, I suppose. At least as secure as the blood banks at most hospitals. Why do you ask?"

"I'm working on a case involving a child whose blood was drained from her body by her murderer. I'm also here with a friend who is a blood donor."

"Oh, you're here with Helen Martin?"

"Yes. So, I have a couple of questions for you."

"Shoot."

"What do you do with old blood?

Dr. Pratt smiled. "We never have old blood. It goes out of here faster than it comes in. We often need to purchase it from private sources. Did you want to donate some today?"

I chuckled awkwardly. "Maybe later. When you draw blood from a donor, how do you prevent it from coagulating?"

"Interesting question. In the old days fresh blood was poured into vinegar, and then the blood could be used for cooking." She laughed. "I know that's not the answer you were looking for." She held up an empty collection bag. Each of these bags contains a chemical anticoagulant. It's a special compound which does not negatively affect the human body."

"I see. Okay, another question: Have you ever discovered blood is missing from the bank? You know, you think you have ten bags and then you discover you have only eight or nine."

"Why yes. Just recently we misplaced one unit of blood. We searched everywhere for it and then decided someone simply must have forgotten to record that it had been used for a patient."

"Is it possible someone might have stolen it?"

"For what purpose?" Dr. Pratt asked.

"For consuming, of course. Certainly, you've heard some people do that?"

"Yes, in medical school I read a research paper about the practice, but it's very rare."

"Are you aware of any blood-drinking cults in the capital region?"

"No, that's more of something from Hollywood, isn't it?"

"You need to get out of the office more often, doctor. It may be more prevalent than you think."

The door to her office opened without a knock. It was Helen, looking a little paler, if it were possible. "I'm done, if you're ready to go."

I thanked the doctor and walked out the door with Helen. She put her left arm around my right as we walked. "I'm always a little weak after these donations."

We walked toward the hospital's main doors. "You want to go back and ask a few more questions of Father Upton?" I asked.

"Nope. I'm feeling a little nauseous. Would you drive me home? I already called my mama. She'll meet us there."

Ten minutes later, we were in Glen Cove, and I was steadying Helen as we walked to her front door. Before we reached her front step, Mama Gracie swung the door open. "Nice to see you again, Jonesy."

I nodded, a little annoyed she didn't call me by my first name.

"Just you give me my little girl and go on about your police business. Helen will be fine once I get some liver and soup into her. We got us a little ritual after these blood donations."

Helen gave me a pat on the arm. "I'll be fine by morning. We've got another interview to conduct, don't we?"

I released Helen's arm into Gracie's. "Mañana, kiddo."

Chapter 30

Edwina Faraday was preparing her notes for the Tuesday noon meeting of the Marshfield Rotary Club when we knocked on her door. She let us into her foyer and asked us to remove our shoes before we walked any further into her Tudor mansion. Located in the most desirable neighborhood, her forty-five hundred square foot home stood like a neon sign that flashed the word "money" to anyone who drove by.

"I guess anybody from Willow Falls is carrying more dirt than desired inside a Marshfield home," Helen whispered.

Edwina ushered us into her greeting room, a space large enough to hold the entire home I had purchased with Rachel. In the center of her floor was a carpet made from a Bengal tiger, head and claws still attached.

"Don't mind Tony," she said with a smile. "My husband's grandfather shot him in India back when tiggers weren't an endangered species.

"Tiggers?" I asked.

"It's from Winnie the Pooh. Pooh and Christopher Robin called their tiger friend 'Tigger.'"

"I'm not up to speed on kid's literature. Disney made a film about Winnie, didn't he?"

Helen gave me a look which let me know how ignorant I sounded. But hey, I never read Winnie the Pooh as a kid, so give me a break.

"Yes, he did," Edwina said. "But you never saw it?"

"No, I guess not."

Helen started in with the professional stuff. "Ma'am, we're here seeking information about the Capital Region Sanguinarians. You're a card-carrying member. Aren't you?"

Edwina sat down uncomfortably on a stuffed chair and pointed to two similar chairs for us to occupy.

"I…I'm not…I'm not sure what you're implying."

Helen placed her notebook on a leather foot stool in front of her chair. Then she opened it. "I have two lists of Sanguinarians from different sources and your name appears on both. The first thing we need from you is verification that you are, indeed, a Sanguinarian."

"I…I wouldn't say I'm a Sanguinarian per se, but I guess if you have the lists, you know I am a practicing Druid."

"Good," Helen replied, "we now have that established."

"Tell us about the Druid meetings," I said. "For example, how often are they held and where do they take place?"

"They usually meet on the full moon of each month. Sometimes we have a blue moon, which means we have two meetings in a single month."

Her response corroborated Roxanne Windsor's. "Do you drink blood at every meeting?"

"I don't, but some do."

"What kind of blood do you Druids drink?"

She squirmed in her seat. "I think beef blood. Sometimes pork or chicken. I think it's whatever kind is available. The Archdruid takes care of arranging for that."

"And who is your Archdruid?"

"I've never seen his face because it's always behind a mask. You know, anonymity is important to Druids. The fact you actually have a list of names is baffling to me."

"We have two lists, ma'am," Helen said.

"Do you know the Archdruid's name?" I asked.

"I've only heard him called an embarrassing name. It's 'Porno Butter.' I'm glad they didn't give me that name."

Helen and I looked at each other. 'Porno Butter' was none other than Robert Upton, priest at Saint Bartholomew's.

"And your name is Fadeaway Drain?" Helen asked.

"Yes, but I suppose you already knew that."

"Yes, ma'am, but we wanted verification," Helen replied.

"When is the next Druid meeting?" I asked.

"Why, our next gathering is in two days, on December 31."

"And where will it be held?"

"At the Great Hall in Willow Falls."

"Do you mean the Great Hall on the third floor of the old Odd Fellows Hall in Schenectady?"

"Actually, no. There are two Great Halls. Regular Druid gatherings are held at the Odd Fellows Great Hall. However, the blood moon gatherings are always held at the Sanguinarian Great Hall. Same city, but different location."

"And when are the blood moon meetings?" Helen asked.

Edwina went to a desk near a picture window and opened her calendar. "After this one, there will be one on

May 26 of this year, called the Total Super Blood Flower Moon Eclipse. But it's really only good if you're on the west coast. Here, we'll just have a partial view. Druids from the capital region have already chartered a plane for that eclipse. We'll be gathering with other Druids from around the world near the Mount Palomar Observatory in southern California."

She paused for a moment. "After that, there will be two next year, one on May 16 and another on November 28, called the Total Frosty Blood Moon Eclipse. And, after next year, there won't be one until the year 2025."

She shut her calendar and returned to her chair.

"Have you ever tasted human blood?" I asked.

"Sure. As a child..."

I cut her off. "Yeah, I know, you licked cuts and scrapes. But I mean at one of your Druid meetings. Have you ever drunk human blood at one of those?"

Edwina's eyes drifted to the floor at her feet. "Yes, I've cut people with razors and licked their blood. And one time I was offered a swallow from a cup of human blood. The Archdruid said it came from a sterile source."

"Like from a blood bank?" Helen asked.

"Yes, I suppose. Possibly one of our members offered it up as a sacrifice to us all."

"How did it taste?" I asked.

"Metallic, I think...Yes, metallic."

Helen leaned forward in her chair. "Did you attend the blood moon meeting in October of this year?"

"No, I couldn't attend the gathering because I was in Belgium purchasing diamonds for my retail store."

"Was there a human sacrifice at the October meeting?"

"I sincerely hope not. There has never been such a

thing at any gathering I've attended."

"Have you spoken with anyone about the meeting?" I asked.

"It's a 'gathering,' Mr. Jones. "Why do you two insist on calling it a 'meeting'?"

"Okay, let me rephrase my question. Have you spoken with any of your fellow druids about what occurred at the gathering?"

"No, I haven't. Should I?

"Would you do so now?" I asked.

"You mean call another druid and ask him or her if there was a human sacrifice at the last gathering?"

"Exactly."

Edwina's hands began to tremble. Splotches appeared on her neck. "You know, I'm due at Rotary this morning."

"Your meeting isn't until noon. You have plenty of time," I said.

"Are you afraid of the answer you'll receive?" Helen asked.

"I'm afraid they'll cast me out if anyone is arrested for murder and I'm the one who has been snooping."

"Well, if we learn from someone else that a young girl was murdered so a bunch of druids could drink her blood, you'll be an accessory to murder and complicit in human torture," I said. "You'll go to jail for a very long time."

Edwina curled into a fetal position and briefly whimpered like a child with a tummy ache.

"I can get the District Attorney to offer you immunity from prosecution if you discover that a felony of any type occurred at the meeting," I said. I was not telling her the truth. The fact was that I could ask the

D.A. to give her immunity, but I could not guarantee he would agree. If he did not agree, a mediocre lawyer would ensure any evidence she provided would be inadmissible in court.

"Could I remain anonymous?" she asked meekly.

"Maybe, but no guarantees. Your testimony may be invaluable to the D.A."

"Or he may ask you to provide a simple deposition," Helen said.

Edwina nodded and then sat up straight. She rose from her chair and took her cell phone from her purse. After taking a couple of deep breaths, she said, "Okay, here goes." She tapped a number into her phone. After a few seconds, she pushed the speaker button on her phone. We heard the phone ring twice.

"Hello?"

"Good morning, R.S. This is Fadeaway Drain. Did I call at a bad time?"

"No, this is a good time for you to call, F.D. I'm getting ready to go to Rotary. Do you need me to bring something or to assist in the meeting in some way?"

"Yes, I do. Would you mind helping at the registration table today? Archie Reynolds is ill, perhaps food poisoning."

"That pompous old fool probably ate something which was two weeks old. I've seen him put things in his mouth I swear he picked up off the ground. Sure, I'll have to go to Rotary a little earlier, but I've still got time to prep my assistant for my usual lunchtime absence."

"I have another question. This one is about the gatherings."

We could hear R.S. moving over the phone and then we heard a clicking sound.

"I just closed my office door," she said, "so our conversation will not be overheard."

Edwina paused a moment and then asked, "I've heard our last gathering included something at a new level."

"Do you mean the sacrifice?"

"Yes. I heard it wasn't an animal this time."

"You heard correctly. It was fabulous. A fabulous high."

"So, you participated?"

"Yes. The fluid was amazing. It carried me to places we've only heard about."

"Was the process performed live?"

R.S. paused. We could hear her breathing. "Yes." She paused again, probably gathering her thoughts to explain. "At first, I thought it would be horrific, but it wasn't. The ritual was orchestrated with class, probably following the way things were done by the Order back in pre-Christian times."

"Do you think I would have been able to watch the sacrifice and then follow through with the passing of the cup? I have always been afraid of being seen as a coward if such a sacrifice were to be offered."

"I think so. Everyone who was there did it. Maybe some were skittish at first, like I was, but, like I said, the high was phenomenal. I got over any personal concerns very quickly. I'm excited about doing it again sometime."

"I'm just so tentative about it."

"From what I hear, you'll have a second chance on Thursday night."

"Really?"

"I've heard P.B. has Adrenochrome tailing another.

Someone who has something unique to offer the gathering. You really shouldn't miss it."

"Thanks, R.S. Maybe so. I'll see you at Rotary."

"Bye. See you in a few."

Edwina canceled her call and threw her cell phone on the floor. "Oh, God," she whimpered. "They've really gone and done it, haven't they?"

Helen reached over and took Edwina by the hand. "It's going to be all right. We'll help you through this. But we need to find out who Adrenochrome plans to kidnap this time. We need to save that person and put an end to this arm of the sanguinarians."

"Can you call in sick to Rotary? Maybe get your vice president to take over the meeting?" I asked. "Then maybe you could spend some time filling us in on the Great Hall and everything you know about the other Druids."

"No, I have an obligation to Rotary and it's the holiday meeting. It's very important I be there."

"Well, you be careful," I said. "Don't say anything more to R.S. except along the line that you're a little skittish about attending on New Year's Eve." I handed her my business card. "Maybe you can give me a call after work, and we can go over anything else you think might help us."

Edwina nodded.

"It's probably going to be best if you don't go to the gathering on Thursday night, honey," Helen said. "It could get ugly."

"I may have to go, if just to alleviate any suggestion I've told you what I have. I need to protect myself from retaliation."

"So, where is the Great Hall located?" I asked.

"It's on the fourth floor of Modern Scientific Supply."

"We were just there last week," I said. "There was no place I'd call a great hall. It was mostly just rooms full of specimens and then the packing and shipping stations."

"There's a false wall behind a stack of shelves in room four-eleven. In case you want to know, the 'four' is the floor level and it stands for 'stability.' And 'eleven' is the number of the spiritual messenger. Anyway, the false wall opens to a hallway. Follow the hallway a short distance and you will see goat's head mounted on the sash above a door. That is the entrance to the Great Hall."

"Anything else we should know?"

"Yes, now I'm very nervous about seeing R.S., but I need to be on my way to help set up the Rotary meeting."

"Yes. Yes," Helen said. "We'll be going now. You've been a great help to us. Perhaps you have assisted us to save a person's life."

Chapter 31

Helen and I drove immediately to Modern Scientific Supply to arrest Horace Modern on suspicion of murder. By bringing him in, we hoped he would not be able to carry out the kidnapping and murder of another innocent person. I brought my car to an abrupt halt, and we hurried into the building.

"We're here to see Mr. Modern," Helen said, flashing her badge.

"Sorry, but you just missed him," the security guard replied. "He's on his way to the airport. He's flying to Bermuda today for a week's vacation."

"Damn," I said. "Let's see if we can chase him down."

I drove quickly to Albany Airport, the only international airport in the capital region. On our way, Helen called her friend Vivian at Triple A. "Can you quickly scan the airlines and see which ones have flights scheduled to Bermuda this morning or early afternoon?"

"I'll try, Helen, but most of the flights to Bermuda go from Kennedy or LaGuardia in New York City, MacArthur on Long Island, or maybe Stewart, Syracuse, Boston, or Newark, or even Philadelphia. It would help me if you could be more specific."

"Let's start with Albany," Helen replied. "After that, we'll be on our own."

Helen held her cell phone to her chest and looked at

me. "Didn't you tell Modern not to leave the area for two weeks?"

I nodded. "Yeah, but I guess he didn't listen."

She put her phone back up to her ear. "There's only one carrier flying to Bermuda today and that's Delta. Plane boards at twelve-thirty and the flight departs at one."

"Thanks, Vivian," Helen said. "Maybe you've helped us catch a bad guy." She turned to me. "Go to the Delta window."

"I'm already on it. I overheard what Vivian said to you. For privacy, you need to hold the phone tight against your ear."

"Humpf. I knew you'd want to eavesdrop, so I held the phone away from my ear, just in case she asked the name of the white guy I was riding with. No brother would be taking me to Bermuda unless I was paying for the flight and the room."

I laughed and continued across town, through Marshfield and Colonie and made the turn into the airport. I parked with a red revolving light on the dash outside the windows advertising "Delta". Helen and I hurried to the desk, where we butted in front of a dozen people and flashed our badges.

"How can I help you?" the ticket agent asked. His almond-shaped black eyes told me he was of Asian descent, but he spoke flawless English.

"We need to know if a man named Horace Modern is on the next flight to Bermuda," I said.

The ticket attendant checked his computer. "Nope, nobody by that name.

I pulled out my pocket notebook, thumbed through it until I found Modern's birth name. "How about someone named Benjamin Middleton?"

Again, the attendant scrolled through his list of passengers. "You said 'Bermuda,' right?"

"Yes."

"Nope. Nobody by that name either."

"Thanks."

Helen and I went through the turnstiles and metal detectors to Gate B-13, where the passengers heading to Bermuda were waiting to board. Modern was not there.

"Let's wait until they announce boarding," Helen suggested, "just in case he's in a bathroom or a lounge getting a pre-flight cocktail."

Helen reminded me Modern was dressed as a woman when he was taking pictures at Laura Moretti's funeral. So, while we waited, we casually walked through the aisles of plastic seats, looking carefully at each passenger in case Modern was in a disguise. No luck, but we managed to annoy a few people.

When the passengers had boarded and the doors to the ramp were closed, Helen and I realized Modern wasn't flying out of Albany. We drove somberly back to the department, where we chatted with the coordinator of uniformed officers and arranged for several teams to assist us on Thursday night, New Year's Eve. The men would happily do anything other than traffic stops and DWI checks all night long. Their team leaders actually looked forward to raiding a private gathering of Druids.

****

At noon Tuesday, Helen and I left the Department and went to Verrigni's, where we both had a cup of coffee and discussed the strategy for the raid on the Sanguinarians. Then I dropped Helen off behind her car in its parking space at the department, and I headed back to Mariaville to clean my forty-five caliber Sig semiautomatic pistol. If it was good enough for the Navy Seals, it was good enough for me. I had had to sight it in only once. After that, it had never failed me. If I put the bead on something, I could blow whatever it was away. I hoped I would not have to use it on Thursday night, but you never know.

On her way home, Helen stopped at the grocery store for some hamburger, a green pepper, and an onion so she could make chili, one of her favorite dishes. When she arrived home, she went right to work on it, so her chili would have an hour to cook down before she ate.

When her dinner was simmering, Helen popped a Bud Lite and sat down to watch the news. Through her living room curtains, she saw a delivery truck pull into her driveway. A man in a brown uniform got out, carrying a small package. He rang the doorbell.

Helen stood up and opened her door. Ice had formed on the glass of her storm door, so she opened it, too, to see what the delivery man had brought her. When she did, her face dropped. "Modern," she blurted at the very moment he hit her in the chest with a stun gun. She blacked out and fell into his arms. He pushed her back into her living room and wrestled her limp body onto the sofa. Then he went into the kitchen and turned off the flame under her dinner.

Modern wrapped Helen in her living room carpet, an old Karastan which was thin from wear, and carried her into his truck. Once inside, he bound her wrists and knees with duct tape and taped a cloth into her mouth, just in case she should come to and begin screaming. Then he went back inside her home, turned off all the lights, and took her home phone off its receiver. On his way back out the door, he picked up her purse and removed the battery from her cell phone. He dropped the battery onto the living room floor but put the phone in his pocket so he could pitch it into the Mohawk River on his way back to Modern Scientific Supply.

It had all gone much easier than he had expected, so much so that he pulled into the drive-thru at McDonald's and ordered the two-for-one Big Mac special which was being advertised on national television. "What a treat," he said to Helen, who was still unconscious and encased in her living room rug. "One for me and one for you, only I also get fries."

****

When Helen woke, she was cold. Her hands and knees were still secured with duct tape, but her mouth had been untaped, and the cloth had been removed. She found herself in a metal cage, bars on all six sides. The bars lying against the floor pushed into her tush and back, sending both cold and pain signals to her brain. Beside her in the cage was a small bag with a MacDonald's logo. Wrapped inside she found a cold Big Mac. She turned on her side and ate the burger to maintain her strength and to feed her body's furnace to fight the cold.

In the dim light of the room, she saw her clothes heaped into a pile and shredded into ribbons. Whoever had undressed her did so with care not to free her hands or feet. She examined the room. It was full of assorted wooden boxes, chains, and pulleys; spotlights were mounted on the ceiling above her. She felt as though she were in an attic or a warehouse or, perhaps, backstage at a theater. She pulled her knees to her chest, partly to hide her nakedness and partly to capture what warmth her body was producing.

When fatigue overtook her, Helen fell asleep. Almost instantly the spotlights above her came on, blinding her, but also sending much needed heat down upon her shivering body. She squinted and held a hand above her eyes while she searched the room for her captor. She remembered it was Modern who had rung her doorbell. *Bastard*, she thought.

Helen sat uncomfortably under the strong lights until fatigue overtook her again and once more she fell asleep, her chin on her chest and her forehead against her knees. In her sleep, she searched for a means of escape. Suddenly, a loud squeal pierced the air, startling her and sending a bolt of fear through her body. She had heard it before, but not so loud. It was Yoko Ono singing "Why." The pounding bass sent shockwaves through her body. The music, if it could be called that, was on a roll, playing over and over and seemingly never ending. It was painful to her ears and worse, painful to her body. Her lips were touching the duct tape which secured her knees. She began chewing at it.

Behind her, a door opened and closed as if on cue. A hook on the end of a stick grabbed the duct tape at her wrists and pulled her arms above her head. She could feel something else being attached. She arched her back to see who it was. It was a man in a theatrical Satan's mask, red with two protruding horns. He had just secured her wrists with nylon Tuff Ties, the kind used by U.S. Marshals when they arrest illegals at the borders.

"I'll get you, you bastard," Helen cried out.

There was no response.

The man in the mask moved to the end of the cage and, using the hook on the end of the stick, forced her ankles toward his outstretched hand. He grasped one ankle and then he wrapped a nylon Tuff Tie to each ankle and secured them to the bars. After unsuccessfully attempting to wrest herself from his grip, Helen lay on her back, the cold hard floor bars beneath her continued to press painfully into her ribs. She had no option to relieve the discomfort of the bars beneath her except to twist her body onto her side, and when she did, the Tuff Ties bit into her wrists and ankles.

The music continued for hours, draining Helen of her strength and urging her to give up her ghost to whomever desired to capture it. Occasionally, a shrill scream, like a woman being tortured came from somewhere to her left. Then the angry calls of apes, lions, hyenas, and trumpeting elephants broke into the tortuous repeating verses of "Why." But the never-ending song continued.

Then everything went silent. Helen's ears pounded from the assault they had been taking. In her mind, the song continued, burned into her subconscious by its loud repetition. Helen waited silently, hoping the torture was over, but in her mental ever-presence, she knew more was in store. But exhaustion overtook her, and she fell asleep again. It was peaceful and healing. As she let herself slip deeper, "Why" began again, only this time much louder and accompanied by strobe lights. It was a phantasmic nightmare. She closed her eyes, but the lights found their way through the thin membranes of her eyelids. There was no escape. she screamed in mental and physical anguish. Then Helen's bowels released.

Chapter 32

Helen did not show up for work on Wednesday, and her cell phone was busy all morning. I figured either she or her mama was sick. But I knew she was looking forward to arresting Modern and Upton and any other Sanguinarians she could fit into a set of handcuffs. So, I expected to hear from her sometime during the day about tomorrow evening's raid. It did not happen.

On my way back to Mariaville after work, I drove by her house. Her car and a late model Chevy were in the driveway, and the lights in her home were on. I called the department and had the Chevy's license plate number traced. The response was back in thirty seconds. "Detective Jones, the car is registered to Grace Martin, age fifty-one. Lives in Schenectady. You want the address?"

"No, but thanks. I know the owner."

So, it appeared that Mama Gracie was visiting with Helen. Maybe Helen was, indeed, sick. I assumed everything was okay and drove home. I called Helen twice before going to bed, but she was not taking calls. Something smelled fishy, but I rationalized that if she wanted to talk with me, she would call.

****

At nine on Thursday morning, Mama Gracie called me. "Mr. Jonesy, I'm sorry to bother you, but it isn't like Helen not to call me every day. I went over to check on her yesterday around five. Her car was there, but when I went inside, she wasn't home. Her supper was still on the stove, but it was cold. She didn't answer at work either. Is she sleeping over at your place?"

"I haven't heard from her, either, and I was beginning to worry. You've just let me know I haven't been worried enough. Can you meet me at her house?"

"I'm on my way over now. Can you come soon?"

"Yeah, Mama Gracie. Try not to touch anything. I'll be there in ten minutes."

I knew Helen too well to wait any longer for her to contact me. She was in trouble, and I had to find her. I called Chief Comstock.

"Go ahead, Jones. I'm all ears," Comstock said when his secretary connected my call.

"Chief, we've got a problem. Helen Martin has disappeared. I believe she's been kidnapped by members of a local Sanguinarian cult. I'm afraid if we don't find her before midnight, she'll be another corpse we have to identify—when and if we find her."

"What do you need from me other than an APB? I can expedite search warrants if you need them."

"That would be great. I know of two places where I think we may find her, Modern Scientific Supply and the Odd Fellows House." I thought I could hear the chief writing. "And I could use a couple of squad cars, maybe eight men, for nineteen-hundred hours tonight."

"I'll call scheduling and order them to give you as many men as you need."

****

After hanging up with Chief Comstock, I drove to Helen's home. When I arrived, Mama Gracie was already there waiting for me in her car. I pulled in behind her and then helped her up the front steps to Helen's duplex.

She handed me the door key. "Here, you do it, Jonesy. I sometimes have trouble with it."

I inserted the key. I had to jiggle it before it would catch the right way and open the door. If I was lucky enough to find Helen, I'd have to tell her to get her mama a new key, one which had been buffed correctly after it had been cut.

When the door opened, I offered Mama Gracie a hand, but she stepped up into Helen's living room like an athlete. "Helen?" she called out. "Anybody here?"

I guess she hoped Helen had returned and she was busy somewhere inside. She turned to me. "Just like yesterday, nobody's home, but her purse is on the floor over there." She pointed to the floor beside Helen's sofa. "Her wallet is in it and her money hasn't been taken."

I reached for Helen's purse and saw a black box-like device under the sofa. I bent down on one knee and pulled it out. It was a cell phone battery. I showed it to Mama Gracie. "This is why she doesn't answer her cell phone. The battery has been removed from it."

I realized I shouldn't have picked it up because I had just compromised any fingerprints which might have been on it. It was a rookie mistake.

"Something else is strange here," Mama Gracie said.

"What's that?"

"I don't know, but I'll figure it out."

She took me into the kitchen and opened the lid to the pot which was on the stove. The air suddenly filled with the aroma of old chili. It was not a particularly nice smell. "Maybe I should just throw this mess out back," she said. "Some neighborhood dog might eat it."

"You might kill that dog. Does Helen have a garbage disposal?"

"Yeah, you're probably right."

Mama Gracie poured the mixture into the disposal, turned on hot water, and pushed the disposal button near the faucet. The noise was loud, especially when the disposal sucked the last remnants of the chili into its gaping mouth.

We then climbed the stairs and checked Helen's bedroom. Her bed was still made and had not been slept in. That was proof Helen was female and not a male in disguise. Most guys I know never make their beds.

Helen's bathroom was pristine. Even the toilet had been flushed. Again, she was no guy.

Mama Gracie ran a little water into the sink. "Gotta keep water in the trap or those little drain flies come out and you gotta pay the Devil to get rid of them."

As we came back downstairs, Mama Gracie turned to me. "I know what it is."

"What what is?"

"I know what's wrong. Helen's carpet is missing. I gave her an old carpet my mama gave to me after I got married. Helen always kept it on the floor in her living room. It's gone."

I didn't know what to make of the missing carpet, but the cell phone battery told me a lot. Whomever kidnapped Helen removed the battery from her cell phone so a smart cop could not call the phone company to find out the phone's location. Whomever it was knew something about modern technology. That narrowed down the list of suspects to somebody under seventy years of age.

I thanked Mama Gracie for letting me into Helen's

home. "I'm going to do my best to find her, Mama. I have a couple of places to look, and I'm going to search them today."

Mama Gracie clasped her hands as though she were praying. "I hope my baby's alive."

I nodded. There was not much I could say. I agreed with her.

****

At seven o'clock, I was dressed in a Kevlar jacket and was down at the motor pool, checking out my Sig while I waited for my eight soldiers. They soon arrived, dressed for possible combat, and Chaquille Bergen was among them. Helen was through with him, so I thought about asking him to stay behind, but I needed the manpower, and he was probably the strongest of us all.

I told the drivers of the two squad cars to travel without sirens or emergency lights because we wanted to be as inconspicuous as possible as we approached our targets. Once we synchronized our watches, we loaded up and hurried out of the parking area.

First on the agenda was Modern Scientific Supply. We arrived at seven-thirty and ours were three of the four cars in the parking lot. I ordered the security guard to open up.

"I'll have to contact Mr. Modern to inform him of the search," he said, shaken by the arrival of so many uniformed and heavily armed police.

"Modern isn't answering his phones," I replied. "Have you seen him at all today?"

"Why, no. But I still have to inform him."

"Go ahead, but we're starting now and if he wants to come down and question me, tell him I'd love to talk to him. Tell him it's Detective Bart Jones." I turned to the two team leaders, Roselli and Bergen. "Let's find room four-eleven. Roselli, your team takes the stairs and the rest of you will come with me on the elevator."

My team reached room four-eleven in under a minute. We entered and began searching the far wall for evidence that it could open. Bergen found a latch below the end of the third shelf. The wall opened like a long door, exposing a corridor. I went first, followed by four men, weapons up and safeties off. When we reached a goat's head mounted above a door, I signaled that this was our target. I pushed on the door, but it wouldn't open. Bergen and I both pushed with our shoulders, but it wouldn't give.

"Stand back," Bergen said. He aimed at the tongue of the door's dead bolt lock and pulled his trigger. The sound was deafening in the confined space, but the full metal jacket round did its job. The door swung open, a gaping hole where the dead bolt had been. The room on the other side of the door was dark and sounded eerily empty. I pulled a flashlight from my utility belt and scanned the wall for light switches. When I saw them, I hit the four switches and the room burst into bright light. The four officers with me scoured the room for any sign of Detective Martin.

Bergen and I checked the area behind the small stage. It, too, was empty.

"Looks like we crashed the wrong party," Bergen said. "You wanna do the other place?"

"Let's do a thorough search here, first. She may be held captive here somewhere and I don't want to overlook her hiding place."

Once we were finished with the Great Hall, it took the eight officers and me thirty minutes to scour the remainder of building, including its basement.

"Tell Modern the department will cover the cost of a new door and dead bolt," I said to the security guard, "if he cares to send us a bill."

"I'll try," he replied, "but he don't answer."

"Leave him a voicemail."

I convened a quick huddle. "Next up, we're going to the Odd Fellows Hall in Schenectady. It's in a dimly lit area at the end of Sirius Street. Same thing. Let me go in first while you guys watch the exits and windows."

It was a ten-minute drive through Willow Falls to the Schenectady City limit. I had not called the Schenectady PD to alert them to our raid. I thought that should be the Chief's job, and I hoped he agreed with me and had made the call.

As we approached Sirius Street from Front Street, we had to wait for a line of twelve cars to pass before we could make the left-hand turn.

The Odd Fellow's Hall was pitch black and its parking lot was empty when we arrived. Roselli held the flashlight while Johnston picked the lock. Thirty seconds later, we were all standing inside. Bergen hit the lights and we began the search. Bergen shot me a look that let me know we both felt like this search was futile. We began on the third floor and worked our way down, searching every room.

When we were finishing the sweep of the second floor, my cell phone beeped. It was a text message from Edwina Faraday. She simply forwarded me a text she had received from someone who left only his initials:

—*Impromptu change of venue:*
Box 3369, Ridge Road
West Glenville

9:00 PM
P.B.—

I checked my watch. It was now eight-forty. I asked Bergen to radio the men and have them reform on the first floor. When we all were together, I told the teams where we were going and then asked, "Anybody here familiar with Ridge Road in Glenville?"

"Yeah," Sgt. Sosnowski said. "It runs from the west end of Scotia to a community called West Glenville. At the Scotia end it's straight, but it gets snaky at the West Glenville end."

"At which end would Box 3369 be?"

"Got it," Bergen said, holding up his cell phone. "We'll get there quickest if we take route five to Rector Road. It intersects Ridge Road about a mile from our destination."

My phone received another text message:

—Hurry—

I pointed at Bergen. "Your car takes the lead. No berries or cherries." I didn't want the Sanguinarians to know we were coming.

****

Redirected by text message to the new location of their blood moon ceremony, the guests arrived at eight-forty-five and entered the barn two or three at a time. As they passed through the sliding barn door, each guest kissed his or her fingers and touched a photograph of a golden goat's head. The real one was still mounted above the sash in the Great Hall at Modern Scientific Supply. Immediately inside, young women dressed in saffron robes and golden goats' masks handed each guest a glass of pink Fleur de Morte champagne. Drinks in hand, the guests circulated among their friends and colleagues, chatting excitedly in anticipation of the evening's event.

When all Sanguinarians had gathered, an unseen hand dimmed the lights to total darkness and a recording of Virgil Fox playing J.S. Bach's *Come Sweet Death* filled the space. Its bass vibrations shook the participants to the bone. When the recording ended, red lights slowly rose at the stage end of the repurposed barn, highlighting sanguine curtains. At stage right, two individuals stood motionless. One wore a glittery silver jumpsuit and a satanic mask. The other wore a similarly glittery golden jumpsuit and a mask representing the fiery sun. In unison they raised their hands toward center stage. A trumpet fanfare echoed throughout the barn and the curtain began to rise. On the emerging stage, swirling spotlights and powerful strobe lights filled the room with increasing energy. A clear polymer sarcophagus was pushed by unseen hands from the shadows to the front of the stage. Inside, Helen Martin lay naked, her hands and feet outstretched and bound by red cords. She turned her head toward the audience. Her face displayed confusion and fear.

At the high priest's command, the strobes stopped. Swirling lights above the sarcophagus and above the audience began to dance around the room to Camille Saint-Saens' *Danse Macabre*. From the shadows, the two maidens who had earlier served champagne carried baskets to the head and foot ends of the sarcophagus. In unison they lifted its clear lid and dumped the contents of their baskets onto Helen's naked body. Tarantulas! The lid closed. Helen screamed and writhed. The massive spiders quickly tiptoed over her body in cadence to the music. Her head thrashed back and forth as she tried in vain to free herself from her bonds. Tears streamed down her cheeks.

When *Danse Macabre* came to an end, the two maidens once again appeared with their same baskets. As they lifted the lid to the sarcophagus for the second time, Helen screamed, "Help me! Somebody, God, please help me!" But her screams and pleas were drowned out by organist Sebastian Heindl's terrifying version of Mussorgsky's *A Night on the Bare Mountain.* In choreographed unison, the two maidens dumped the new contents of their baskets onto Helen's naked face and legs. The strobe lights immediately began their rapid pulsing again, adding to the terror. Eight snakes quickly slithered across Helen, reaching upwards, but not able to escape the clear polymer prison. The lid closed. The snakes slithered quickly back and forth, spiders riding the backs of three. Helen screamed again and again. The maidens disappeared momentarily and then reappeared, dancing in circles around the sarcophagus with live boa constrictors across their shoulders. When the music reached its crescendo and the maidens disappeared to re-cage their boas, Helen's chest heaved and spasmed. Then suddenly nothing.

The two high priests raised their hands toward heaven. Slowly, Helen's body rose feet first from the sarcophagus. Two snakes slid from her belly, across her face, and dropped back into the clear box. A tarantula clung to her hair but one of the maidens quickly swept it away. Hanging like a side of beef, Helen's body glided by cables to stage left, where the maidens positioned it over a crystal chalice which had been placed on a small rolling altar. The golden cross on its green altar linen hung upside down.

The audience watched in silence as the silver-clad

high priest quickly punctured Helen's neck with a sharp medical instrument from which a clear plastic catheter dangled. Blood flowed instantly from the catheter in Helen's neck into the crystal chalice below.

****

The trip to West Glenville took longer than I had estimated, and we didn't reach Box 3369 until nine fifteen. We'd have driven past it if Bergen had not kept his cell phone on until its female voice said, "You've reached your destination on the left. Turn now."

The driveway was almost a quarter of a mile long, and we proceeded slowly with only the dim light of the rust-colored full moon to guide us. We approached the only structure we could see, an old unpainted barn, probably Amish made in the thirties or forties. Its windows were shuttered, and its main door pulled closed. More than a dozen vehicles were parked in front of it.

We got out of our cars but did not shut the doors because we didn't want the sound of slamming doors reaching those inside the barn. Sgt. Sosnowski quickly passed among the parked cars taking pictures of their license plates with his cell phone, while the seven others surrounded the structure, ensuring nobody would be able to exit unseen.

The barn door was bolted from the inside, so I walked along the barn's left side until I found a door near the rear. I used my radio to call Roselli. "Send Johnston back here. He's got another lock to pick."

"Ten-four."

A few moments later, Johnston was beside me and I was holding my cell phone's flashlight so he could see what he was doing. A scream emanated from somewhere inside. It might have been Helen's voice, but I was not sure. Another scream.

"Hurry," I said to Johnston.

When the door swung open, Johnston rejoined Roselli near the front of the barn. I waited ten seconds and then went inside.

As I silently crept through a stall area, I could hear a man's deep voice breaking the silence of the night like a fundamentalist preacher. "The sons of Satan have done their work. Raise the sacrificial lamb."

I could hear the clanging rattle of a chain hoist. Through a door I could see the thin body of a black woman being raised out of a glass container. *Helen!* The glass container was full of large snakes and spiders. *Goddammit!* I stepped backwards and then smashed my shoulder against the locked door. It must have been old or decayed because I fell through the doorway and onto a wooden floor, sprawling in surprise. Several screams came from an unlit area in front of me.

I stood and looked to my left. A man in a silver jumpsuit was inserting something into Helen's neck. I turned in the direction of the screams. "You are all under arrest. Get down on your knees with your hands in the air."

Almost instantly I was tackled from the side by the man in the glittery silver jumpsuit. His matching cape and a vermillion devil's mask were frightening. I found myself on the floor again, this time with two-hundred pounds of flesh on top of me. The guy I was wrestling punched me twice in the face. His third swing missed me and hit the floor. Hoping I could blind my attacker, I pulled at his cape until it covered his mask. Then I punched him twice in the throat. That seemed to stun him briefly. We rolled, me on top and then him on top again.

I thrashed with my feet and brought my right leg around his head and pushed him backwards toward the floor.

A shot rang out. Then another. Screams erupted from the gallery. The energy of the masked man became dead weight, and he was no longer resisting me. I pulled my Sig from its holster and looked in the direction of the two gunshots. Another man, this one in a golden jumpsuit with a red cape and a theatrical sun mask, shot at me again. A few splinters hit my face as his bullet drilled a hole in the wooden floor less than six inches from my head. Instinctively, I shot. A third eye appeared in the sun mask. The man's arms dropped to his side, he staggered backwards into a wooden post, and then fell face forward onto the floor. The golden tip of one of his balsawood sunbeams broke off and skittered toward me, coming to rest against a silver-clad leg.

I rolled the man in silver off me and tore off his mask. It was Modern, bleeding heavily from his left side, where one of the bullets must have entered his body.

Lights came on in the space where the women had screamed. More than twenty people were standing in shock at the scene which had played out in front of them. Five policemen began processing them, securing their hands with Tuff Ties. Multiple voices were reading Miranda Rights: "You are under arrest. You have the right to remain silent…"

I turned my attention to Helen, who was hanging by her feet totally naked, her head level with my belt buckle. A clear plastic IV tube was hanging from the right side of her neck. The end of the tube had been inserted into a clear crystal pitcher containing more than two cups of her blood. I pulled the tube out of the pitcher, squeezed two feet of blood back into Helen's neck and tied the tube into a double knot. "I hope I'm not late," I told her, though she was unconscious and unaware I was there beside her.

I followed the electric wire leading from the ceiling-mounted winch until I found the small control panel mounted on the side of the barn wall. I flipped the switch and watched as Helen's body began descending. I hurried to her and cradled her head until her entire body was resting on the floor. I removed my coat and covered her chest and abdomen. Then I called for assistance.

"Bart Jones, Willow Falls. Officer down. Repeat, officer down. Eleven-forty-one. Second victim with gunshot to abdomen. Third victim with gunshot to head. Request two ambulances at Box 3369, Ridge Road, West Glenville."

"Ten-four," the dispatcher said. I waited for what seemed like five minutes. The dispatcher returned. "Copy your eleven-forty-one. Two West Glenville ambulances responding."

"Ten-four," I replied.

Good. The ambulances were on the way and, thank God, the dispatcher did not send them from Willow Falls.

In less than a minute, I could hear the sirens of the two ambulances as they found their way to the site of the emergency. They pulled in behind our squad cars and four paramedics hurried into the barn.

"Which one is the officer?" one paramedic asked.

I pointed at Helen, still lying unconscious on the floor. "Her name is Helen Martin... Detective Martin. Her blood type is 0-negative. When she isn't naked, she's not bad looking."

"Where we gonna get 0-negative blood?" the EMT

asked his partners.

"Probably fly it in from Syracuse or the City," one replied, shrugging his shoulders.

"Where are you taking her?" I asked.

"Schenectady or Albany," the EMT replied. "You got a preference?"

"Yeah. Schenectady. Maybe I can get some o-negative delivered there."

I watched as the ambulances were loaded with the two living victims, Helen in one and Modern in the other. The large trucks appeared clumsy as they bounced down the driveway to Ridge Road, heading with sirens blaring for Schenectady Memorial Hospital. Once they were gone, I pulled out my cell phone and called Mama Gracie. "We found her. She's alive."

"Oh, praise Jesus," she cried.

"Do any of your other kids have the same 0-negative blood as Helen?" I asked.

"No, but Cousin Nadine does."

"Can you get her to the Schenectady Memorial Hospital as soon as possible? The ambulance is taking Helen there and she needs blood."

"Oh, dear. Maybe. Nadine, well, she's afraid of needles. She never donates her blood like Helen does."

"Tell her if she doesn't donate a little blood, Helen will die, and I will hold her responsible. See you at the hospital soon."

After I hung up, I asked Bergen if he would oversee the processing of the Sanguinarians we had arrested.

"Got a meat wagon on its way. How do you want them booked?"

"Accessory to kidnapping and attempted murder. The live one who's gone to the hospital is no accessory.

He's the kidnapper and murderer of Laura Moretti. Be sure to assign a guard to ensure he stays there."

"The way he was bleeding out, he might not arrive alive. What about the dead one?"

I walked over and tugged the sun mask off the corpse. It was Father Upton. "Deliver the good Father to the morgue. His parishioners are going to need a shrink when they find out what he's been up to."

"We're good here," Bergen said, "except maybe I've got to call Fish and Game to come and get those snakes and spiders."

"Can you imagine being naked and tied in a glass container full of those things?"

Bergen shook his head. "Think she'll be okay?"

I nodded.

"Go ahead and look after your partner," he said. "She owes you her life."

I went outside, put the blue flashing light on my dash, plugged it in, and headed down Ridge Road to Schenectady.

Chapter 33

Mama Gracie was sitting in the emergency room waiting area at the hospital when I walked in. She stood, tears in her eyes. "She's still unconscious."

I gave her a hug. "Our girl is strong. She'll pull through in no time." I was not sure about that. Helen had just lived through a ghoulish experience, testing both her physical and mental stamina. It was something which would kill a lot of people on the spot. I had no sense of her vital signs when she left the barn, but I knew she was breathing, and she was in the good hands of experienced paramedics until she arrived at the hospital.

"Nadine didn't want to do it, but I told her what you said. She's in there now, giving her blood to her cousin."

"Be sure to tell her if she ever needs blood for any reason, Helen will undoubtedly be there for her. She's doing the right thing."

Mama Gracie nodded. Then we sat down together and waited for the doctor to give us the news. I hoped it would be good.

An hour later a young woman in physician's garb approached us. "Are you with Officer Martin?" she asked Mama Gracie.

"Yes. Is she…?"

"She's lost a lot of blood, but it appears the transfusion is working. She has regained consciousness. You can see her, but only for a minute. Tomorrow you can enjoy a longer visiting period."

"Can I come, too?" I asked, motioning I was still in uniform. "She's my partner, and I'd like to report on her condition to the Chief."

"Sure, but only for a minute."

I nodded. "Thank you, Dr. Prentice."

"Do I know you?"

"You're wearing a name tag."

She laughed. "I can see why you're a cop."

"Don't tell anyone. It's a trade secret."

We walked down a hallway from the waiting area. Its vinyl floor tiles were blood red, but tan subway tiles climbed halfway up the walls. The hallway emptied into the emergency room, a large square with a nurses' station on one wall and curtained patient cubicles on the other three walls.

"How many patients can you handle at one time?" I asked.

"We've handled as many as fifty. That was last year when the aftermath of a high school basketball game was a riot."

"Albany versus Schenectady? I remember when it happened. Fortunately, I was off duty. You'd think kids would know better than to fight over a game."

"It wasn't kids. It was parents."

"Where is my little girl?" Mama Gracie asked.

"Right in here," Dr. Prentice said. "Now remember, only a minute." She left to tend to other patients.

I held the curtain for Mama Gracie, and she walked in ahead of me. Helen still had a portion of a unit of blood to receive. Then, I was certain, she'd need saline solution. Her face showed signs of stress. Her hair was matted to one side.

"You look great, Helen," I said as her mama kissed and hugged her.

"I'm gonna be all right, Mama," she said to Mama Gracie. Then Helen looked at me. "You get those bastards?" she asked in a raspy voice.

"Yeah, Upton is DOA. Modern caught a couple of rounds and is getting put back together. Maybe you'll get to see him while you're in here."

"I do and he's a dead man."

"That's no way for a Christian girl to talk, sweetheart," Mama Gracie said.

"Where'd you get the blood?"

"Nadine," Mama Gracie said.

Helen nodded. "Thank her for me."

A nurse came into the cubicle. "Time to go, folks. Come back tomorrow. By then she'll be in a room."

I turned to leave.

"Hey, Jonesy," Helen said.

I turned back to look at her.

"Thanks for saving my life."

I smiled and saluted her with my pointer finger.

"But don't think just 'cause you did, you get something special from me. You were late."

"Not late enough, I think."

She smiled and winked at me.

Mama Gracie and I walked through the waiting room together. "That little girl of mine has it bad for you, Jonesy."

"She *is* special, isn't she?" I replied.

"You could do worse."

With Rachel, I think I already had.

****

The next morning I spoke with Chief Comstock

about the raid and the individuals we had arrested. "They were participating as observers during an attempted murder," I said. "And it was voluntary. Nobody forced them to be there, and they came by invitation. We overheard one woman tell our confident she was excited about being there and drinking Helen's blood. Well, not quite in those words."

"And who was your confidant?"

"Her name is Edwina Faraday. She owns a small jewelry store on Main Street. Hell, if it hadn't been for her, we'd never have known the dates of the upcoming blood moons and certainly we would never have known the revised location of the ceremony where Helen was guest of honor. Edwina deserves a break."

"So, I'll put in a good word about her with the DA and get the charges dropped."

"Thanks, I'd appreciate that."

The Chief smiled. "I imagine she will, too."

But the chief had a surprise for me. "I want to thank you profusely for solving the Laura Moretti case."

"It wasn't just me," I replied. "The case never would have been solved without Helen Martin."

"Yeah, I know," the chief replied. "She's getting a commendation and a medal."

I smiled. Helen deserved a medal for performance above the call of duty. And maybe a purple heart, if the department offered one.

Then the chief's expression changed. "But you're getting thirty days suspension without pay."

"Why? What did I do?"

"I've caught wind you've been moonlighting as a private dick without official approval."

"You know about my upcoming divorce, don't you?

I wouldn't have had a place to lay my head if it weren't for Joey Astor. I needed a few extra bucks, and I only worked for one client. That's all."

"You know the rules. You violated your union contract. I could fire you, but I'm not doing that. Give me your badge and your city-issued sidearm. I'll see you in thirty days. On your first day back, bring your union rep with you. That's the way it's written in your contract."

I unloaded my Sig Sauer and placed it on the chief's desk along with my badge. "This is bullshit, Chief. I helped solve a really important case involving a number of highly respected people in our community, and this is what you do to me?"

"Got to, Jonesy. I got to play by the book and your union contract is the book I gotta follow."

****

I dropped by to see Helen for a few minutes before heading back to Mariaville. It was going to be my first of thirty days off—and without pay. How was I going to meet my obligation to keep a roof over Rachel's head?

Helen looked better. Her mama had washed and done her hair into a conservative Afro, and she was wearing purple lipstick.

"What you doing here? Don't you have reports to write? How many peeps did you arrest last night?"

"The chief gave me a few days off," I lied. "I have to rest up after yesterday's ordeal. You know, we searched for you in three places before you showed up."

"I heard. Chaquille Bergen stopped by." She pointed a vase full of colorful flowers. "Brought me those, like he's my boyfriend or something. What did you bring me? Nothing but your ugly face." She smiled and winked.

"Got something in your eye?"

"Doc says I have to stay another day or two in the hospital."

"Is your blood count low?"

"No, I have to debrief with the 'Flight Surgeon.' You know about them?"

"Yeah. It's a military term for 'psychiatrist.' Just tell him you want to kill Horace Modern, and he'll have you out of here in no time."

Helen laughed. "Sure, and you'll be visiting me in the nut house."

"Where's your mama?"

"She's gone home to make me some liver."

I knew Helen was going to be okay. She seemed in good spirits and had her wits about her. She was also going to be in Mama Gracie's good hands until she started back to work.

I said goodbye. I even kissed her on the cheek and told her I'd be back soon.

****

I was in my car, driving back toward Mariaville against a thirty mile per hour headwind when my cell phone rang. It was Diego Cisneros.

"Hey, gringo, I heard you got a couple days off."

"Yeah. It's a miscarriage of justice. You calling to rub it in?"

"Nope. I got another job for you to do, if you're interested."

I looked in my rearview mirror and saw nobody was behind me. I pulled onto the right shoulder of the road and put on my left blinker. After an eighteen-wheeler passed by heading toward the city, I rechecked my side view mirror and then did a U-turn toward Cisneros' office and the possibility of a payday.

A word about the author...

Born in Massachusetts, Edward Baker traveled widely as a child because his U.S. Marine father was transferred on a regular basis to new assignments across the U.S.A. By the time Ed was twelve, he had crossed the United States three times. And as a licensed driver at the ripe old age of sixteen, he drove a stick shift Ford across the nation, following his dad, who was pulling a camping trailer behind the family's station wagon.

An English major at Elon College, Ed earned a master's degree at Appalachian State University and a doctorate in Educational Leadership at the Sage Colleges' Esteves School of Education. After thirty-five years in higher education and after retiring as Interim President of a public community college, he turned his attention to his first love, writing, while continuing to teach undergraduate and graduate courses on an adjunct basis at a private college in upstate New York.

During the cold months, Ed and his wife "hole up" in their winter quarters in Saratoga Springs, New York. However, during the warm months, they reside in their cabin on Galway Lake, New York. When he's not writing or engaged in a woodworking project, Ed can be found on the lake or playing with his grandchildren or his four-legged canine companion Sudsy.

His web site and blog can be found at: www.edwardsbaker.com